I0625672

Repercussions

Qiana Rae

Princess of Erotica Books

ISBN: 978-0-9916187-5-0

Dedication
I dedicate this novel to everyone who has supported and believed in me thus far.
Love,
Qiana Rae

Table of Contents

Acknowledgments

Whew! I did it again, of course only with the help of my lord and savior Jesus Christ. I thank Him for helping to make my first published novel, *Tempted*, HAWT! The reviews don't lie! I thank my husband, Devon for motivating me every day, and not complaining when I spend an entire day writing. I also thank him for promoting almost as much as I do, and that's hard to do! Devon, thank you for always being there. I love you baby!

I also thank my family for supporting me and giving me words of encouragement when they are most needed. Even though my momma read the end of *Tempted* first, ruining the whole book for herself, I still love her and appreciate her loving support. Thank you to my sister, who was one of the first to read *Tempted* and gave me great feedback! Teuwuna, I love you girl!

Last, but definitely not least, thank you to all my true friends, and all the new fans I've gained in this short period of time, whether it be from Facebook, Twitter, or Instagram. I truly appreciate each and every one of you for picking up my book out of all the books you could've chosen and having so many wonderful things to say. I can't even express how that makes me feel! All of you are a big part of my motivation. I write to please my readers, and so far I've been successful in doing so. Thank you to everyone who is reading this book and for all future support! Believe me when I say that there will be plenty more. Thank you for believing in Qiana Rae, and enjoy your read.

Peace and many blessings,
Qiana Rae

Chapter 1

I've been lounging around my condo for the past three days, staring out the window at the beautiful view of the lake, and enjoying peace and quiet. I turned my ringer off on both my house and cell phones because I just wanted to spend time with me, myself, and I, with no interruptions. I want to get to know myself, what I want, what I don't want, my dreams, my aspirations, my desires, my strengths, and my weaknesses. People stop by and ring the doorbell. I don't answer. I don't even look out to see who it is. I really don't care. If no one important to me is dying, it's not important. Having time to myself is top priority right now, so I can clear my head and get my priorities right. This was long overdue.

My new place is perfect for me and only me. I moved in five days ago. The first two days I spent moving stuff and unpacking with the help of family and friends. I haven't spoken to anyone since. Not that I didn't appreciate the help. I truly did, but I couldn't wait 'til everyone was gone so I could get some much needed me time. Especially after everything I put myself through. I had a completely new perspective on life and was gonna try to make it my point to only surround myself with positive things and positive people. After the fuchsia sky turned dark, I took one last look at the beautiful water as the light from the moon hit it and lit up the small waves. I closed the blinds to my large picture window and turned around, admiring what I now called, my home. My condo was open concept, so I had a lot of wide-open space without the obstruction of walls. I had a spiral staircase that lead to the upstairs hallway. From there, you could overlook the family room. I only had two bedrooms, which I wasn't used to, but I didn't need any more than that. I bought all new furniture so I could start fresh, and everything was in order. Now, all I needed to do was go grocery shopping, but not until I was ready. Until then, I would be ordering take-out.

The doorbell rang, and even though I knew I had ordered a pizza, I looked out of my back window that overlooked the parking lot to make sure I saw a pizza delivery car. I didn't need any surprises. I pressed the button to let the pizza guy in. When I opened the door, it was actually girl who was around seventeen or eighteen. She was Caucasian with pink hair and a lip piercing. I wasn't the one to stereotype, but surprisingly, she was very pleasant and seemed very free-spirited like I once was. She carried on a conversation telling me how I was her last delivery for the night and she was going to the movies with her boyfriend when she got off. While she kept talking, I went and found my purse so I could pay for my food and, of course, give her a tip. She was nice and all, but I really wasn't in the mood to talk. I hoped I didn't come off as being rude. I did manage, however, to tell her to enjoy her night.

I went and sat my pizza on the island in the kitchen, and pulled a champagne glass out of the cabinet. I made sure I always had some Welch's sparkling white grape juice, to at least give me the illusion of having a glass of wine, since I couldn't really have one. I filled my glass halfway with crushed ice, which I craved all the time, and filled it to the rim with what I pretended to be Moscato.

I always loved picnics, so I laid a blanket across my hardwood floor in the living room and planned on watching TV, but then I remembered that I had forgotten to schedule for the cable to be hooked up, so I put in my Jill Scott CD instead, and the first track was the song "Blessed." That song helped me through a lot of dark, gloomy days.

I picked up my landline while I ate, so I could check a few of my million messages. I knew exactly who the first message would be.

"Kel, this is Momma. Just worried about you baby. I came by a couple of times. I know you probably just don't wanna talk, but you can at least let somebody know you're okay! I even called crazy Tasha and she said she hasn't talked to you either. Just know you have people who love and care about you! And remember, you're gonna need a babysitter! Love you!"

After hearing my momma's message, I grinned a little. She always knew how to make me smile, even when I didn't feel like it. I texted her a message that read: *Hey, ma. Got your message. I'm fine. Just spendin' some time alone right now. I'll call you soon. Love you.*

The next couple of messages were from my girl Tasha. She basically said the same thing my momma said, but in her own little way.

"Girl, yo ass better call somebody. I'm sick of worryin' about you! I ain't got no kids, but I feel like I do with you acting so crazy. You know everybody been askin' me about you. Love you girl! Call me!"

I put down the phone so I could fully enjoy my meal. I had to make sure that my baby ate good. I was only three months pregnant, but I already had a baby bump. I sat on my blanket Indian-style in the middle of my beautiful living room, reminiscing on how I got to this place in my life. In the eyes of people who were on the outside looking in, only three months ago, I was happily married, living in a beautiful home with my "wonderful husband." Truth be told, I wasn't that happy, and what you do in the dark always comes to light. While I was out cheating on my "wonderful" hubby, Terrance, he was fucking one of my best friends, Tif!

Even though I was doing wrong, it hurt me so bad when I walked in on them while trying to surprise him on his birthday. I had thought about it over and over and over. Each and every time, it seemed like the pain just got worse. I never wanted to be in a place ever again where I felt like taking my own life would be the solution to all of my problems. I never would've thought Terrance would've been out there acting a fool. He never gave me any indication that he was cheating, or any reason to not trust him, but I guess it was a lesson learned. I didn't think I'd ever be able to trust or even love a man again.

When I think about that night when I drove to Whitebeach Park with intentions on killing myself after walking in on Terrance and Tif, it was almost like I was watching a movie. Like an outer body experience most probably wouldn't understand. I didn't feel like myself at all that night. The real Kelicia would've never even thought about killing herself, but when a person allows certain bad spirits into their life, those spirits are given access to take over their life. I not only would've ended my life, but also the life of my unborn child. I can and will admit that was very selfish of me.

Terrance may have thought he and Tif were gonna live happily ever after, but in the words of my momma, I threw a monkey wrench in that shit. They would not have the last laugh at my expense. On top of me finding out he was messing around with Tif, he was also messing with his co-worker, Stacy, which I figured out on my own . . . Just a little too late.

That emotional night, I called Stacy to meet me at Whitebeach Park and wrote her a letter as I sat in the car, preparing to end my life. The letter read:

Dear Stacy,

I now know the reason you wanted to meet with me and talk, and I feel so naïve to not have figured this out before now, but Terrance hid everything very well. Not only did he hide things from me, his wife, he also hid things from you, who is only one of his mistresses. Yes, you are ONE of his mistresses. He is cheating on you, just like he's cheating on me, so you shouldn't walk around thinkin' you did some shit! He don't care about your ass, and if you think he does, you a damn fool! If it had only been you, I would fight to keep my man! But now, knowing everything that I need to know, he's not even worth it. You can have his sorry ass if you want him! All I want is for him to suffer like I'm suffering as I write this letter, and he will, once I do this one last thing! Have a happy motherfuckin' life you stupid bitch!!!

Yours fuckin' truly,
Kel

Oh yeah, I'm sure you wanna know who his other woman is. Her name is Tiffany Lucas, and her phone # is 555-785-9282. Give her a call. I hope both of you rot in Hell, right along with Terrance! Fuck you Stacy!

My plan was to be dead by the time she got there to make the gruesome discovery and for her to be troubled by the thought of me for the rest of her life. I stuck the letter outside my car window, and while the gun was at my temple, held by yours truly, I felt empty inside. All I thought about was how good it would feel to no longer feel any of the pain or emptiness that I was feeling at that time. I was numb to everything that was happening and acting on pure impulse. I suddenly understood how people could do such a thing without fully thinking it through, or thinking about all the consequences and all the people who would be hurt behind it. What I still couldn't understand was how people premeditated such a grueling thing, and actually went through with it.

I slowly pulled the trigger and nothing happened. I began rapidly pulling the trigger repeatedly, and when I finally came to the realization, nothing was happening, I started crying uncontrollably. I open the gun's chamber, and saw that there were no bullets inside, then threw the gun on the passenger seat, and laid my head on the steering wheel. My entire, quickly-thought-up plan failed due to that one detail of the gun not having bullets. Terrance hadn't put bullets in it like he had told me he would. The best thing Terrance probably had ever done for me was not putting bullets in the gun that he bought for me.

Before initially pulling the trigger, I saw what I knew were Stacy's headlights shining through my window, so I knew she would be walking up soon. Still crying, which felt like a release of all kinds of anger and frustration that needed to come out, I could barely hear Stacy on the other side of my window calling my name. I lifted up my head, hair stuck to my face, from tears and sweat. Black streams of eyeliner ran down my once perfectly made up face, which I had done for Terrance on his day. I had made sure

I looked my best for him that day. I rolled the window down halfway, grabbing the letter before it fell, and Stacy said, "What the fuck?"

Voice trembling and body shaking, realizing that I had just cheated death, I told Stacy to get in, motioning for her to go to the passenger side. She hesitated, but walked around the car and opened the door. She jumped back when she saw the gun sitting there in the passenger seat, which I had completely forgotten about. Stacy slammed the door, about to run until I stepped out of the car and started crying even harder. I was supposed to be beating this bitch's ass, and there I was, crying like a big ass baby!

"What? Are you planning on killing me?" she shouted.

Foolishly, she slowly walked toward me, looking confused as I continued to cry. When she finally stood only inches from me, she grabbed and hugged me. At that point, I think I was even more confused than she was. I didn't know what to feel. *Should I hug her back or should I slap the shit out of her?* I thought. I calmed down a little bit, but was still breathing hard, and bottom lip quivering like a little kid who just got her ass whooped. Stacy led me over to the beach and we sat in the sand. She watched me inquisitively as I stared out into the water with a blank expression on my face. I opened my mouth to speak, but nothing would come out at first. I tried again and said in a low tone, "I wrote you a letter." Stacy waited for me to say more.

"Since we're both here, I guess I can tell you what I need to tell you face to face."

Stacy said, "Wait a minute. Let me go first, since I was the one who came to you and said we needed to talk. I don't know what you know, or if you know everything, but it looks to me like you just might. Terrance and I have been seeing each other for almost a year. When he first came to work at the bank, we found interest in each other, and it went from there. The nights he would come home late, he was with me. Before you think this was just a fling, believe me when I say it wasn't. Men don't take flings out in public. We went on actual dates. Something he told me y'all hadn't done in a while, and frankly, he didn't have any desire to do with you anymore. When he told me he was marrying you, I was distraught. I felt like I think you feel right now. I couldn't eat, sleep, or barely get up to go to work and face him every day."

I sat there attentively listening to Stacy tell her side of the story. I couldn't believe they were together before Terrance and I even got married. My entire marriage was a lie. All this time, I thought I started this whole infidelity issue in our marriage, but I didn't. It was him, and maybe I subconsciously knew he was cheating, but like the other dumb hoes, tried to ignore it. I thought about how he cried as I walked down the aisle towards him on our wedding day, realizing it was all a façade.

"A few months ago, Terrance told me he caught you cheating and got some information from another source about you and some other guy, but he hadn't confronted you about it. He didn't give me any specifics, but I really didn't care to know anyway. I know this part is gonna hurt, Kellie, but I want to tell you the entire truth. Terrance told me he was going to leave you and he wanted to be with me permanently."

At that moment my heart dropped, and as she put her left hand out in front of me to show me the small princess cut diamond on her long slender married finger, I felt like snatching that long thick hair straight out of her scalp. In my mind, I jumped up and choked the shit out of that bitch right in that white sand, but I didn't move. I didn't say a word. I didn't have the strength. I thought she was finished, so I could tell her what I needed to, but she opened her mouth to say something else. Whatever it was, by the look on her face, I could tell she really didn't want to.

"Kellie . . . I'm pregnant. About a month."

"And whose baby is it, Stacy?"

"Terrance's."

I suddenly got the strength to say a whole mouthful and I don't think Stacy was prepared for it.

"So Stacy . . . You're gonna sit here and tell me that you've been fucking my husband, and he planned on leaving me to marry you, and you're pregnant by his ass?" I stood up and began pointing my finger at her while she sat there looking like a poor little Yorkie.

"Let me tell you something Miss Stacy! You are even dumber than I thought you were! You stuck around even after he got married on yo ass? Dumb bitch! You can have his ass cuz guess what . . ." I continued without even giving her a chance to ask what. "He's fuckin' one of my very good friends. His so-called source where he's supposedly getting information about me. I just caught them in my motherfuckin' bed sweatin' like some damn pigs going at it! Nasty dogs! Both of them! I pray for you and your child, sweetie, because you got pregnant by the wrong man! Obviously, he wasn't with you EVERY night he came home late! How about that? And how about my so-called girl has been living with us and they were at my house together alone on numerous occasions, so don't even think you're special, sweetie!"

Stacy was in tears, but how was I supposed to feel sorry for her when I was sitting there feeling sorry myself? I was glad I didn't give any of them the satisfaction of killing myself. Just then, Stacy stood up and the craziest thing came out of her mouth.

"You lying bitch! You're just mad 'cause you messed things up with a good man and now he don't want your ass no more! Don't be mad, boo. It's okay. I'll live a great life with him for you. Me and our child!"

I felt like hittin' that hoe in her goddamn stomach, but again, she wasn't worth it, and if she really was pregnant, the baby didn't do anything to me. His or her stankin' ass mommy and daddy did it. I also knew that there was a chance that I may be pregnant by Terrance too. I definitely wasn't gonna tell her that. Especially knowing that I wasn't sure if Terrance was even the father.

"You know what, Stacy?" I said as I looked down at her short ass. "I think we're done here. You've told me what you needed to say and I've told you what I thought you needed to know! Why don't you go ahead and stop by my house to see what your man is up to?"

Stacy stood there looking dumbfounded as I walked to my car and drove off. I hadn't seen or talked to her since that day. That was two and a half months ago. I never went back home that day. I stayed at a hotel for a few days, not talking to anyone, so no one knew what I was going through. Terrance called me a few more times, in addition to the time he called me right after I ran out of the house after seeing the wretched sight of him and Tif. He left a message and I deleted it after I let it sit in my mailbox for a few days without listening to it. I didn't know if I even wanted to hear what he had to say. There was no excuse for what I saw, especially after he told me, his wife, to leave and for Tif to stay. People may say how could I get mad and I cheated a couple of times too. I fully understood that, but I couldn't explain it. It just wasn't supposed to happen to me. Especially with it involving my so-called friend who tricked me into believing she was there for me.

I went to the house with a small U-Haul a few days later. My girl, Tasha, and I went during the middle of the day when I knew no one was around. Including Terrance. I was praying that Mike, my next-door neighbor who was obsessed with me, especially wasn't around. I knew he would've been trying to be in my face to make sure I was okay, but I wasn't trying to hear it. I wasn't feeling anything that was going on at that moment. The only reason I was talking to Tasha was because I needed her help to get my shit. We packed up as many of my things as we could. I left the furniture. I definitely didn't want that bed. I took my expensive china, the two plasma TVs that I bought, and of course, my clothes and shoes. Whatever I didn't get was just gonna be there. Maybe Tif's raggedy ass could put some use to whatever I left.

While I was packing up my clothes, I was hoping that I didn't happen to see any of Tif's things in my house. I think that would've pushed me over the edge. Surprisingly, I didn't see as much as an earring that didn't belong to me. The house looked exactly as it did when I left, except no one was in the bed, and it was perfectly made as if I had made it.

Tasha and I pulled up at my momma's house with the U-Haul. I was not looking forward to seeing her, since she tried to pound in my head not to trust my girls. She had no idea what had been going on with me, or what had happened a few days prior. I had no other choice though. Tasha only had a one-bedroom apartment, and I wasn't trying to sleep on anybody's couch. My other girl, Bri, had abruptly moved to Texas with her momma because she lost her job and needed her momma to help support her, which I thought was a damn shame. She probably wouldn't have been an option anyway only because I didn't want too many people knowing my business, and she never knew how to keep her mouth closed!

My momma opened the door before I even got to the porch. She squinted her eyes and wrinkled her forehead, watching me as though she was trying to read my thoughts. She came out and stood on the porch, folding her arms. I thought Tasha was right behind me, but when I looked back, I saw that she had started grabbing stuff out of the U-Haul. I told her to wait. I didn't know how this was gonna go with my momma, and might've had to come up with a new plan.

"So, what happened?" My momma asked, with anger in her voice. "Please don't tell me you then went and did something stupid and Terrance put you out. Let me go put on my shoes so we can go fix this."

As she was turning around to go back in the house, I grabbed her and said, "No, Ma. He's with Tif."

"What?" she exclaimed. "What in the world is he doing with her?"

"Let's just go in. I need to sit down, and you do, too."

I motioned for Tasha to follow us. I sat there with my momma and Tasha, telling the story all over again of my recent revelation. I told her everything from when I got home from Atlanta, to my talk with Stacy, excluding the part that Terrance had told her that I was cheating on him. The whole time, Tasha sat there shaking her head and rolling her eyes as she listened for the second time. I could tell how much it irritated her that Tif would do something so scandalous to me, especially after we were all there for her through her rape incident. It was really surprising to me, especially after Tif shared so much with me about her family that she had never talked to anyone else about. I knew one thing for sure: I wouldn't put anything past anyone else. Tif was the only one who I told about my affair with my old friend from school, Reggie, and now I was kicking myself. I was just glad that I hadn't shared everything with her, which I almost foolishly did. She didn't need anything else to go around spreading about me. At least I had ruled out Reggie being the father of my baby since we only had sex once, and the time from when that happened, and when I got pregnant, fortunately didn't add up. I didn't need anyone else on my list for paternity tests. I already knew Tif would probably tell people she ended up with Terrance because I didn't know how to treat a good man, and that I stepped out on him. What Tif didn't know was the part Stacy told me about Terrance cheating on me way before we were married, and way before Terrance started messing around with her. My life was more of a mess than what I knew. When I got on the plane leaving Atlanta, coming back to Chicago, I planned to leave my promiscuity behind, and work hard to preserve my marriage. That plan changed in a matter of seconds.

After my momma heard the story, minus the fact that I'd had an affair with Reggie and the man I had really fallen for, Ty, I could see the rage in her eyes. I had cried so much the past few days, I couldn't cry anymore.

"Didn't I tell you not to be trusting these women out here? Especially your supposed friends!" she said, glancing over at Tasha.

Tasha sat back in her seat and took a deep breath. I glanced over at her and quickly shook my head letting her know not to take it personal. That's just how my momma was. She didn't take no nonsense, and whatever she had to say when she had to say it, she did just that!

"So what is your plan, baby?" she said in a more subtle tone.

"I was hoping that I could stay with you until I get things figured out. I'll pay you rent. That's no problem. I just need to look around so I can find me another place, because I'm surely not going back there!"

"You know you can stay with me as long as you need to. I just can't believe that happened! I feel like going over there myself! What did he say when you took your stuff?"

"He wasn't there, thank God. I can't face him. I may end up in jail. But let's not talk about him anymore. There's a much bigger issue."

I didn't want to tell my momma I was pregnant. I actually didn't wanna tell anyone, but I knew everyone would find out soon, so I knew I might as well said something right then and there. I would keep the additional info that there were two possible fathers to myself, until I felt it was necessary to share that information, which I was hoping was never.

"What's that?" she said nervously, trying to imagine what could've been bigger than what I had already told her.

Tasha had a confused look on her face, since I hadn't even told her.

"I just found out I'm pregnant. While I was in Atlanta for the hair show, I took a pregnancy test."

If there had been a fly in the room, it would've flown straight into my momma and Tasha's mouths. They wouldn't say a word. They sat still and quiet, causing the atmosphere to be very uncomfortable. Suddenly, my momma's entire expression changed. Her bright red lips began to turn up at the corners and all I could see were her beautiful, freshly whitened teeth. This was not what I was expecting at all. I was expecting her to sit there and lecture me about being a single mother, and how tough it was going to be, and how expensive babies are, blah, blah, blah!

"I'm gonna have a grandbaby, huh? I had a feeling. I told you last time I saw you that it looked like you had put on a little weight. Well, at least you got one good thing out of the deal!"

Tasha didn't know what to say, so I tried breaking the ice. "So, what do you have to say Auntie Tasha?"

Tasha jumped up smiling, gave me a hug and said, "Congratulations, ma!"

I don't think this would've been such a happy occasion if they both had known that Ty could be the father. A man who they didn't even know was a special part of my life. I fell deeply in love with Ty, but after finding out he was a big-time drug dealer, and all the expensive and fancy things he had came from dirty money, I knew there could be no future for us. That's some hood shit, and don't get me wrong, I did come from the hood, but I worked damn hard to get away from it and that lifestyle. I still thought about Ty. Did I still love him? Of course I did, and there wasn't a day that went by that I hadn't thought about him. Love don't go away overnight. Ty was like a drug and I gave him up cold turkey. Between losing my husband to that bitch, and giving up my drug, I was definitely going through withdrawal. Ty was so mysterious, yet fun to be around. I was in love with two men at the same time. If someone would've ever asked me if that was possible before it happened to me, I would've said "Hell naw!" But now, since I've experienced it for myself, I know it's real . . . and it's real fucked up! In the end, it leaves you lonely, just as I was right now.

I didn't even know if Ty was still alive. I figured he was probably dead or locked up somewhere, only because he never tried to contact me after I left his ass in Atlanta after finding out about his grimy lifestyle. He had upset some of his clients who came after him while I was trying to enjoy my vacation. They ended up in my hotel suite, while I hid underneath the bathroom sink. Ty thought he was smart, but he obviously wasn't that smart when it came to hiring people to deliver product for him. They switched the good stuff for some bad shit, and probably went and made a profit for themselves, unless they were dumb enough to smoke it all up. Anyway, then Ty had people coming after him, thinking he purposely did the shit. I had to get out of there quick, so I was on the next flight home. That made me realize the grass wasn't always greener on the other side. I could've been killed just for being in the wrong place at the wrong time. Ty said he was staying to tie up some lose ends. Whatever happened to Ty after that, I didn't know. I never tried to contact him again. I did know that Ty cared for me, so if he were in any condition to call, I knew he would've.

I figured as long as I could keep my pregnancy quiet from Terrance, my baby and I could go on living our lives without him. If it was Ty's baby, it didn't look like I had to worry about him being a part of its life. There would be a whole lot less drama if things could just go my way. I got a call from Terrance's cell later on that night after I went and got my stuff from the house. Of course I didn't answer because I still didn't wanna hear his voice and probably never would. That time, he didn't leave a message.

I lived with my momma for three whole months and it was not fun! I then remembered why I moved out when I did! She tried to run my life and was always nagging about something. She wanted to tell me what to eat, what not to eat, when to eat, when to take a nap, when to be in the house, and when to go to bed. My closing date for my new home didn't come soon enough!

Chapter 2

I laid flat on my back, rubbing my belly, while staring up at my vaulted ceiling after finishing my pizza. I was so stuffed I didn't feel like moving. I took the whole week off from work, just so I could get situated in my new place, but I would be due to go back into that madhouse in a couple more days. As I continued daydreaming, I drifted off into a deep sleep with Jill Scott still playing in the background.

I could feel a ray of heat on my forehead. I slowly opened my eyes and squinted. The sun still managed to beam through my closed blinds. I laid there for a while, but there were things on my to do list that had to be done before I went back to work. I knew once I went back, I wouldn't have time to get things done that needed to be done. That was one good thing work did for me: occupied my mind. Working as a hair stylist, everyone told me their problems, which made it seem like mine weren't that bad.

The hardest part of my days these days was trying to find something that fit. All of my jeans were skinny, and my baby bump wasn't too happy about that, so today was the day I decided I would go shopping for maternity clothes. I refused to be one of these heifas out here who didn't buy maternity clothes and just wore their pants unbuttoned for the entire nine months! My morning sickness phase had finally passed, so I hadn't been putting on much weight before because everything I would try to eat would come right back up. Now I could eat any and everything, and that scared me! I definitely didn't wanna have a ton of weight to lose after I dropped my load.

I picked up my blanket from my overnight picnic, folded it up and put it in the linen closet. I opened the blinds and it looked like a cool fall day, even though it was winter. The sun was shining bright and the leaves on the trees had just begun changing colors. I could tell the wind was strong by the way the leaves blew from the branches into the yellowish-green grass. It seemed we had an extra long summer, and autumn was coming late.

Before I got in the shower, I stared at myself in my bathroom mirror, noticing my glow for the first time. My caramel skin was clear and golden, my hair, jet-black and stronger than ever, my hips starting to round out, breasts fuller than they had ever been, and center attraction was my small round belly. This sometimes seemed like a dream, but I knew it wasn't. I would soon be a mother to someone who would love me unconditionally.

I closed my eyes in the shower and let the water run down my face. I reminisced about how Terrance and I would make love in the shower. I missed the feeling of someone caressing me, making me feel like everything was okay. I didn't like sleeping alone, without strong arms wrapped around me as I slept. I missed the smell of breakfast in the morning, kisses for no reason, and looking up just to see my man staring and smiling at me. I wish I could erase the last memory of Terrance, and just remember him the way that he was before, even though he was being deceptive. I loved that Terrance. In my mind, he was the perfect man and would've never done me any harm. He always wanted what was best for me, and always told me how much he appreciated and loved me.

I didn't know how long I had been in the shower, but I could feel the water getting cold as it washed away the tears from my eyes. I knew I shouldn't have been crying over Terrance, but I couldn't help it. Every time I thought about him, I felt a lump in my throat, even though I felt so much hatred towards him. I felt like I could never forgive him. I knew there would be a day when I would, but it wouldn't be any time soon. My momma always told me that things get better with time. I was just wondering how much time.

When I opened the garage door, I noticed how much my red BMW was in need of a car wash. That was another thing I didn't have to worry about when I had a man around. Terrance kept my ride clean. Everything seemed to remind me of Terrance, and I knew it would fade, but I was just hoping sooner than later. I decided my first stop of the day would be Chicago Ridge Mall, which wasn't too far from where I lived. It was early, but this mall was always packed, especially on Saturdays. It took forever to find a parking space, but after driving around the parking lot for nearly fifteen minutes, I saw a black Porsche pulling out of a spot. After it completely pulled out, it hesitated to move so I could pull in.

"Move idiot!" I said and blew my horn.

I was very annoyed at this point, and my raging hormones weren't helping! The person driving the Porsche finally switched gears and pulled off. I flew into the parking space just in case that asshole wanted to come back and try to pull back in. I moved slowly trying to take my seatbelt off and ease the door open. I knew for a fact this would be my last day wearing my skinny jeans. I couldn't function at all. My pregnancy wasn't very noticeable, but I was to the point that I was starting to feel uncomfortable in regular clothes. I rolled to one side, trying not to pop the button off my jeans, and eased out of the car, grabbing my Coach bag.

As I was walking through the parking lot to get to the mall's entrance, I heard a car's engine behind me, sounding like it was getting closer and closer. I didn't bother to look back. I just moved closer to the parked cars so the car had room to pass. As soon as I did that, I could see someone pulling up on the side of me in the corner of my eye. I could suddenly hear music playing, as if the driver had rolled down the passenger side window trying to get my attention.

"Hey, stranger." I heard a familiar voice say.

I slowly turned to look, hoping it wasn't who I thought it was. As soon as I looked in the direction of the voice, I saw the black Porsche, and that's when I realized that it was Mike, my old next-door neighbor's car. He was another person who I had been trying to avoid. I tried my best not to act standoffish, but I have to admit, I wasn't the best actress.

Mike was the last person I saw, immediately after running out of my house in tears, right before I met with Stacy. At that moment, he was still trying to profess his love for me. No matter how good of a man Mike seemed to be, I knew we could never work out, even if Terrance and I didn't work out. Mike saw and knew too much about me, and the things I did while Terrance was away, being my next-door neighbor and all, so he was definitely disqualified. Mike had just been a good shoulder to cry on when I didn't have anyone else to vent to.

"Hey, you!" I said, smiling, trying my best to sound excited.

"How are you? I've been thinking about you, but had no way of contacting you. I hope everything has been okay with you. Last time I saw you, you weren't doing too well. What happened between you and Terrance was really messed up."

He just had to bring that up, and just then, a gold, older model Malibu, trying to get around Mike's car honked its horn.

Saved by the bell! I thought. "Okay then, Mike. It was good to see you."

I gave him a phony smile and before I started to walk away, he put his index finger up and told me to wait, then sped off. I looked back at the woman in the Malibu who was shaking her head with an irritated look on her face. I stood there with my hand on my hip in my pissed off stance and stared her down until she realized she better not play with me today, and she drove off. I was wasting too much time. I needed to get inside of the mall and get lost before Mike found me. I started power walking in my black pumps, and as soon as I got to the double doors to go inside, I heard Mike, sounding like he was out of breath, and his reflection appeared through the glass in front of me.

I didn't turn around at first. I just stood there staring at the glass on the doors, fixing my face to seem like I was elated. I slowly turned around to find Mike Jogging, trying to catch up to me. I can't even lie. He was looking scrumptious which was even more reason for me to run as fast as I could! I didn't need to be around any good-looking men at that time, as horny as I had been lately! It had been three months since I'd had some, and when you're pregnant, it's even worse because those hormones have a sista going crazy! Mike had on an ocean blue fitted Aeropostale T-shirt, which he probably intentionally bought a size too small, so he could show off his huge biceps and perfect abs on that sexy 6'2" physique.

When he finally reached me, he swept me up off the ground, hugging me and twirling me around. When he put me back down, he just stared at me with a sneaky grin on his high yellow face, and shook his head.

"Girl, I don't care what you've been through or where you've been, you are still sexy as hell!"

He licked his juicy pink lip just like L.L. would do. He was fine as hell. Even finer than I had remembered. He still had his sexy goatee, but had grown out his black wavy hair a little bit. I always liked men to have short low cuts, but the change looked good on him.

We walked into the mall together as if we were a couple, with him not being able to take his eyes off of me. The last thing I had said to Mike the last time I saw him was that it should've been him, meaning, if I was gonna cheat on Terrance, I wish it would've been with him. I truly meant it when I said it, but now was a bad time. I didn't need any distractions in my life right now while I was trying to pull everything together and make sense of it all.

"You look like you've put on a little weight since you've been away, but it looks good on you," Mike said, as I browsed the shoes on one of Nordstrom's shoe tables.

Obviously, he hadn't noticed my baby bump, which I was glad of because I really didn't want to discuss that with him, especially since he knew that I had cheated on Terrance. I was glad that I decided to wear my black and silver halter-top that flared at the bottom. On top of that I wore my short red leather jacket, so I concealed what Mike may have otherwise noticed.

"Yes, I did put on a few pounds. Thanks for the compliment. You were always good with those," I said, blushing a bit.

"No problem. An attractive, smart woman always deserves for someone to tell them how nice they look. You have that natural beauty that not too many women are blessed with."

I could feel my clit swelling, and I knew this conversation was not leading to anything nice, but I didn't know how to get rid of him. Out of all the calls that I had been getting, my phone wouldn't ring for shit! At least then I could say I had an emergency and leave his ass standing right there. He made me feel so weak. Even though we had never had any sexual contact, while he was talking to me, all I could think about was the day I sat on my patio and he came over, massaged my shoulders, and we shared that one kiss that felt like Heaven. That's as far as it ever went with Mike, and I planned on it staying that way. If his kiss felt that good, ain't no telling what making love to him would do to me. He would probably be able to get me to do whatever the hell he wanted, since he was older, and probably more experienced in the sex department, so I definitely knew I didn't need to go there! My first priority was going to be my baby!

I kept walking, browsing the racks, hoping Mike would abruptly say he had to leave. He owned his own business, in which he had good workers holding it down, so I knew there wouldn't be a possibility he would be called in to work, unless things had changed within the past few months. Living next door to him, it seemed like he never worked, but he was living well.

"What you out shopping for, Kel?"

He would ask that, I thought. I couldn't be honest and tell him maternity clothes. Well, I could've, but that would've just opened another can of worms. I didn't even know why I cared if he knew I was pregnant, but all I did know was that I wasn't ready for him to know.

"I'm really just lookin'. I haven't been out shopping in a while, so thought I'd enjoy my Saturday off."

"Well, if you haven't had lunch, why don't we go sit down somewhere and eat so we can talk? I'd love to hear what you been up to."

I wanted so badly to say that I had eaten lunch already, but to be perfectly honest, WE were starving. I hadn't even eaten breakfast and my stomach was growling like crazy!

"Okay. Sounds good."

We walked out of Nordstrom's into the rest of the mall and people were everywhere. I had to think about what time of the year was. Was it tax time or the first of the month? It was neither of those, so I just figured the economy wasn't bad for everyone, but then again, some people had their priorities all messed up and would buy up everything in the damn mall, then couldn't pay their rent or mortgage.

As we walked towards the food court, I could see Mike glancing back and forth at me in the corner of my eye. It kinda made me nervous because it made me think he had figured it out.

"Why do you keep lookin' at me?" I exclaimed.

Mike at first looked startled. I guess he wasn't expecting that, but a person can only take so much of someone constantly staring at them. He grabbed my hand and held it gently, and without looking at me said, "I'm just admiring your beauty, but I'll stop if it makes you uncomfortable."

"Yes, it does."

We arrived at the food court, and I was glad because as soon as Mike had mentioned food, my stomach started turning flips.

"What do you have a taste for?" he asked.

I looked around at all the different choices. I hadn't eaten at Sbarro in a while, and Chicken Parmesan sounded great, so that's where we went and stood in line. After ordering, I went and saved us a table, while Mike waited for our food to come up. When he came over with a tray in his hand, he sat across from me, and I knew I would be forced to look at him throughout the entire meal. The scent of his cologne was captivating. He always did smell good, which I loved in a man. Especially a sexy one.

"Kel, I just wanna tell you again, it feels so good seeing you. I would say I've been miserable not being able to see you, but you probably wouldn't believe me anyway. Oh, I just said it, sooo . . . do you believe me?"

He gave me that little cute side grin showing only a few of his gorgeous white teeth.

I stabbed at my chicken with my fork, and said, "Now you know that's going a little overboard. Like I used to tell you before, I know there are plenty of women out there who you can have. We both know you are not limited!"

"And like I used to tell you, they are all about money. That's all a lot of these women look at. I'm not afraid of much, but one of the things I am afraid of is being with a woman who doesn't love me for me, and is only with me for my money. I need to be with someone who is sincere. Someone who I can feel I can trust."

I knew exactly where this was going, so I quickly changed the subject.

"So, how is Travis Inc. doing?"

Mike's last name was Travis, and Travis Inc. was the brokerage firm that he owned.

Mike laughed, knowing what I was trying to do since I made it quite obvious. "Kel, you are a trip, but since you wanna know, Travis Inc. is doing very well. The economy is doing a little better, the client's stock is doing better, they're happy, so we're happy. Matter of fact, I had just left the office when I got here. I had to tie up some lose ends with a new client."

"Whaaaat! You were actually at the office? I need to write this down! You know you never used to go to work," I said while I laughed joyously.

"What? I go to work. Just not as much as the average person. I'm blessed to be able to do a lot of work from home. That's why I would be the perfect family man."

There was that sexy smirk again! I didn't know how much more of this I could take! I was almost done with my Chicken Parmesan, taking the last few sips of my Coke. Mike had been done, and was just watching me eat while talking. He finally asked me the dreaded question.

"I don't mean to pry, but what's the current status of you and Terrance? Don't feel obligated to answer that if you don't want to."

Me, feel obligated? Yeah, okay. Mike must've really not known who he was talking to. Since we had broken the ice and it really wasn't a secret, I told him that I had filed for divorce, but I hadn't spoken to Terrance since the incident and he wouldn't sign the papers. Mike wasn't clear as to everything that had actually happened, so I felt comfortable enough filling him in on that.

"So basically, he slept with your friend, and now wants to contest the divorce?"

"Exactly," I said, clicking my nails on the table. "I was given a trial date in which he's supposed to prove the reason that I want a divorce is invalid, when the law clearly states that one of the valid reasons is adultery. And he clearly committed adultery! I asked that the date be rescheduled just because I feel the whole thing is ridiculous! I just don't understand why he's putting me through all of this. He made it very apparent that he wanted Tif to stay and for me to leave."

"Well, I don't see much of Terrance these days. I may see him once a week, if that."

I didn't want to seem like I cared, but I just had to ask. I lowered my voice as if I didn't want anyone else to hear, because I felt ashamed for even asking. "Do you ever see . . . her?"

Mike scratched his head before he started to answer the question and I already knew what that meant.

"If you're talking about that chick that don't got nothing on you, then, yeah, I do. Actually every time I do see him, he's with her."

Mike glared at me as though he was trying to study my reaction to what he had just said.

All I could say was "Oh." I then took a deep breath.

"Personally, I don't understand how he could've cheated on you with her. I truly mean it when I say she has nothing on you. She's one of those women I was talking about who wasn't blessed with natural beauty."

Mike's phone rang and he looked to see who it was and excused himself from the table. I sat there trying to get my mind off of Terrance and Tif, and Tif living it up in what used to be my house. I tried my hardest to focus on something else. I saw Mike standing near a window in the food court still on the phone. He caught me glancing over in his direction and winked at me. I wondered if he had someone in his life who he was dating. I definitely wouldn't be surprised if he did. It was probably her who he was talking to. A minute later, he was walking back towards me not looking happy.

"What's wrong?" I asked sounding concerned.

"Unfortunately, I have to cut our lunch short. My client that I was telling you about is back at the office with some questions he would like answered, and he would prefer to speak with me rather than any of my well-educated, and overly qualified employees, so I guess back to the office I go."

I have to admit, I was a little disappointed. I was enjoying Mike's company, and it felt good talking about things and getting some stuff off of my chest. He really seemed like he cared about what I was going through and how I was handling things.

He grabbed the tray from in front of me, and went to a nearby trash to dispose of everything. I was standing by the time he came back. He grabbed me and hugged me again, whispering in my ear how he wished he could stay longer. He said that he would like it if we could keep in touch. He didn't want to risk losing contact again, so he asked for my telephone number. I pulled out my cell phone and asked for his number. As he recited the number, I dialed it in my phone. I heard his cell phone ring, then hung up.

"Make sure you save it," I said with a grin.

"I will, and you do the same," Mike said as he kissed me on the cheek, leaving it slightly moist.

I watched Mike as he walked away. Once I could no longer see him in the distance, reality kicked in, and I started on my way to Motherhood, hoping to find some flattering maternity clothes.

Chapter 3

Getting out today really made me feel good. Maybe that's what I needed instead of trying to hide from the world, feeling sorry for myself. I even found some stylish maternity clothes that I wouldn't feel ashamed to be seen in, and they were a lot more comfortable than my regular clothes that I had been squeezing in to. I would finally be able to let my belly breathe! I was amazed to see that there were maternity skinny jeans in all colors, and plenty of cute tops to choose from that didn't make me look like a balloon! I guessed these fashion designers finally figured out that pregnant women wanted to be sexy too! I know I did!

While I was out and feeling good, I decided to drive around a little bit and see what I hadn't been missing. I took a ride near the beach, which of course was empty because summer was long gone and the cool weather had set in. I rode past Hair Haven, the shop that I worked at and it was packed, like it always was on a Saturdays, but most of the clients were mine most of the time. I knew I had better hurried my ass up and got back to work before they found them someone else to do their hair, but I knew if they had, they would come runnin' back. I was the baddest bitch in the Chi when it came to hooking up some hair. I didn't only style hair. My clients were assured with me being their stylist that they would also have healthy hair.

I thought about riding past my old house, which now belonged to Terrance, but I was afraid of what I might've seen. I was more afraid of how I would react, so I decided against that. Maybe another day in the near future I would be ready to face my fears. Seeing Terrance and Tiffany together would probably be way too much for my mind to handle right now. I drove in circles for a while, not wanting to go in because I felt so good. I thought everything would go back to normal and I would fall back into my state of depression once I got home but I knew I couldn't stay out forever.

As soon as I walked up to my door and put my key in, my cell phone started ringing. I couldn't grab it because my hand was full of bags from Motherhood. I got in the house, slipped off my black pumps with a sigh of relief, and took my bags upstairs to my bedroom. Forgetting my phone even rang, and not realizing how tired I was, I dove onto my king-sized bed, and drifted into the wonderful world of sleep.

I was in such a deep sleep that when my phone started ringing again, I thought it was in my dream. My mouth open, I finally realized it wasn't a dream, and cracked open one eye. Without moving anything, except one arm, I felt around for the phone and by the time I reached it, it had stopped ringing. My call history showed it was Mike calling, and it was him who had called earlier when I first got home. If he did leave a message, there was no way I was gonna check it because I had a million others and it would've probably taken over an hour for me to listen through all of them to finally get to his.

I laid there, contemplating on whether or not I wanted to call Mike back. I really didn't know what to expect from him. What else did we possibly have to talk about? I didn't think he would ever settle for being just my friend, and that's all I really needed right now. I knew one thing for sure about Mike, and that was he was very persistent. I may have made a big mistake just by giving him my number. I didn't wanna lead Mike on causing more drama than necessary in my life, so I decided to go ahead and call him and tell him the truth.

The phone rang one time and Mike answered. "Hey, sexy. I was worried about you."

"Worried about me? Why?"

"I've been trying to call you as I'm sure you can see."

"Just because I don't answer doesn't mean I'm laid out on the side of the road somewhere in harm's way. If you didn't know, I do have a life!" I said sarcastically.

I think Mike realized he had offended me and he backed off and tried another route. I didn't know why men felt like every time they called, we, women were supposed to answer. I'd had enough of that shit. No man was about to run me! My man or not! Some may think I blew the whole thing out of proportion, and maybe I did, but I blame it on the hormones. That was the nice thing about being pregnant. I could blame everything on the hormones!

"I was just calling to tell you again that I really enjoyed lunch with you and I apologize that I had to suddenly leave. I wish I could've spent the whole day with you, baby."

I suddenly felt this strange flutter in my stomach. I didn't know if it was the baby, or butterflies, but it was a wonderful feeling, however, I couldn't let Mike get in my head. I had to be strong, but I knew if he had been in my presence at that very moment, it would've gone down!

My dumb ass responded, saying, "It would've been very nice spending the day with you. I would've really enjoyed that."

"Well, it's not too late."

There was dead silence in the phone. I didn't know how to respond, because, actually it wasn't too late. It was only a quarter 'til seven, and we didn't have anything but time and opportunity on our side. I just kept picturing those big, muscular arms, those sexy lips, those abs . . . Shit! Everything about him was arousing! I then remembered what I was calling to tell him. I had second thoughts, since that minor detail may have changed the whole mood. I would tell him, just not now.

"Kel, you there?"

"Yeah."

"So, is it okay if I come by? Or I can come by and pick you up."

"Um, I do have a car!"

"I know, babe, but it's getting late, and I wouldn't want you out driving by yourself once we go our separate ways. At least if I come get you, I can make sure you get back home safely."

I didn't know whether or not Mike was just that considerate, or he was really trying hard to get in my head so he could get him some. Some men think they are so slick, but I couldn't quite read Mike's sincerity yet.

"You can just come by here. I really don't feel like getting back out tonight."

I thought I heard Mike smile through the phone. I gave him my address and he said he was already out and not far from where I lived, so he would be here in about ten minutes. That gave me just enough time to find something sexy, yet discreet and comfortable to put on before he got here.

My heart was beating out of control, as I ran around the house, making sure everything was perfect. I threw on my black leggings and loose black top that hung off one shoulder, and put a little of my Vera Wang perfume behind each ear. As I walked past my full-length mirror in my bedroom, taking a final look, the doorbell rang. I spoke through the intercom making sure it was Mike. As soon as I heard his seductive voice, I buzzed him in.

He, of course had the same thing on from earlier. I guess his clients didn't mind him being casually dressed while he talked money with them. He must've been really good at his job. I was sure he was probably good at a lot of other things too.

I opened the door wide, welcoming him in. Before he was able to get in the door, just by looking at Mike, I was ready to open my legs wide and welcome him in. I turned around to close the door behind him, and when I turned to face him, he was standing in the middle of the living room with his hands in his pockets looking around in amazement.

"Wow, Kel. This is really nice. I'm really proud of you for moving on the way you have."

I told him I appreciated that, and he walked over to me with his arms open wide. I fell right into them, and he kissed me on the top of my head. He held me tight and I felt so safe and secure in his arms. He took his hand and put his index finger under my dimpled chin, lifting it until we were looking into each other's eyes. He slowly eased his face towards mine until our lips met. His perfect lips were softer than I had remembered. I wrapped both of my arms around his neck, pulling him closer to me and holding him tighter as our tongues intermingled inside each other's mouths. As we continued kissing, we both moaned as though we were making love. Mike began walking, forcing me to walk backward toward the sofa. Once I felt the back of my leg hit it, I slowly sat down trying my best not to let our lips part.

Mike let go of me, and I watched him quickly pull his T-shirt over his head. As soon as I saw what was underneath, my clit began to throb, calling for Mike to relieve it. I didn't wanna seem desperate, so I tried not to be aggressive. I knew how bad I wanted him, but he sure as hell didn't need to know.

He laid me back and gently sucked my neck and earlobes. His touch was so tantalizing. He just didn't know what he was doing to me. Or maybe he did.

"I want you to be mine. Can you be mine, Kel?"

I heard what he said, but I was lost in the moment and unable to answer. He continued to talk, telling me how long he had waited for this moment, as his hands wandered up and down my spine. I felt my titties relax as he unclasped my bra. He slid his body off of me onto the floor, and I could feel a breeze on my belly as he attempted to lift my shirt with his teeth.

That was my reminder that I hadn't shared my little secret with Mike yet, and I sat up and hurriedly pulled my shirt down. The look on his face asked what he did wrong. He hadn't done a thing wrong. Actually, he was doing everything right, which was the problem.

"Mike, I'm sorry, but we can't do this," I said in a shameful tone.

"Why not this time, Kel?" he asked in an irritated tone; one in which I had never heard him use. I understood why he was using that tone when I looked down at his jeans and saw the huge bulge that I had helped create.

Seeing that just made me wanna give him some pussy even more, just because I kind of felt sorry for him. I didn't want him to think I was leading him on, and I definitely didn't want him to go home with blue balls. I really wasn't trying to seem like a tease, but it felt so good to be close to a man, I got lost in the moment. Mike rubbed his forehead like he was stressed, and continued with what he needed to say.

"You said you couldn't do it before, but at least you had the excuse that I was your neighbor and you were with your husband! As far as I know you're single. Not single-single, but you know what I mean. Maybe I should say readily available. I have feelings for you, and I would like to think that you have feelings for me. When we kissed, I felt it, and I know you felt it too. You can't run from this. It's fate that we ran into each other today. I'm not the one to beg, but just give me a chance. I'll show you a whole nother world. You won't have to seek no other cuz I'll be all that you need. I care about you and that shit ain't gonna change!"

Damn! This man had just poured his heart out to me, and I had to turn around and break it. As he spoke to me, I realized he was an exceptional man. He had it all. A business of his own, beautiful home, nice car, compassion, and he cared abundantly for me. What would he want with someone like me? He could have any woman out there, and there were plenty of thirsty ones! Mike had no children, so what would he look like being with me and raising some asshole's child? I wouldn't even feel right allowing him to take on that responsibility.

"Mike, I know you're a really good man. I really do, and everything you just said is of value to me, but right now is just not a good time."

Mike opened his mouth to speak again, and I raised my index finger signaling for him to let me finish.

"Please trust me on this one. I don't wanna get into it right now, but just know I'm doing this because I do care for you. I really wish this could work, but it always seems to be bad timing for us. Maybe that's a sign that it's not meant to be."

I thought Mike was gonna try to talk me out of my decision again, but without saying a word, he got up, put his shirt on, and walked out the door, slamming it behind him. I sat there in shock, staring at the door, knowing that he was gonna walk back in. I realized he had really gone when I heard his car door slam and his Porsche speed off.

That night was a rough one. While I lie in bed, attempting to get some sleep, I smelled the scent of Mike all over me. I kept thinking about how close I was to satisfying my hunger with one of the sexiest men I had ever seen. I was restless. I kept my eyes open because every time I closed them, I visualized his chest, arms, lips, and smile. I could even feel his touch for a brief moment. I had to do something to relieve this feeling so I did something I hadn't done in a long time because I refused to tease myself, but right now I was both desperate and beyond anxious.

I got up and stepped into my walk-in closet, hitting the light switch. I looked up at the top shelf and saw my favorite pink box, where I knew I would find Mr. Ultimate Indulgence. If you'd like to know, he was my purple dildo that had 8 speeds and 8 different functions. I paid a lot of money for him at one of Tasha's "Erotica" Parties. Erotica was a sex toy company, and Tasha's freaky ass was an "Erotica" consultant. Mr. Ultimate finished off many of my nights with a bang while I was with Terrance. That's why I didn't complain much about Terrance being a minuteman, because what he didn't do, Mr. Ultimate indulgence was sure to do! I was so wet thinking about Mike, I didn't even have to pull out the K-Y jelly. I spread my legs and my man on batteries went to work! He moved in circles, forward, backward, and whatever else my heart desired. As he worked, I closed my eyes imagining it was Mike satisfying my every need. After having the best and only orgasm in three months, I was in such a deep sleep, I felt comatose.

Chapter 4

It was Tuesday morning, which was a hair-stylist's Monday, and it was time for me to get back on the grind. It wasn't just me I had to think about now. My savings was dwindling from having to make such a sudden, drastic move, paying attorney's fees, and then needing to take some time off didn't help either. Bills certainly didn't pay themselves, which would've been quite nice at this point in time!

When I walked in the shop, someone was already sittin' in my chair. She wasn't one of my regulars. In fact, I had never seen her before, so I figured she must've been a walk-in. The other three stylists, Cameron, Rhonda, who was the owner, and Isis, all had clients they were working on. I was actually surprised to see them at work so early. I was normally the first one there to open up shop. I didn't have any appointments for about another hour, so a little extra money in the meantime was always good.

"Hey! I'm Kel," I said, introducing myself to the client in my chair.

She barely smiled when she told me her name was Jada. She was a very pretty woman, but seemed kinda quiet, so it was a bit uncomfortable. I don't think she ever read the Beauty Shop handbook which clearly stated that you must gossip and tell all of your business when you go get your hair done. There's no better place to vent. No information is too much information in the beauty shop. Tell it all or go home!

"Kel, you look mighty sassy today with your thick self!" Cameron said as she curled her client's hair.

I had put on one of my new maternity outfits, which I must say, was pretty sassy, since I vowed that I would not be uncomfortable during this pregnancy another day.

"Thanks Cam, but I know you're not calling anybody thick with that big ole badonkadonk. Just give me a little bit of that!"

Everybody in the shop busted out laughing, including Jada! Something about her seemed so familiar, but I just couldn't put my finger on it. Cameron did have a big ass, but she had the smallest waist I had ever seen. It seemed strange, but she worked the hell out of it! Even though Cameron was older than the rest of us, she still fit in. She had the best style out of all the stylists. She wore her hair in a cute, short asymmetrical bob-like cut, resembling Megan Good. She reminded me of Queen Latifah in the face, with beautiful high cheekbones, and a jet-black mole on the left one. She always found clothes that complemented her shape well. I got along with the other stylists. I just didn't trust them. Just like I didn't trust Cameron. She could be cool as hell, but could turn around two seconds later and be a bitch. That was the Gemini in her!

"Girl, you can have it all! I've been trying to do me some Zumba to get rid of this big ole thang!" Cameron said, turning her ass towards the mirror and smacking it.

"I wish I did have an ass!" Jada said.

"Girl, you got you a cute little shape. Be careful what you ask for! Actually, you remind me a lot of Kel!" Cameron said.

Everybody in the shop nodded in agreement. Maybe that was who she reminded me of. Myself. Not to sound arrogant, but she was very pretty, just like me, and we had a lot of the same features. While I was finishing Jada's hair, she had finally opened up a lot, telling me she was a teacher's aide at one of the elementary schools in the area. She grew up in the same part of Chicago I did, and we went to the same high school. She graduated two years before me, but I didn't remember her. She didn't have any kids, but she asked about my pregnancy, and whether I wanted a boy or a girl. I really didn't have a preference, although, I thought about how I was growing up and was a bit concerned about having a girl. You know the saying, "What goes around comes around!"

When I finished her hair, I realized this chic was a bad ass bitch! She didn't look like anybody's teacher's aide. She was gorgeous! She was a tad bit lighter than me, around 5'6" and thin, but had a few curves. She also had thick, perfectly arched eyebrows. Her dark brown hair with golden blonde streaks came a little past her shoulders, so I gave her some of my famous "Kim Kardashian" curls. The style fit her perfectly. She was so impressed with my work, she asked for my appointment book so she could write down her next appointment. I could tell she was real cool and down to earth. Even somebody I might've been able to hang out with.

As soon as Jada walked out of the shop, almost every woman in there did exactly what women do! Tried to hate! They knew that they didn't have anything to say about that girl, so they talked about how thin she was. Each and every one of their asses wished they could've been her size. It wasn't like she was anorexic thin. She just had a small frame. Matter of fact, Jada wasn't much smaller than me, minus being pregnant, so that had me wondering, what the hell they said about me when I wasn't around??? Women just couldn't seem to compliment each other. I give credit where credit is due, and Jada was beautiful. If I was a man, she could get it!

A few minutes later, a car jetted past the shop window and Jada was the driver. I noticed she was driving the new 2012 Audi R8 Spyder. I only knew what it was because I had looked at it, before realizing it was a one-hundred-thirty-thousand-dollar car! I walked out of the dealership that day holding my head down in shame! Hers was silver and clean as hell. It seemed strange because I knew a teacher's aide's salary wasn't paying for no Audi! Especially that one. Hell! A teacher's salary probably couldn't afford that, and she was just the help! I worked on my next client, still thinking, trying to make it all add up, saying in my head, "Teacher's aide, Audi, teacher's aide, Audi." Then I thought, maybe she just grew up in a family with money. That was certainly a possibility. I wasn't the one to hate on anybody, so, however she got it, she got it.

The next few days went by extremely fast, and were very profitable. My customers were so loyal that they waited for me to return so they could get their hair done instead of going to someone else. I knew one thing. They must've been a lot more loyal than me, because the way their heads were looking, I would've let anyone else do my hair! I had to ask a few of my clients if they had really been walking around with their heads looking like that. They laughed, but I was so, so serious!

I was surprised that I hadn't heard from Mike since he had sped off without saying a word to me. Maybe he had given up on me, but if so, I didn't know how I would feel about that. I enjoyed having a man pursue me the way that he did with such conviction, even though I knew I wasn't ready for a relationship with him. Honestly, I felt like I really wanted Mike, but I wasn't ready to be rejected once he found out the truth. What I didn't understand is how I felt this way now, but never wanted to give Mike a chance before. Maybe I was just vulnerable at the moment. I knew constantly wondering what he was workin' with was also influencing how I felt.

Leaving work for the evening, I decided to overcome my fear of seeing my soon-to-be ex-husband and Tif together. I had been going way out of my way, so I didn't have to go anywhere near the home Terrance and I once shared, afraid of seeing them. I was mostly afraid of what I might've felt or even did. I felt a nervous feeling in my stomach because I knew this would be a huge step for me.

When I finally got a block away from the house, I felt like turning around and going my normal route home, but I was determined to do this. I didn't know if it would do any good, or make me feel any differently, but I was definitely hoping so. I needed something to help me get past this. In a strange sort of way, I was hoping that I actually saw them outside together because maybe then reality could really set in, seeing that he was happy without me. Not saying that it wasn't reality catching the two of them fucking in my bed! I just needed more of a closure. I had been depressed and angry for long enough. I knew there was no future for Terrance and I, and I wouldn't take him back for anything in the world. I just wanted to have more peace with it.

As I slowly started driving down my old street, a few of my old neighbors saw me and waved. I honked my horn, and when I approached the house, coincidentally I saw Mike standing in his driveway talking to Terrance. I looked around to see if I saw Tif's car, since Mike had told me at lunch the other day that every time he saw Terrance, Tif was with him. I didn't see her or her car, and the next thing I knew, I felt like I wasn't in control anymore. Instead of continuing to drive, I pulled up right in front of Mike's house. Both Mike and Terrance looked over at my car, still talking as they both stared.

I took my time getting out the car because I didn't know what the hell I was doing there and what I was gonna do next. Walking up the driveway, I held my head up high and attempted to put on a fake smile. The expression on Mike's face didn't look very inviting. I assumed he was still upset from the other night, which, I didn't know if I could blame him. He probably went home with blue balls, because I know I would've been in bad shape if I hadn't had my battery-operated man.

I could tell Terrance was very uneasy, because I could see the sweat building up on his nose. That was always a sign that he was nervous. I walked up to Mike and gave him a hug, still smiling. I looked directly into his eyes with my arms still wrapped around his waist, and saw he was still looking lost. His arms remained at his sides.

"Hey, baby!" I said enthusiastically.

Thank God he decided to cooperate and didn't leave me out there lookin' stupid. That would've been a disaster, but I probably deserved it after what happened the other night. He held his head down and gave me a peck on the lips. Even though this was a game, that kiss still felt so real. Every time Mike kissed me, I had this indescribable feeling move through my body. My back was still facing Terrance, and I wished that I had eyes in the back of my head because I would've given anything to see his face!

It became completely quiet. All I could hear was the sound of cars flying down the street. Terrance and Mike must've spoken with their expressions because next thing I knew, Terrance told me to go wait for him in the house. I complied. As I walked further up the driveway, towards the front door, which was open, I felt like all eyes were on me. I went in and everything was exactly how I remembered it. I peeked out the window and saw the two of them talking, and it looked like they were in a deep conversation. I wondered what Mike would tell him. Would he lie and say we were in a relationship, or tell him the truth, which was he had no idea what I was doing there?

I sat on Mike's brown leather couch observing all of the pictures he had, which I had never paid attention to before. There were lots of old pictures with an older man and woman who I assumed were his parents, and a few pictures were of Terrance with a woman. They looked happy. I wondered if it was an old girlfriend, or maybe a current girlfriend who he failed to mention. Either way, I knew I would get it out of him. He didn't seem like the type to lie if I asked.

After about twenty minutes, I heard Mike come in and close the front door. When he finally appeared in the entryway to the living room, I still had a picture in my hand, which I quickly sat back on the table. Mike had the most serious look on his face that I had ever seen.

"Sooo, what happened?" I asked inquiringly.

Mike walked briskly towards me, grabbed me, threw me down on the couch, and laid on top of me kissing me intensely. I wrapped my long legs around his and held him tight. He stood up and pulled my pants down to my ankles, and carefully pulled them over my feet. I spread my legs to let him know I was ready this time and there was no turning back. I wanted to experience him inside of me. Mike got on his knees and tenderly kissed the inside of my thighs. I gyrated my hips and moaned, already able to feel what was coming next.

He all of a sudden stopped, and I opened my eyes to find him standing in front of me staring at me.

Please don't tell me the tables have turned and I'm the one being rejected this time! I said in my head.

It was almost as if he was reading my mind, because at that moment he relieved me of my insecurities and said, "I don't want to do this here. I want this to be perfect. I've been waiting too long for it not to be."

He picked me up and carried me upstairs to his master bedroom. It was huge . . . The room, that is! He had a king-sized, oval-shaped bed that had a million pillows on top of it. He sat me on the bed and before he could do anything else, I unbuttoned his jeans and pulled them down, exposing the bulge in his burgundy boxer briefs. He quickly stepped out of them, showing me how anxious he was to have me. I laid back while he pulled down my floral print thong, and spread my legs. I soon could feel his warm breath near the lips of my pussy. Moments later, I felt his tongue moving up and down the edges of my labia, nice and gentle. His smooth tongue felt heavenly. He slowly moved his tongue inside my pussy, and back out, tickling my clit with the tip of it. Mike knew exactly what to do and how I liked it. It was almost like he had trained for this moment.

He must've known I was about to climax from the way my body was shaking and the way I moaned, because he stopped, came up from my wet pussy and started moving up towards my stomach.

"I'm not ready for you to come yet, baby. I got a whole lot more to show you," he said in a low, soothing tone.

He put both hands on my hips and moved them up my body until he had raised my shirt as far as it would go. I raised my arms so he could pull it over my head. His huge hands moved up and down from my titties back down to my stomach. The last time he did it, I noticed that his hands remained still on my stomach. Suddenly, he got up and walked away. The moment the light came on, I tried to hurry up and grab something to throw on top of me, but I wasn't fast enough, and at that moment, I knew the truth was out.

Chapter 5

Mike stood at the light switch staring at me, while I sat there naked looking like a lost puppy.

"Kel, are you keeping something from me?"

I sat there quiet, not knowing what to say. I definitely couldn't lie about it, but still wishing I could. There was no way out of it. I should've just been straight up with him and told him the truth from the beginning. Then I wouldn't be sitting here looking stupid now. He would've told me he didn't wanna see me anymore, and that could've been that. But no, I always had make things more difficult than they had to be.

"Mike, I was gonna tell you, but I didn't know how you'd react. I was really feelin' you, and I didn't want this to change anything between us. That's why I left you hangin' the other night. I was fearful of the end result. I am so sorry. I thought it would've just been best if I stopped it right there, so I didn't have to explain anything, and go through the hurt of you finding out and leaving me alone."

Mike still stood in the same place, not attempting to come any closer to me. I had said my peace and couldn't think of another word to say. I got up and started putting my clothes back on, so I could get out of that uncomfortable situation quick, fast, and in a hurry.

"So did you think I would never find out?" Before I could answer, even though I didn't have a thing to say, he continued on. "I understand now why you did what you did the other night, but I'm not understanding why you would come over here today and start this up again, when you knew you were carrying around a lie."

"Hold up! I'm not carrying around a lie! I'm carrying a baby! My baby. This baby may be a part of someone I don't wish to have in my life, but it's also a part of me!"

After correcting him, he looked at me with no remorse in his eyes for what he had said, and said nothing. I understood him being upset, but he had no right speaking of my child like it was nothing. I finished getting dressed, then hesitantly walked towards him.

"Look, if you want me to leave, I'll leave. I'll understand. I wouldn't be happy if you lied to me about something so serious either."

"I think that would be the best thing for you to do right now."

When those words came out of his mouth, my heart skipped a beat. As I walked past him, he couldn't even look me in the eyes. I should've expected that, but I didn't. He was serious. Not the cool, laid-back, sympathetic Mike that I knew. I thought he'd at least follow me down the stairs, but he didn't budge. I wanted to at least know what was said between him and Terrance, but I guessed I'd never know. Mike was officially done with me and that was some hurtful truth for your ass.

What hurt so bad was that Mike was the only person able to get me out of my pitiful slump. After seeing him, my whole mindset changed, and I liked the way I was feeling. Before I walked out the door, I looked back one more time, hoping that Mike was coming up behind me. The room was empty, and I didn't even hear the sound of Mike moving around upstairs. It was quite apparent now that he wanted me to leave, so I did.

A couple of weeks had gone by, and I was getting out more and more, and going back to my normal routine. Business was back booming for me, and Jada had sent a lot of clients my way. She had even come back for her second appointment. I didn't know what it was about her, but we really clicked. We exchanged numbers and said we would have to go out soon. I had been spending time with my girl, Tasha, when she wasn't busy. Since Tasha and I were best friends, I didn't want her to get jealous seeing as though I was spending more time with someone else. Women could sometimes be petty like that, but I didn't know if Tasha would click with Jada the way I did. Tasha had a very strong personality that you just had to get used to. She never had many friends because she was a little intimidating at first and would scare people off.

I still hadn't heard from Mike, and wasn't expecting to. I wouldn't want anyone to be a part of my life who couldn't accept my child anyway. I did think about him a lot though, hoping deep down that he would come around, so that we could be friends again, at the least. I didn't want our friendship to end like this, especially when we were just reunited. If he never did contact me again, I really couldn't blame him. I wouldn't wanna be with anyone who had a baby on the way either, because I wouldn't wanna deal with the baggage of baby mama drama, among other things.

Because it had been such a busy week for me, I had been too tired each evening to stop at the bank to make a deposit, and I had way too much money on me. I didn't like to keep money on me because I was more prone to spend it. Terrance used to work at the bank not too far from my shop, but he should've finished his internship for law school by now, so I figured it was safe to go without seeing him. When I walked in the bank, it was crowded as hell, and I started to walk back out. Instead, I waited in the long line, and checked my email on my phone to make the time go by.

Finally I was called next, and what did you know. There was Stacy's pregnant ass. I almost said never mind, I'll wait for the next teller, but I didn't want to be so simple. As I was walking up, she stared at my belly, like she was analyzing it to see if it was just a beer belly. Hers was a lot bigger than mine. It made me wonder if she was having twins, and if they would be my baby's siblings, or if they really were Terrance's.

"Hello! How are you today?" Stacy said, trying to smile at the same time.

Since she wanted to be fake, I would be fake right along with her.

"I'm great! How about yourself?"

"Oh, hanging in there!" she said, rubbing her belly with a devious grin.

She just didn't know I was laughing at her ass. I knew Terrance wasn't thinking about her, while she was sitting up there trying to act like she was about to have a big happy family.

"That's good." I handed her my money and deposit slip.

"Will that be all for you, Ms. Armstrong?"

This bitch was really trying to get under my skin by calling me by my maiden name. She knew damn well what she saw on her computer screen with those big pretty brown eyes.

"I'm sorry you're sadly mistaken, but it's Mrs. Moore, due to my husband not wanting to sign my divorce papers. He just can't let me go!" I chuckled. "That's men for you! But no sweetie. That will be all! Have a great day and be sure to wipe the egg off your face."

I turned around and walked out of the bank with more pride than I had walked in with. When I got in the car, I checked my bank receipt to make sure that bitch didn't try to pull some slick shit, and put it in a safe place for future reference. She needed her job now more than ever, so she had better not tried to play any games with my account. I pictured Stacy putting her closed sign up to her window to go to the bathroom and cry. People need to be well prepared when they call themselves going in on me. I laughed at her ignorance the whole way home.

Once I got in the house, I called Tasha to see what she was up to since I hadn't talked to her in a few days, and to see if she wanted to go with me and Jada to the movies and out for drinks tomorrow night after work. Well, Jada would have drinks, and I would have a few non-alcoholic daiquiris, I supposed.

"Hey, Kel girl!" Tasha said excitedly.

These days, Tasha, always sounded upbeat when I called her, so whenever she didn't, I knew something was seriously wrong.

"Hey, Tasha. What are you doing tomorrow?"

"Lemuel is takin' me out tomorrow. He said it's a surprise and I can't wait! Why? What's up?"

"I was just gonna ask you if you wanted to go to the movies with me and the girl Jada I've been telling you about. We're goin' somewhere to just chill afterward, but since you're going out with your boo, I understand!"

We both laughed. I was so glad to see Tasha finally had a good man, from what I could tell so far! He treated her good and accepted her loud, ghetto ass for who she was. Actually, she had calmed down a bit since being with him. I would get jealous sometimes because it used to be whenever I wanted to go out, Tasha was always available, but now, Lem took up a lot of her time, but that was cool because she was happy.

I heard a knock at the door and said, "Girl, let me see who this is at my door. I'll talk to you later," I said rushing Tasha off of the phone.

It was strange because no one had rang the doorbell so I could buzz them in the building, so I figured it was one of the neighbors. I opened the door and my eyes got so big they felt like they were gonna pop out of my head. My heart was beating double time.

"So, what's up for dinner beautiful?"

Mike stood there with a dozen yellow roses in his hand, and extended his arm to give them to me. I grabbed the roses and stood in the doorway not inviting him in. This was exactly what I wanted, but now that it had happened, I was pissed.

"I know how I reacted was wrong, and I just wanna apologize for that and make it up to you however I can. I've been rehearsing what to say to you over and over again, and realized it was a waste of time. You can't rehearse what's already in your heart. Sorry it took so long."

I just stood there with my arms folded, trying my best not to smile, or show any other type of emotion. I was waiting on him to keep going, while he was waiting on me to tell him to come in. I was gonna make him grovel, even though I knew I was wrong too, but I had already apologized, and didn't know what else to do or say. I was pregnant, and that wasn't gonna change.

"I'm sorry, Kel. Can I please come in so we can talk?"

I moved from the doorway so he could walk in. He looked at me like he wanted to hug me, but I think he looked at the expression on my face and decided against that. He sat down in the living room and waited for me to come over. He patted the seat next to him on the couch, signaling for me to sit there. I decided to sit in the chair across from him.

"Look, I know you're mad. You have every right to be. But you have to understand where I was coming from too. A lot was sprung on me at once, and I didn't know how to react. Again, I apologize. I'm so embarrassed for the way I acted. I was very immature, and you know that's not the man that I am. I took too much time pursuing you to just let it end like this. You know how I feel about you."

Whenever Mike spoke, it was with so much sincerity. I couldn't even stay mad at him. He still hadn't addressed the baby though. That's the part I was waiting for. It seemed like he was only expressing his apologies about the way he had acted. I figured I would bring it up, so we could fully discuss the entire issue before getting my hopes up.

"I accept your apology, Mike. And again, I apologize for keeping the pregnancy from you. So what does the future hold for us?"

"I was actually hoping I could take you to dinner and we could discuss everything over a nice meal. But if you prefer, we can discuss it right here, right now."

I agreed to go out to dinner, since I hadn't eaten yet. Maybe this would be our last date. I didn't know what Mike's thoughts on this situation were. He waited for me while I showered. I hated going anywhere after I left the shop because I always felt like I smelled like hair spray, spritz, and relaxer. On the way to dinner, I asked Mike what he and Terrance were talking about when I went in his house the day he found out I was pregnant. He said that Terrance asked him if we were we together, and he told him we were just good friends, waiting to see what happens. He said Terrance got upset and called me a few names and tried to bring up the fact that I had cheated on him and I would do the same to Mike. Mike said that he stopped him before he could go any further and told him that even though we were going through some

things, we needed to respect each other since we once both once
loved each other enough to get married. After Mike told me that
much of the conversation, he asked that we didn't talk about
Terrance anymore. He said he just wanted to enjoy the ride with
the most beautiful woman in the world sitting next to him. I
obliged.

Dinner started off quiet, as we both looked through the menu at
the Olive Garden. The high yellow waitress, with the cutest short
haircut came by the table and asked what we'd like to drink, and
went over the wine specials. She raved about one of their red wines
that I could tell she loved. She got excited just by talking about it.
Mike and I caught each other's eye and smiled, as she continued.

"So would you like to try that, Ma'am?"

I rubbed my hand over my stomach and said, "I would've
loved to. You make it sound so good, but I'm expecting."

"Oh, I'm so sorry. I hadn't noticed, but congratulations to the
both of you," she said, sounding embarrassed.

I glanced over at Mike, and he smiled and told her thank you.
He looked a little uncomfortable, but I was just glad he wasn't an
asshole and said something like it's not his, or something else
stupid that a man might've said. We both ordered Cokes and
continued to look through the menu.

"Here you two, or should I say three, go!" she laughed loudly,
exposing her cute dimples as she sat our glasses down and took our
orders.

When she walked away and I picked up my glass to take a sip,
Mike obviously had something on his mind.

"Is that good for the baby?"

"What, Coke?" I asked, cracking up.

"Yeah," he said without even a hint of a smile. "I didn't think it
was good to drink pop while you're . . . you know . . ."

"**PREGNANT?!?!?**" I said, enunciating each letter. "Why
does it seem like you're scared to talk about it? I'm pregnant, I'm
pregnant, I'm pregnant!"

I guess I got a little loud because our neighbors sitting in the
booths in the front and back of us turned around in their seats
trying to see what was going on.

Lowering my voice, I said, "I'm sorry, Mike. These hormones get me to acting crazy sometimes. I know it's hard for you to accept, and if you can't, then we probably should go our separate ways."

"Kel, quit trying to push me away. It's just gonna take some getting used to. I brought you here so we can talk and that's what I wanna talk about. I know you won't believe it, but I love you. I know I don't know everything about you, but I know enough to know how I feel. I wanna be there for you and the baby through this, but in order for me to do that, I need for you to be honest about everything, so first and foremost, who is the father?"

I knew that question would be coming soon, and I should've been prepared to answer, but of course I wasn't. I could've just said Terrance's, but I knew if it wasn't his, it would come out one day, and there would stand another lie on my track record. I had just started over with Mike with a clean slate, and I didn't wanna start off with a lie, but how do you say, I don't know who the father is, without sounding like a hoe? I guessed I would just have to do my best.

"Well, as you already know, I wasn't faithful when I was with Terrance . . ."

"So, it's the other guy's?"

"Not exactly. Let me finish. Not the guy you saw me with that day. It only happened with him once, and no, there's no possibility it's his."

Mike was referring to Reggie, assuming it was his because of the day he saw us leaving my house together, while Terrance was supposed to be at work. He watched me intensely, anxiously waiting on every word that came out of my mouth.

"There was a guy I told you a little bit about . . . Someone else I was involved with. It was much more serious. You probably remember me telling you about Ty, but didn't believe me when I told you how serious it was. I'm gonna be completely honest with you. I don't know if the baby is Terrance's or Ty's, and I don't wish to know."

Mike was very quiet, and I asked him did he have any more questions or anything to say.

"So, what do you plan on doing once you start getting bigger, and Terrance or Ty sees you, and asks you if the baby is theirs?"

"I haven't thought that far ahead yet, but from what I know, I don't have to worry about Ty. I think he's dead."

Mike sat back in his chair, looking like he was asking himself what the hell he had gotten himself into. I told him it's a long story, and he responded by saying all we have is time. Our food came, and as we ate, I started from the beginning of my relationship with Ty. I also told him why I believed Ty to be dead. Mike said that we would just have to take it day by day, and he was willing to accept full responsibility of the baby if no one asked questions or stepped up. He wanted to show me how loyal and dedicated he was to me. I couldn't believe him. Did he understand what he was saying? The rest of our meal was a lot more relaxing since I got a lot off my chest, and Mike and I talked about a lot of things that needed to be discussed. I even asked him about the woman he was with in the picture at his house, and was relieved with his explanation. It was his sister, Michelle. I was relieved because I didn't have it in me to deal with any other drama. I just wanted everything else to go smooth without any kinks, but who was I kidding? We were talking about my drama-filled life!

Mike and I really enjoyed the night. There was something powerful that came over my mind and body when I was around him. It felt like I had not a care in the world. I wished that I had met him before I met Terrance. If I had, I could've avoided everything that I had gone through and currently going through. We rode around the Chi, admiring all the beautiful lights and skyscrapers. Chicago was so beautiful at night. We drove down Lakeshore Drive, and when I saw one of the brightly lit ships out in the distance on the water, I knew we were close to Navy Pier. They had Firework shows every Friday night, and we made it just in time to watch. We sat in the car which seemed much more enjoyable and romantic.

Mike and I pulled up in front of my condo after watching the vivid firework display, and being the gentleman he was, he got out, opened my car door, and grabbed my hand to help me out. I put the key in the keyhole, and before I could turn it, Mike lightly grabbed my waist and twirled me around towards him. The wind blew a strand of hair in my face and Mike gently placed it behind my ear.

"I love you, Kel, and I'm gonna work hard, keep everything how it is and how we feel right now at this moment, so you'll never be able to say you want it how it used to be. All of the other women I've even come close to taking seriously have all been superficial, but you're different, and I've always been able to feel that."

The next thing I knew, our lips met, and Mike slowly drew back, taking my bottom lip with him part of the way. He then knelt down and raised my blush pink blouse slightly and kissed my round belly. I felt myself inhale the cool air, then exhale with my eyes closed. When we finally made it into the house, after our cherished moment, Mike carried me up to my bedroom, completely undressed me, admired my body, and made passionate love to me. It was something that had been greatly desired by the both of us for a long time, and it was very evident! He showed me things I had never seen before, and made me feel something that I had never felt before. I had an idea of what I had been missing out on, but now I truly knew. I was missing out on a whole lot more than I could've ever imagined.

Chapter 6

When the alarm clock started beeping loud as hell in my ear, I opened my eyes unable to see anything with all of my hair covering my face. The sheet covered half of my torso, and I lay there limp, with one leg hanging off the bed. I slowly lifted one arm up to shut off the annoying noise and I felt movement behind me. I turned around facing the most gorgeous man I had ever seen. Mike was so enticing, even with morning breath. I couldn't think of any better word for him besides exceptional.

"Well, you know what that means," I said to Mike, dreading the fact I had to leave and go to work, but again, the bills definitely weren't paying themselves.

"Do you gotta go, babe? I wanted to spend some more time with you."

"We have plenty of time," I said and smiled, as I kissed Mike and raised my naked body out of bed.

While in the shower, singing Tamia's "Beautiful Surprise," which I felt was very appropriate for the moment, I heard the faucet to the bathroom sink turn on.

"You have a gorgeous voice. I never knew you sang."

"It only sounds that good in the shower!" I said as I laughed.

"So, do we have a date tonight?"

"Sounds good! What do you have in mind?"

Before Mike could start, I said, "Oh shit. I forgot. I have plans tonight."

I heard the faucet turn off and it got very quiet. I peeked out of the shower and Mike was standing in the mirror washing his face with my face scrub! *Oh well. If he was gonna be my man, he had to have clear skin,* I thought.

"Yeah, I'm still here. So you gonna tell me what kind of plans you have?"

"I'm just going to the movies with a friend of mine, Jada."

"Okay. So how late do you plan on being out?"

I couldn't believe Mike was asking me all these questions. I had just gotten used to being single, not having to answer to anyone, and it was still too soon to be answering to him! I wasn't interested in anyone else, but I also didn't wanna feel tied down either. I still felt we needed time to get to know each other better. We knew how we felt about each other and that was enough for now. Maybe I was just still paranoid and had my guards up a little, but I thought that was normal, under the circumstances. Not enough time for me had passed yet to just open all the way up to Mike. For now, I just wanted to take things one step at a time. Whether he liked it or not, I was going out and was gonna have a good time with one of my girls. I just hoped he understood just because I gave him some pussy, didn't mean he owned me.

"Ummm, I'm not sure what time. Do I have a curfew?" I asked sarcastically.

"No, you don't have a curfew. I just wanted to see if maybe we would have time to do something once you got back. Sorry if I offended you."

Now his ass wanted to make me feel guilty, but I wasn't falling for it.

"No. Probably not. We'll just plan something for another day," I said, as I stepped out of the shower and grabbed my towel off the rack.

Mike tried to hide it, but I could see right through him. He
looked pissed, but I knew he'd get over it and be okay. He didn't
come this far for nothing. We both finished getting dressed and
walked out together. We shared a kiss and parted ways to begin
our day. Me, working, and him, whatever the hell he wanted to do!
Must've been nice was all I could say.

I knew today was gonna be a busy day once I got to the shop
and counted out sixteen appointments in my appointment book.
That didn't include the walk-ins I knew I would have. I hoped that
I wasn't too tired to go out once I finished up for the day. I knew
Mike would've just loved that!

"Girl, you really got that pregnant glow going on! You look so
purty!" Cameron said, as she was yanking the mess out of this little
girl's hair. She wasn't the gentlest!

"Thank you, lady! And I feel great!" I said grinning from ear to
ear.

I knew my pregnancy had a lot to do with my glow, but what
Cameron and all the rest of the stylists didn't know was I had a lot
more to glow about. Mike had hit my G-spot so many damn times
the night before! I didn't think I had ever had so many orgasms. I
had to give it to him. He knew what he was doing in the bedroom!
I didn't know if it came from a lot of practice, or it came natural to
him. Whichever it was, he was blessed with what he had and his
knowledge on how to work it. I was already whipped by the dick,
but he wouldn't know that. Deep down, I did wanna ditch Jada and
go out with Mike, but I couldn't seem like I was desperate, even
though I was just a little.

I had finished half of my clients, and was sitting on the couch
in the waiting area, awaiting my next client, who was due in the
next half hour. I glanced out of the window and saw a colorful van
pulling up that had "Chuckle's" on the side with big bubbly letters.
I got up to open the door, and there came a clown, jumping out of
the driver's side. I was a little taken aback, not knowing what was
going on.

"What in the hell?" I said aloud.

Cameron and the other stylist's immediately stopped what they
were doing and ran over to the window, about to trample each

other trying to see what was going on. By that time, the clown was in the back of the van, getting something out.

"Y'all, that's Chuckles!" Cameron said excitedly.

"Okaaaay?!" I replied, waiting on that to mean something to me.

"Girl, she brings gifts! Maybe my new boo sent me something!"

I really hoped it was for Cameron because she got so excited she began rapidly clapping her hands. She bumped everyone out of the way with her wide hips, including me, to open the door for this big idiotic looking clown.

"Hey, Chuckles! What do you have there?" Cameron asked nosily.

Chuckles spoke with the cutest, shrieky, animated voice. She sounded a whole lot like Minnie Mouse. She held what looked like three dozens of roses in all colors, in a beautifully sculptured glass vase. She also held a box of my favorite Belgium chocolates. Whoever it belonged to was definitely gonna have to share!

"I'm looking for Kelicia Moore! I have a special surprise for her!"

"She's right there," Cameron said awkwardly, and walked back over to her station to continue working on her client who was sitting there, not so patiently, looking at her watch. Chuckles came and handed me the flowers and candy. She then said she would be right back. She came back in with another vase, that had its own individual design, but the roses in it were identical to the other.

"Someone must think you're really special! He's a keeper!" Chuckles said.

Was I really getting love advice from a clown? I giggled to myself and walked Chuckles out. I went to open the card, which was attached to the box of candy. I didn't know that Mike even knew that they were my favorite, but it was amazing what a man could find out about a woman he loved. I procrastinated for a minute before I opened the card, because I already knew everyone in there was waiting and were secretly watching. *Nosey heifas!* I thought.

I looked down to open the card and could feel everyone watching. I twirled around in my stylist chair until I got a little dizzy, and began opening it. The card was so nice and Mike always knew what to say to make me feel like the most special person to him in the world._Some people were_better expressing themselves in person than on paper, but Mike was apparently good at both. The card read:

Dear Kel,
I just wanted you to know that I think about you morning, noon, and night.
> **I love you and always will. I got you one for home and one for work, so you'll always be thinking of me. (Wink)**

Everything was so beautiful, thoughtful, and so on point. I was in a daze as I held the card and twirled in my chair again. All I could think was, *Damn! My pregnant pussy must be that oooooh weeee. It made that negro buy up the whole floral shop!* I smiled and laughed to myself. My concentration was broken from the sound of Cameron's voice.

"Stop before you make that baby dizzy. That can't be good for her!"

I didn't know whether I was having a girl or a boy, but Cameron was so determined for me to have a girl that she always referred to the baby as such.

"So you gonna tell us who the flowers are from?" Rhonda asked, without any shame.

Cameron said, "Quit being so nosey, Rhonda! Maybe she don't want us to know! Or maybe they're from a secret admirer! It's a secret, isn't it, Kel?"

Cameron knew damn well she wanted to know who they were from more than anyone else in there. I tried to keep a lot from Cameron, because like I said before, she could sometimes be a hater. When she felt like things were going too good for someone, she always had to put her negative two cents in, but I thought, maybe now since she had a man, she would have more compassion.

"No, y'all. It's not a secret. They're from a friend of mine who I've recently been seeing. His name is Mike."

"Awww! That's so nice. So how does he feel about the baby? There ain't too many men out there who are willing to accept another man's kid. And speaking of which, are you even divorced yet?"

I guess I had given Cameron way too much credit. She was still the same ole Cameron! Even on my wedding day when I was about to marry Terrance, she gave me a male-bashing talk, telling me and the rest of the shop how men were good at hiding things and I shouldn't trust Terrance because he was just like the rest of them. Well, I can't lie. What she said ended up being the truth, and yes, she threw it all up in my face the first time she got the chance. She, nor anyone else in the shop knew the specifics of what happened between Terrance and I, but they all assumed that he cheated. They weren't bold enough to go as far as asking me what happened between us. Not even Cameron.

"Not that it's any of your business, but I am still working on the divorce, and Mike isn't any ordinary man. I have explained to him everything that's going on, and he's willing to be a part of the baby's and my life. He is truly an exception to the rule."

Everyone in the shop was quiet as a mouse. They all knew when I was irritated, and when not to say another word to me. It remained that way until I left for the evening. Maybe Cameron would be more selective next time with the types of questions she asked. She didn't have any type of filter and that drove me nuts! Before leaving the others in the shop, I grabbed the vase with the prettiest design to take home, and my box of chocolates that I planned on devouring before the end of the night. Even though I was still mad . . . let me change that. My momma always taught me that only dogs get mad. So, even though I was still furious at Cameron, which resulted in me having an attitude with everyone, I was still cordial enough to tell everyone to have a good night.

I got home in just enough time to shower, put on something cuter than what I had on, and call Mike. He didn't pick up, but I left him a message telling him how sweet and thoughtful he was, and thanked him for the roses. He probably didn't answer, trying to play hard to get since he knew I was going out tonight. I had given him my house key just in case he wanted to stop by and wait for me to get home, so I figured he'd be good and ready for me once I came back from with Jada. I hesitated on giving him my key, but I trusted him. A few minutes later, Jada called telling me she was on the way. I had assigned her as the designated driver for the night, only because I wanted to ride in that bad ass Audi! I even made sure to wear some silver, just so I could match it and look good in it.

When I got in the car, I could smell Jada's perfume. It was a sweet, soft scent, which was quite familiar. Then it clicked. Ty had given me some perfume that smelled exactly like that when we were together and he felt like he had to shower me with gifts. Her makeup was flawless, and her outfit and shoes were on point. She still had her Kim Kardashian curls, but she had one side pinned up with a cute diamond barrette. The style was so cute, I just might've had to steal it. We stylists were always looking for something new to try on our clients or ourselves. Jada and I both looked like a million dollars. I really knew now that we would get along just fine. I wouldn't have to be worried about being embarrassed by something she wore or said, like I sometimes felt when I was with Tasha. Girl had class!

"Girl, I love that perfume you have on. I think I have the same one on my dresser somewhere."

"Thanks girl! It's called 'Captivate.'"

"Yep, that's it. I don't know why I stopped wearing it. I may have to try it out again."

I knew damn well why I had stopped wearing that perfume. I loved it, but after I left Ty alone, I couldn't wear it anymore because it reminded me of him too much, and he was one of the last people I wanted on my mind. I guessed I would have to deal with it tonight.

We finally made it to the movies and it was packed! I should've known better than to go to the show on a Saturday, but it was cool. Before we could even get out of the car, all eyes were on us. Men who were with their women intentionally walked behind so they could secretly look back at us. It was so crazy how bold men were. I actually felt bad for the women, but Jada and I just shook our heads at them and giggled. The women were just so naïve. They never once looked back to see what their men were behind them looking at. Their crazy butts probably thought they were looking at their asses.

Mike texted me during the movie just to tell me he loved me and was just thinking about me. Even though he did always seem sincere, I made sure to still keep my guard up so I didn't get hurt again. Quite frankly, I wasn't ready to throw the "love" word around yet, and I wouldn't until I was ready. Jada and I both enjoyed the movie, but I must be perfectly honest and say I loved the original version of the movie "Sparkle" a whole lot more, and Jada agreed. But what can you say. The original is better probably ninety-eight percent of the time.

Even though I had eaten popcorn, nachos, and a box of sour patch kids during the movie, I was still starving, and Jada thought it was funny! My appetite had increased so much during the past month and it wasn't funny at all. I would be big as a house before I knew it, which I definitely didn't want. I prayed so hard that I would bounce right back to my pre-pregnancy size after I dropped this load. We headed to La Fajita, which was a Mexican Restaurant/Bar in the city. When you wanted to get an excellent Margarita that was definitely the place to go. I was jealous because I couldn't have one, but somehow, I felt good watching Jada sip hers, imagining that my non-alcoholic frozen daiquiri was the same thing.

That night I found out when Jada got liquor in her, she talked a whole lot. I figured this would probably be the best time to get all the information I could out of her. I especially wanted to know how she could afford that car. I wondered where she lived. I would find out all of that tonight. *Keep 'em coming!* I thought.

Jada mostly talked about her boyfriend and I told her a few things about Mike. She told me how she thought her man would soon be popping the question. I asked her why she thought that, and she said because they had been going to jewelry stores looking at rings, and he would try to get an idea of what her taste was. She said he was from this area, but a few years older than her, which would've made him around twenty-eight. I asked his name, since I did know a lot of people, and she said his name was Silas Cooper. That name didn't ring a bell at all, so I moved on to a more important topic. I could tell Jada was really tipsy by looking at her glassy eyes, and she kept this little silly grin on her face the whole time we sat there, especially when we talked about Silas. I could tell she was in love.

"Jada, you have to tell me if your job is hiring! Maybe I can be a part-time teacher's aide!" I said as I stirred my third slushy drink."

"Why in the hell would you wanna do that?" she asked, with the grin disappearing from her face.

"I want that car, damnit!" I replied playfully.

"Girl, you'll never get that car in my line of work! Silas bought my car. He owns his own company, so I'm sure he and your boo would get along great. I remember you saying he owns his own too. They could relate to all that business talk. We should double date sometime."

"That would be fun! Mike is available most of the time. He works mostly from home, so just see when Silas would be available."

Jada was finishing up her last drink as we continued talking and laughing. She was a cool chick. When she finished, we grabbed our purses to leave, but before we did, Jada dug in her purse and threw a bill on the table. I looked and saw that it was a fifty. This girl had hit the jackpot and the jackpot's name was Mr. Silas Cooper.

The next morning, I woke up to the smell of pancakes, bacon, and eggs. I threw on my robe and went downstairs. There, I saw Mike at the stove, in a nice, navy-blue suite, white dress shirt, and matching tie.

"Good morning, sexy." Mike smiled as he watched me coming down the stairs.

"And where do you think you're going, looking all good?" I said as I walked over and wrapped my arms around his neck.

"Going to church. I need to thank God as much as I can for bringing you back into my life. It is such a blessing."

Mike was so mature, and his maturity was such a turn-on for me. I didn't like dealing with little boys. He was ten years older than me, but there were still men his age that I knew, and they still weren't as mature as he was. Most men his age would've tried to take advantage of a woman who was younger than them, but I wasn't having that. Mike wasn't the type to treat me like I was inferior in any way.

"How was your night out?"

"Oh, I had a great time. We will definitely have to hang out again. She would love for us to double date. She has a good head on her shoulders, and from what she said, sounds like her beau does too. He even owns his own business like you, so I'm sure you two would have a lot to talk about."

"Sounds like a plan. Just let me know when. I hope you didn't mind me texting you while you were out. I just missed you so much."

"Not a problem. It was nice to know I was being thought about," I said as I sat at the dining room table waiting to be served.

My roses were still sitting in the middle of the table where I had placed them. The card was sitting on the table next to the vase, which was not where I put it.

"Were you reading the card that you sent with the flowers?"

Mike was facing the stove, scrambling the eggs, and didn't respond. I figured he didn't hear me, so I repeated myself.

"Oh, yeah. I ordered them over the phone and told them what to put in the card, so I just wanted to make sure they did everything I told them to do, and put every word verbatim."

"So, did they?" I asked.

Mike came back with, "Did you like the message?"

"I sure did. I loved everything, from the cute clown, to the vases, to the flowers, right down to the lovely card."

"Well, then, yep, everything was perfect!"

Mike fixed our plates, and as soon as I cut my homemade pancakes and put a piece in my mouth, I chewed slowly with my eyes closed, savoring the delicious taste. I was never a big fan of pancakes, but after that, I became a huge fan! Mike had earned another brownie point. Brotha could throw down! I was so full, I couldn't get up out the chair. I leaned back, closed my eyes, and just rubbed my belly. I heard Mike's chair slide from underneath the table, and next thing I knew, he was behind me, giving me a massage, starting at my temples, down to my shoulders. He then pulled his chair up in front of mine, and lifted each leg one by one, messaging them, then my feet. I was in Heaven. After all that, he did the cutest thing and put his head to my stomach and started talking to the baby. He referred to himself as "Daddy Mike." I assumed he didn't wanna just say daddy, because it was such a touchy situation. I appreciated all the effort Mike put into making sure I was comfortable and happy.

Chapter 7

The next few weeks, I stayed in constant contact with my divorce attorney, trying to get that part of my life done and over with. I didn't feel completely free, and Terrance was driving me insane, not wanting to sign the papers. Why was he holding on? I couldn't understand. Maybe he knew it was driving me crazy and he was getting off on the thought of it. Frankly, I was tired of the back and forth, and I knew Mike was too because he would ask me questions about the progress every other day.

Ever since I had started pursuing the divorce so heavily, I had started getting lots of private calls on my cell phone. Whoever was doing it would just sit on the phone and listen to me asking who it was, until I would finally hang up. I figured it was Terrance playing games, but who knew. Maybe it was just a coincidence. Mike told me just to change my cell number, but I definitely couldn't do that. Everyone had my number, which included all of my clients, which in my eyes was all of my money. I would just have to deal with ignorance until they got tired.

After almost a whole month, my lawyer called me with a new court date, which would be almost another whole month away.

Now, there was no hiding that I was pregnant, and by the time my court date came around, I would almost be a full six months along. I was nervous about going into court, and Terrance seeing me. He still had no idea that I was expecting, and I wasn't thrilled to see what his reaction would be. I was hoping he wouldn't ask any questions, so that I wouldn't have to answer any. The best thing he could do for me right now was to leave me the hell alone.

Mike and I grew closer and closer and he confirmed many times over that he was all the man that I needed. I didn't look at anyone else, and I had no desire to be with anyone else. We did everything together. I enjoyed having a man who had time to spend with me, and not always having to go to work, or school like Terrance did. I think that's where our relationship went awry. We didn't make enough time for each other. Mike had practically moved in. His clothes filled up half of my walk-in closet, and the majority of the time, he spent the night with me. I enjoyed every minute of it, but believe it or not, I still hadn't told him that I loved him. He didn't pressure me though. He knew I would when I was good and ready.

Mike talked to the baby three to four times a day, and was sure to go to every doctor's visit with me. We found out that I was having a little girl, which I wasn't looking forward to before the doctor told us, but all of a sudden, a huge excitement came over me when "girl" came out of her mouth. I think Mike was more excited than I was. He had the biggest smile on his face that I had ever seen, and immediately began calling her his little princess. Now I just had to focus on thinking of a perfect name. It couldn't be anything over the top. I wanted her to have a name that would help her land one of the best jobs in the world. A lot of people don't think before they name their children. They give them all of these ole exotic names, and when executives run across that person's resume, it gets skipped just because they couldn't pronounce the shit. It's sad, but it was the truth. Her name would have some flavor to it, but flavor that everyone could relate to. I would think long and hard, because in my eyes, naming my baby would be one of the most important things I would do in my life. I was aiming for a name that guaranteed my daughter everything she deserved.

When I told the girls at the shop that I was having a girl, Cameron jumped her big ass up and down, screaming, "I told you! I told you!" What can I say? She was right again. First, about Terrance not being the perfect man for me. Now, she had correctly predicted the sex of my baby. Maybe I should've start listening to Cameron more often. I knew that wasn't even about to happen!

Tasha, my momma, Jada, and the girls at the shop all wanted to throw me a baby shower. I didn't wanna hurt anybody's feelings, so I told all of them they had great ideas and that they could all work together to throw me one big shower. I knew Cameron would still probably put something together to have at the shop. She was just like that. She had to always feel extra important. I hadn't yet introduced Jada to Tasha and my momma, and I was kinda worried. I was worried about my momma meeting her just as much as I was worried about Tasha meeting her. I knew my momma definitely didn't have a filter and didn't care what the hell she said. Especially if she thought someone or something was a threat to me, her only child. She was a protector by nature, and I loved her for it, but sometimes she did cross the line.

Jada and I had been out a few more times, but still hadn't had our double date, so I mentioned it to her one night we went to dinner.

"So did you set up our double date yet? Mike and I are excited to go out with another couple."

"Girl, you must've been reading my mind. I can't wait either. Silas has just had to go out of town on business so much lately. I've actually gone on a few trips with him, but with him being so busy, it's not a lot of fun hanging out in big cities by myself. He took what would be his last trip for a while a few days ago, so maybe we can go out within the next week or two. I'll let you know."

"Okay. We're waiting on y'all!" I said, slicing up my grilled chicken. "It'll be nice to be able to go out with another no-drama couple. I know we'll have a great time."

I don't think I was as excited about actually going to dinner with Jada and Silas as I was about seeing Mister Moneybags Silas. From the way she had described him, he was fine as hell. As much as she talked about him, I was surprised that she didn't carry any pictures around of him. I had to give it to her. The girl had it made. He gave her everything she wanted and more. Not to say that Mike didn't give me everything I wanted, but I knew it would be a while before he would even probably consider buying me a car. Especially something as nice as Jada's car. She told me that they had been dating only for a few months and he had bought her that car only about a month ago. I figured Jada must've had that good-good and had that negro pussy-whipped! I liked that in her!

Jada had met Silas at a party that a mutual friend of theirs had thrown. She was actually with her boyfriend at the time, who she said she was with for five and a half years. The party was held at the friend's house, with a lot of drinking, getting high, dancing, chilling, whatever! When she was describing the setting, it sounded to me like anything went that night. That night, her boyfriend got really drunk, and high off of something. She said she wasn't sure what it was he was high off of. She just knew he kept disappearing, and when he would come back around he would be acting extremely strange.

The last time he slipped away and came back, he became really aggressive towards her. He grabbed her by her hair and started pouring liquor all over her. When she tried to snatch away, he slapped her down to the ground, looked at her helplessly laying there, spit on her, and as soon as he lifted his foot to kick her, her knight in shining armor arrived to the scene. Jada said Silas beat the shit out of that man. She felt bad for him at first, but he deserved it. After Silas beat him unconscious, he picked Jada up, put her in his car and drove her home. After that night, she said she's loved him ever since.

Jada and I had become real cool, and we shared a lot with each other, but I was still very careful about what I shared because I learned that it can all come bite you in the ass later. She knew I was in the process of divorce due to irreconcilable differences and that's all she needed to know for now. As far as she was concerned, the baby was Terrance's, but Mike was sticking around to be a part of our lives. She was on the outside looking in, and in her eyes, everything going on with me was crystal clear. That's the way I wished it to be. Maybe one day I would feel she was a good enough friend to tell her the real story, but for now, what she knew was sufficient.

Jada felt comfortable sharing things with me, which was true of most people. I felt like I was in the wrong line of work a lot of the time because people loved to talk to me about their problems, but I guess that came along with the business I'm in too. She told me she was pregnant once by her ex and miscarried. That's when she told me the whole truth about that relationship. The night at her friend's party wasn't the first time he had been abusive towards her, and I had already figured as much. I knew abuse didn't just come out the blue, so as long as they had already been together, I knew there had to have been a history of it. She and the ex, who I had learned name was Isaac, began living together only after about a month of dating.

The abuse started shortly afterward. It began as mental abuse. He would always talk about how skinny she was, and how it was unattractive. He would also always throw it in her face about how he always dated light-skinned women, and she was kinda dark for his taste. What I got from what she told me was that he was one insecure negro who wanted to tear down her self-esteem because he knew she was gorgeous, but didn't want her to think so. I knew that type all too well. I saw my co-worker Phelecia go through it with her boyfriend, Duwan, and he ended up killing her. I couldn't believe that Jada took that from a man, but I did believe that love is blind.

Jada became pregnant by Isaac after about two years of living together and taking the abuse. She said when she found out she was pregnant, she was excited, not due to the fact that she was gonna have a baby, but because she felt like pregnancy may have been her shield from the violence for the next nine months. Isaac seemed just as excited as she was, and that was all he would talk about. He would still get angry at Jada during the pregnancy, and get anger in his eyes like he was going to hit her, but instead, would go punch a hole in the wall, or something else to relieve the anger inside of him.

Jada made it through five months of pregnancy without being beat up on like a punching bag, and she thought that maybe it was a breakthrough for Isaac. One day, she and Isaac went to the mall together and she ran into a close guy friend from high school who she hadn't seen in a while. They hugged, and she introduced him to Isaac. They shook hands and even engaged in conversation about football. The guy even congratulated them on their addition. Everything seemed fine, and they went on their way and finished shopping.

All hell broke loose when they got home. Isaac started throwing shit all over the place, asking Jada whose baby she was pregnant with. He told her that he knew she had been fucking around with the dude from the mall and they tried to play him right in front of his face like he didn't know what was going on. Jada said she had never seen him get that bad, but he completely lost it! At first she just stood back, and tried to stay out of his way while he ripped through everything, but she couldn't stand seeing him like that. She walked closer to him to try to calm him down so they could talk. She said she just wanted to try to bring him back to reality because he was in another world.

While Jada was telling the story, tears began forming in her eyes. She said, his breathing was hard, there was evil in his eyes, rage in his face, but she loved him so she was still willing to be there for him. She knew he had problems, but wanted to try to fix him. She rubbed his back gently and told him to calm down. She kept telling him over and over again that she loved him and she didn't want anyone else. He told her to get the fuck away from him, turned around and punched her dead in her stomach as hard as he possibly could have. What hurt even more was that immediately after doing it, he told her that's how he felt about her and the fuckin' baby. That's when she knew that what he had done was intentional. She immediately started bleeding profusely and had to drive herself to the hospital because he refused to. That night, she lost her precious baby girl.

Even after that, Jada still managed to stay with the muthafucker. I didn't understand how she could've even stood to look at him after that. She said he never talked about that day again, and never spoke of the baby. Things were as if she had never been pregnant. She knew the right thing to do would've been to go to the police and press charges, but even after what he had done, for some reason it hurt her to think of him going to jail. He had her mind all fucked up. She now regretted staying with him, especially after that, but he had broken her down so much mentally, she couldn't think on her own, and felt like she had no one else but him. After the fact, she realized that there were a lot more people out there who loved her and Silas made her realize that. The past few months, he had shown her how to love herself again, and she was once again enjoying her life. I hadn't met Silas yet, but I was already thankful to him for saving Jada and taking her from that dangerous life.

Chapter 8

It was an exceptionally slow Saturday at work, so I sat in my chair thinking about some things I needed to get done in the little bit of free time that I had. Since my momma and Tasha would soon be planning my baby shower, and Jada definitely wanted to be a part of it, I decided to call my momma and set up a time for us all to meet up at her house so they could all get acquainted with each other. My momma always sounded so excited to hear from me as though it had been months since she'd last spoken to me.

"Hey, baby!" My momma said as soon as she answered the phone. She obviously had looked at the caller ID before answering. Plus, she didn't get many calls from anyone except for me anyway. She was like me, or I should say, I was like her when it came to friends. We both had only a select few.

"Hey, momma. I was thinkin' . . . Since my girl Jada wants to help with the shower, y'all need to meet, so everyone can be on the same page.

"Okay. So y'all gone come by today or what?"

"Today? I wasn't planning on it today . . ."

"What you mean not today? My grandbaby is gonna be here very soon, so we need to get this show on the road! This may be my only time I get to plan a baby shower for my baby, so you know momma gonna hook it up!"

I didn't know what my momma meant by this being the only time she'd get to do this, so I asked, "Why do you think this will be the only shower you'll get to plan for me?" She made me nervous with that statement, making me think something was wrong with her. She hadn't mentioned anything to me about being sick or anything, but I knew how when people got older, they kept things from their kids because they didn't want them to worry. I'd be heartbroken if my momma was ill and kept it from me, then something happened to her.

"I say that because your grandma only had one child, making me the only child, I had one child, making you the only child, so I figured you'll probably follow suit. This little girl gone be a spoiled only child just like her momma!"

Whew! I was so glad that was the answer. I wasn't ready to accept anything happening to my momma. I knew she would always be there for me no matter what, and I didn't know what I would do without her. I still had my daddy, but he was busy trying to keep his wife, who was almost twenty years younger than him, happy. All I could say for him and that situation was "Gone with your bad self Daddy!" Even though we didn't talk much, I still knew he loved me. How could you not love your one and only child?

"Since you wanna do this today, let me check with Jada and Tasha to see if they're available. I'll call you back in a few minutes."

"They better be, or you know I can do this by myself! That is no problem. I ain't got time to waiting on nobody."

There she went on her power trip! My momma loved to be in charge. I always thought she would've made a great manager somewhere because her employees would've been too scared not to do whatever she told their asses to do.

I called Jada first to see what she was up to for the day. Hopefully, she didn't have plans with Silas because dealing with my momma, this little meet and greet thing could end up being an all day event.

Jada answered, sounding lively as always, "Hey, Kel. What's up? You must not be busy at work today."

"No, not very, but it's a nice little break from the norm."

"I hear you! So what's going on?" she asked curiously.

"I know it's last minute, but my momma wanna start planning this baby shower so she wants to meet up with you and Tasha at her house today. Hopefully, you don't have plans because she don't like to take no for an answer."

Jada started laughing, not understanding the seriousness of this. I wasn't joking at all. Everyone who knew my momma knew she could be crazy and unreasonable, but that was my momma. You either loved her or couldn't stand her ass. There was no in between and she would tell you that.

"Well, luckily, I don't have any plans. Silas is gone for the day, so I was just lounging around doing nothing. I'm glad you called so I can get out this house!"

"Good, even though I don't know how you deal with your man being gone all day, but he's a businessman so that's understandable."

"Girl, I know right, but what can I do? Tell him to quit? It's okay. He still makes plenty of time for me. Believe me, we get ours in!" Jada said, laughing joyfully. She was always so happy, so I knew Silas was doing something right, and I was happy for her.

"I know y'all probably do, just like the saying goes, absence makes the heart grow fonder, so sometimes it's good to have a chance to miss your man, cuz you know when he returns, it's going dowwwwwwwnnn!"

We both busted out laughing. I told her I would text her my momma's address and the exact time of the meeting. I then proceeded to call Tasha, hoping things went as smoothly with her. Knowing her, she and Lem probably had plans. They were always going somewhere and doing something. If that were the case, I was just gonna have to ask Mr. Lemuel to grant me a little of my friend's time.

It seemed like everyone was in a good mood today. Tasha answered her phone sounding more upbeat than Jada had, and that was hard to match!

"Hey, Tasha! Please tell me you don't have plans today."

"It depends," she said.

"Depends on what, Chile?"

"On what you tryin' to do. You know my time is limited these days. My boo is stingy with me! He wants all my time to his self."

Lem had really blown up my girl's head, but that was okay. She was feelin' herself, but we all do sometimes. I considered it normal.

"Well, my momma . . ."

Before I could finish what I was saying, Tasha said, "Oh lawd! Yes, I'm busy, girl!"

"Girl, it's not that bad! She just wants to meet up with you and Jada today. She still hasn't met Jada, and she wants to start discussing the shower."

Tasha hesitantly said, "Okay. I guess I can make time for that. Have you already warned Jada about Momma Armstrong?"

"I've told her a little bit about her, but it's not gonna be bad! Trust me!"

"Okay . . . I'm just making sure because I've known her for more than ten years and some of the things she say still shock the hell out of me! I just hope Jada is ready to experience us both at the same time, and she better not be no phony ass bitch, cuz you know I can see straight through that shit and I'll call her out!"

I couldn't believe Tasha was worried about Jada meeting my momma. I didn't want to tell her that I was more worried about Jada meeting her. She started talking crazy and when she did that, I knew it was time to let her go so she could calm herself down. I swear sometimes I thought that girl was bipolar! Poor Jada! She was in for a ride. I ended my conversation with Tasha by telling her to meet me at my momma's at four. I then texted Jada with the info, and called to tell my momma to be expecting us.

At three o' clock, the shop was completely empty. The other stylists and I sat around chattin' it up for a little while, then I headed home to clean myself up. I was so worried about making sure Jada and Tasha didn't have any plans, I forgot all about calling Mike to make sure he didn't have anything planned for us. When I got home, fortunately, he wasn't there. I tried to hurry and get changed so I could leave out before he got there. I didn't want him trying to come along when he found out I was going to my momma's house. I wasn't ready for that quite yet, and I was sure my momma wasn't either.

On my way to my momma's, Mike texted me, just to tell me he loved me, as usual. I texted him back and told him I missed him. He probably figured I was still at work since the shop was normally slammed on Saturdays. When I pulled up in front of my momma's house, she was looking out the screen door. Neither Jada nor Tasha had made it yet, but I was a few minutes early.

I walked up my momma's walkway, watching her smile bigger and bigger the closer I got. She held the screen door open for me and as soon as I stepped in the house onto her hardwood floors, she knelt down rubbing my belly addressing the baby before she said a word to me! It didn't bother me. It was cute. It was so amazing to me how a baby could bring so much joy and delight into everyone's lives.

After doing a whole lot of baby talk, my momma stood up and gave me one of her rough hugs. She literally would grab you by the neck and almost choke the shit out of you, but they were all in love. My momma and I sat in the living room while we waited on the girls, having a little girl talk. She talked mostly about how she couldn't wait 'til her grandbaby was here so she could spoil her rotten.

A few minutes later, through the big picture window, I saw Tasha pull up. I thought she would be the last to arrive, but then again, knowing her, she was probably anxious to see what Jada was all about.

When my momma glanced over to see what I was looking at out the window, she said, "Oh Lord."

I laughed at the fact that Tasha and my momma had the exact same reaction towards each other.

"What you laughin' at, girl?" my momma said with a slight grin.

"Nothing at all!"

At that moment, Tasha walked in the door.

"Girl, I know you didn't just walk in my house without knockin'!"

"I'm sorry. Would you like me to walk back out and knock this time?" Tasha said sarcastically, not thinkin' my momma would respond the way she did.

Tasha knew how my momma was. I didn't even know why she thought she would go there with her.

My momma responded by saying, "As a matter of fact, yes! Y'all young girls need to learn some manners. You gone learn today!"

Tasha turned towards the door, getting ready to walk out, trying her best to hold in her laughter. Suddenly my momma grabbed her from the back and turned her around, giving her a hug.

"Now girl, you know I'm just messin' with you. Y'all say I'm crazy, so I'm gonna start acting crazy!" We all laughed hysterically.

Just then, I saw Jada's Audi pulling up. "Here Jada comes y'all!"

Tasha looked out the living room window in awe. "You didn't say she was ballin'!"

"Hey, she's not the one ballin'. Her man is and I'm not mad at her!"

That slipped out of my mouth before I knew it. I didn't wanna give Tasha anything negative to say about Jada. What I said wasn't really negative, but if Tasha didn't wanna like someone, she could turn anything someone said into something negative.

"Well, does her man have any friends or brothers?" Tasha asked.

"Now you know Lem got you under lock and key. You ain't goin' nowhere!"

"You got that right!" Tasha said, smiling so big I couldn't help but to see that nasty rotten tooth in the back of her mouth that I wished she would get pulled or somethin'!

My momma opened the door for Jada and I bowed my head to pray.

"Hello, Ma'am. I'm Jada. It's very nice to finally meet you," I heard Jada say from the living room.

Tasha sat on the couch across from me, rolling her eyes and chewing the shit out of her gum. She hadn't even met the girl yet, but already had in her mind that she wasn't gonna like her. That was Tasha for you. My momma didn't make things any better.

"Tasha, you hear this girl in here, saying 'ma'am' and 'nice to meet you'? Now she has manners! She might be able to teach you somethin'!"

Jada and my momma made it to the living room, where Tasha and I were sitting. I stood up and gave her a hug, then introduced her to Tasha.

Without standing, or even looking at her, Tasha said in her nasally, uninterested tone, "Hey, how you doin'?"

"I'm good. I've heard so much about you! It's nice to finally meet one of Kel's other friends. She's such a sweetheart. I know if you're a friend of hers, you're good people."

Tasha finally looked up at Jada, and with a smile said, "Thanks girl. It's good to meet you too."

My breathing eased up a little bit, seeing that Tasha wasn't gonna act a complete fool. Jada was a hard person not to like. She was just one of those likeable people. If anyone had beef with Jada, something had to have been wrong them. Just when I felt I had Tasha under control, my momma would start.

"Jayla, I'm just sittin' here looking at you wonderin' if you always looked like that or started lookin' like that after you met Kel."

Oh God! I thought.

Jada, looking lost said, "What do you mean by that Ms. Armstrong?" without even addressing the fact that my momma called her by the wrong name.

"Well, you look a whole lot like my baby. You know how some of these women out here want so badly to be like somebody else that they . . ."

"Momma, Jada, not Jayla, is her own person. Not like some of the other friends I've had. We just have a lot in common, including style."

Jada looked back and forth at my momma and me. She was gonna learn very fast that my momma said whatever was on her mind. Tasha sat there with her legs crossed and a grin on her face just enjoying the fact that it wasn't her that time. My eyes connected with Jada and I just shook my head letting her know not to mind my momma.

"Oh, Jada, I didn't mean no harm. I just have to make sure Kel ain't hangin' with no wannabes, or no fake, jealous women. I've seen too many of them during my day and they are out to destroy anyone in their way! So just don't let me find out you're one of those scandalous ones! Stay on my good side now, Chile."

"Ms. Armstrong, you don't have to worry about that at all from me. I'm here for Kel, just like y'all are. I consider her a very good friend."

I interrupted and said, "Well, since we've had a very interesting introductory session, we should probably get to planning."

The rest of the evening went pretty well. We enjoyed a lot of laughs and I believe Jada ended up enjoying herself as well. She and Tasha began to get along very well. When my momma left out the room, Tasha told her to just act like my momma was in charge at all times and she'd be fine. Jada laughed, but she would learn real quick that Tasha was giving her the best advice when it came to dealing with my momma. They all had good ideas, and surprisingly, my momma was willing to listen to the girls, and not just try to incorporate her own ideas. My mission was to make sure that they got along well enough that I would feel comfortable with all of them being in the same room without me being around, and that was accomplished. Even though I had a good time with all the ladies in my life, I was ecstatic when the evening was over so I could spend some time with that man of mine.

Chapter 9

My court date with Terrance had finally arrived and I was anxious to get it over with. Nothing seemed to be going right that morning, while getting ready to go. Everything I tried to put on just didn't fit right. Mike said everything looked fine, and it was just my nerves, but I didn't believe it. I tried on around ten different outfits, and I looked fat in everything. I was having a bad hair day, and I couldn't get my makeup to go on right. Mike had worry in his eyes. He didn't like seeing his baby like this, and I didn't like feeling like this.

I was pacing back and forth, throwing clothes all over the place as if I was going to magically have a whole new wardrobe. Mike stopped me in my tracks, grabbing me by my waist and told me to calm down, and everything was gonna be all right. I already knew that. I didn't know what had come over me. My attorney told me that Terrance had no grounds for contesting the divorce, so I didn't have anything to worry about, and this would all be over after today.

I went in the bathroom, just to sit down for a moment to calm my nerves, splashed some cold water on my face, and told myself to get it together. I was okay after about a half an hour. I threw on one of my prettiest maternity dresses that had pink, black, and white diagonal stripes, and form fitting on my cute little belly. It came to my knees and flared at the bottom. I pulled my hair up in a bun, threw on some matching earrings and necklace, and of course, a pair of black pumps. Mike had finished getting dressed before I did, of course, so he was waiting on me out in the car. He made sure he didn't schedule any appointments or anything for this day, because he wanted to make sure he was there to support me. He had also been anxiously awaiting this day as much as I had. I knew Tif probably wouldn't be there because I was sure that Terrance wouldn't have wanted her to know he was trying to contest the divorce. She probably didn't even have any idea that we were still going to court. His lying ass probably told her the divorce was already final or made it seem like I was contesting the divorce. If she didn't think we were already divorced, I was sure her ass couldn't wait 'til we were so she could try to move her ass all the way in, but as far as I was concerned, she could have his black ass. I just hoped there was enough of him to go around to share with Stacy and her baby!

When Mike saw me walking out the house, he got out the car so he could open the passenger side door for me.

"Baby, you are the most beautiful pregnant, about to be divorced woman I have ever seen in my life!"

He always knew how to make light of every situation. I laughed, gave him a hug, and whispered a sincere "thank you" in his ear. I appreciated him for always being there for me, no matter what.

When we pulled up to the courthouse, the parking lot was so crowded we couldn't find a parking space. Mike pulled over in front of the building to let me out, so I wouldn't have to walk a long distance. I don't think that would've been the problem, compared to the flight of steep stairs I was about to climb just trying to get to the entrance of the building. There had to have been around fifty steps. As I began stepping it, I heard someone coming up behind me.

"You think you gonna make it?"

I held on to the handrail, and looked back to find Terrance's ass grinning like something really amused him. I wish I could've taken a picture of the expression on his face when he looked down and saw my full body. Now that was a Kodak moment.

"Yeah, I'm gonna make it just fine," I said mischievously, and turned around and kept walking.

I heard complete silence for a minute, then heard him coming up behind me again.

"Looks like you got something to tell me, Kel. This is gonna make things that much more complicated," he said.

This was exactly what I was afraid of: things becoming more complicated. I didn't need any more complication in my life than I already had.

"Terrance, why are you doing this? I just want this to be over and done with so you and I can both move on. We obviously weren't right for each other and we both found something better for the both of us. You don't want me, so what's the problem? Just let it go."

By the time I finished saying my peace, I had finally made it to the top of the staircase, along with Terrance right beside me.

"So, are you trying to tell me that's not my baby?"

I wanted to tell him badly that it wasn't, but I couldn't lie. If Terrance was the father, my daughter had the right to know him. No girl should grow up not knowing who her father is. I always believed fathers were an essential parts of a girl's life. I know mine was. I knew just because Terrance and I didn't work out, didn't mean that he would be a bad father too.

"There's a possibility, but I refuse to talk about this right here, right now."

"I know one thing. You will not keep my child from me," he said and walked briskly like a bitch towards the glass double doors, shaking his head.

After that undesirable conversation was over, Mike came running right up behind me.

He grabbed my hand and said, "I saw you up here talking to Terrance. Is everything all right? He didn't come at you wrong, did he?"

"Everything's cool. Let's just go get this over with."

As we walked into the courtroom, I noticed that there were more people there than I had imagined. I wondered if they were spectators just wanting to be nosey, or were they waiting to see the same judge. It seemed like everyone looked back as soon as Mike and I stepped one foot inside, including Terrance and his lawyer, who were already seated at the front. Mike kissed me on the cheek and found a seat in the back of the courtroom with all the nosey folks. As I got closer to the front, I saw that my attorney, Malcolm Dunlap, was also already seated next to the empty chair that belonged to me. The court reporter had a small table in the middle of me and Terrance's tables, directly in front of where the judge would sit.

Once I sat next to Malcolm, and he gave me that reassuring nod and smile, I felt a lot better. Malcolm was one of the best divorce attorneys in Chicago and I had a lot of faith in him. He was always so calm, and didn't seem to have a nervous bone in his body. He didn't seem to be worried about a thing, so I figured, why should I be? Sitting there, looking straight ahead, it seemed as though the bailiff was staring straight at me, but it could've been my imagination getting the best of me. I kept trying to make small talk with Malcolm, just to give me a reason to look away from where the bailiff was standing.

Finally, the time came when court was called to order and everyone was instructed to stand. As I stood, I looked back at Mike nervously. He nodded and winked letting me know once again that everything would be okay. The judge, who was a woman, like Malcolm had told me, walked in with a stern look on her face. This didn't look good at all! She was a very petite black woman, with very short curly hair. She was older, maybe in her late fifties, and still very attractive. I could tell she was probably something else back in her younger days. She told everyone to be seated, and didn't waste any time getting to business.

Since I was the one who filed for the divorce, Malcolm and I were up first. Malcolm grabbed his thousands of notes and stood up to give my side and reasons for requesting a divorce. He began by sucking up to the judge, telling her how lovely she looked and thanking her for taking the time to hear our case. Surprisingly, he did get a slight grin out of her, and her light skin turned a slight pinkish color from blushing.

"Your honor, my client, Mrs. Kalecia Moore has requested a divorce from her husband, Mr. Terrance Moore due to infidelity issues. Mrs. Moore caught her husband in bed with another woman, who, might I add, was a very good friend of hers. Mr. Moore is now contesting the divorce, and in all my years as an attorney, I still don't know what kind of grounds he has for doing so."

I glanced over at Terrance and his lawyer to see how ridiculous they looked. I couldn't even believe that his lawyer would take on such ridiculousness. He knew Terrance didn't have any right to do what he was doing, but I guess they'll do anything to get paid.

"Mr. Dunlap," the judge began, "rest assured that I know how long you've been an attorney, and a quite reputable one; however, you should also know that Mr. Moore and his attorney have not yet had their turn to speak, so if you could please keep your opinions to yourself, I would greatly appreciate it."

Damn, I thought. She wasn't cutting poor Malcolm any slack. When he had initially found out who the judge was, he told me she was tough, but he felt he would be able to crack her wide open.

"Now, Mr. Dunlap, is there anything else, you would like to add, or anything your client would like to say?"

"Yes, your honor. I do deeply apologize for my last statement. I just also want to add that Mrs. Moore's friend was not the only woman Mr. Moore was cheating with. He was also having sexual relations with his co-worker, which my client later found out about, and there is also a chance the young lady may be carrying Mr. Moore's child."

"What!" Terrance stood up and shouted.

Everyone in the courtroom started whispering amongst each other and laughing at my so-called life. It felt so humiliating putting all of my business out in front of the public eye, but because of Terrance's stubborn ass, this was the only way.

The judge hit her gavel on the desk and said, "Order in the court! Order in my courtroom! Mr. Moore, sit down before I have you put out!"

As Terrance slowly sat down, he looked over at me and gave me the evilest look ever. I couldn't believe he tried to act as if he didn't know Stacy was pregnant by him. If she wasn't pregnant by him, then all I could say was he needed to get his bitches in check. After all the ruckus was over, the courtroom became so quiet you could've heard a pin drop. Malcolm finished by giving the judge the rest of the history of me and Terrance's relationship, and added that I just wanted to leave this painful part of my life behind.

Terrance rubbed his hands together grinning at me when it was time for his side to approach. His lawyer, who was a tall, lanky white man, who I assumed probably worked with him, whispered a few things back and forth to Terrance before he stood. He didn't try to suck up to the judge the way Malcolm had. He got straight to why he was there.

"Your honor, my client, Mr. Moore and I are here because his wife has requested a divorce, as Mr. Dunlap has already stated, however, it is not that simple to my client. That is why we are here to contest it. My client also witnessed Mrs. Moore engaging in an adulterous act with one of her long time male companions. This was before Mr. Moore was caught in the act."

As Terrance's attorney spoke, the judge wrote several notes. More than what she did while Malcolm pled my case, but once he stated that I was caught cheating too, she looked up from her paper and glanced first at Terrance, then at me, and shook her head.

"My client knows that two wrongs don't make a right and regrets the actions that he took to get back at his wife. He wants to try to reconcile their differences, and she won't give it a chance. He even tried to call her on several occasions so they could talk, but she wouldn't answer his calls and never even called him back. Mr. Moore has the phone bills to prove it. In fact, she has moved on with a man who was their neighbor at the home they once shared together."

Malcolm stood up and said, "Objection! Hearsay!"

"Sustained," the judge replied.

The tall, lanky lawyer tried to continue, fumbling through his notes, looking for more dirt on me. I couldn't believe he had told the judge that Terrance had called me to fix things between us!

Now I knew the only reason he had called me was so that he'd have proof for court that he had tried.

"Your honor, the bottom line is that Mr. Moore wants to at least try counseling before giving up. Unlike a lot of couples that are going through divorce, this man still has hope. He still loves his wife and married her not to divorce, but to be with her until death do them part."

Are you fucking kidding me! I thought to myself. What the hell was Terrance trying to do? Was he just that desperate to make my life miserable for as long as he could? I was really praying to God now that this baby was not Terrance's. I could not see myself tied to this man for the rest of my life!

Terrance's lawyer sat down after he did what lawyers do best . . . Lie!

"Before I rule, I just have a few questions and comments to make things a little clearer, because this entire situation is . . . What do you young folks say today? Messy! The two of you got married because obviously you thought you loved one another. That may be true, but just because you love someone doesn't mean you're ready to marry them! You both look young and that could pose a problem right there, even though it is possible to be young and everything work out just fine. I've seen it happen. However, in this case, I don't care who has and hasn't moved on. What' s clear is that you both cheated and I'm sure hurt by it. It's hard to come back from that because it's extremely hard to regain trust after it's lost. Mr. Moore, clearly, your wife does not want to try to make it work and just wants to move on. Even if I do rule for you two to go to counseling, I feel it just may be a waste because it takes two to make it work, and both parties have to give one hundred percent. Not fifty-fifty like a lot of ignorant folks say."

I started getting antsy, curious of how the judge would rule. Everything she said made a lot of sense, and if nothing else good came out of this, I was sure there were people in the audience that needed to hear some, if not all of what she was saying, so that they didn't make the same mistakes Terrance and I did. Suddenly, I no longer felt embarrassed. I began to understand that life isn't perfect and people go through things. I wasn't the first and wouldn't be the last woman to go through a nasty divorce, and as far as I was concerned, it could've been a lot nastier. While I was in deep thought, the judge continued.

"There is one other thing that I need to have cleared up. Mrs. Moore, it's hard not to notice that you're expecting. With the infidelity that occurred, I have to ask, are you pregnant with your husband's child?"

As soon as the question came out of her mouth, I became extremely warm and felt as though I had to throw up. Even though I knew I would have to answer that question today, and no matter how much I had "prepared" to answer it, I still wasn't ready.

Voice trembling, I said, "Ma'am . . . I mean your honor, unfortunately, under the circumstances discussed, I'm not sure if Mr. Moore is the father of my child. There is a possibility, but I can't confirm."

A sudden relief came over me as soon as I got it out. I was ashamed of not knowing who my child's father was, but it was what it was, and it wasn't like I could go back and change anything. I think I was so ashamed because I felt like such a hypocrite. I always talked badly about women who didn't know who their kid's father was, and here I was in that same situation. I had learned a lot through this whole ordeal. No one is immune to bullshit. Shit can happen to anyone, and no one is invincible.

"Thank you, Mrs. Moore. I know that took a lot of courage, but I do respect your honesty."

The judge looked back down at her notes, reviewing everything, while the courtroom remained quiet. I think everyone was just as curious as I was to see what the judge's ruling would be.

"After looking over all the facts and hearing all of your statements, I have decided to grant the divorce between the two of you. I don't see any reason for putting it off any longer. Mr. Moore, unfortunately you have no grounds for contesting this divorce, however you do have rights to the child if it is, in fact, yours. In saying that, Mrs. Moore, I am ordering that a paternity test be completed as soon as the baby is born, which I assume would probably be within the next couple of months."

"Yes ma'am . . . Your honor."

"Both of you seem like nice young adults who have made some mistakes. I hope you have learned some things from this and use them to better yourselves. I wish both of you luck with everything. Court dismissed."

I was grinning from ear to ear. I looked back and saw Mike smiling and nodding his head. I gave Malcolm the biggest hug and told him thanks for everything. While Malcolm and I were grabbing all of our belongings, Terrance walked over to our table with his lawyer and said, "I guess I'll be hearing from you in a couple of months, Ms. Armstrong." That was right. I would no longer be Mrs. Moore, and the first thing I was going to do was change my name back to Kelicia Armstrong.

After Terrance's lying ass got out of my face, I made it to the back of the courtroom, where my baby, Mike was. I think he was cheesing harder than me. He grabbed me, wrapping his arms around my waist, and kissed me like he was the happiest man in the world. When our lips parted, Mike said the words I had been waiting to hear for what seemed like a very long time.

"It's finally over, baby."

It felt good to hear that, but I knew this would only be the beginning if Terrance and I shared a baby together.

Chapter 10

"Hey, girl!" Jada said eagerly when I answered the phone.

"Hey, Jada. What's goin' on?"

I could barely hear Jada because all I could hear in her background were a bunch of kids. She must've been at work, but she should've waited 'til those bad ass kids went to lunch or recess before she called me. As I tried holding the phone slightly away from my ear, I told her she needed to speak up, feeling like I was screaming.

"Girl, I am so sorry. These kids then had too much sugar today or something. Anyway, I talked to Silas today and we don't have anything going on this evening if the two of you are free. If not, I understand. I know it's short notice."

"Well, I'll be finishing up early at work today, but I'll have to check to see if Mike has anything going on, but I'm curling a client right now, so once I finish, I'll call him and give you a call back."

"Okay. I'll be waiting to hear from you."

When I was hanging up the phone, I could hear Jada screaming at the kids, telling them to sit down and act like they had some sense. I didn't know how she did it. They couldn't pay me enough to babysit someone else's kids. Especially fifth graders, which is what grade she had. That's when kids start thinking that they're grown and wanna talk back and shit. Ain't nobody got time for that!. With everything Silas did for her, I didn't know why she was still working in the first place. I could see if she had a great job she didn't wanna leave, but the little money she made for babysitting some bad ass kids wasn't even worth it. Maybe she just wanted to have her own money to do stuff with, or maybe she just liked her job. She did seem to like kids.

To my surprise, not even ten minutes after hanging up from with Jada, Mike came walking into the shop. We hadn't officially gone public with the seriousness of our relationship, but obviously he must've felt it was time. The girls in the shop knew about him only because of the flowers that he sent, but had never met him, and I wasn't sure if I was ready for them to meet him. He shocked the hell out of me, and I stood there wishing that I could've been better prepared for the occasion.

When Mike walked in, I didn't say a word. I continued curling my client's hair and acted like I hadn't noticed him.

"Hey, cutie pie. What brings you in today?" Cameron said, batting her long, fake lashes.

Before Cameron said something to him to really piss me off, I stopped it right there and acknowledged Mike.

"Hey, baby. What are you doing here?"

Cameron looked at me with her hands on her hips and rolled her eyes. The other girls held their heads down trying to hold in their laughter. Mike said hello to everyone and walked towards me.

"I just thought I'd come by and surprise you. I thought about the fact I've never seen where you worked and I was just curious." He lowered his voice and put his mouth near my ear and said, "Is this okay? I'm not overstepping my boundaries, am I?"

I spoke even lower when I said, "It's fine, but you could've let me know."

Everyone in the shop was super quiet, which meant they were trying their best to ear hustle. Nosey ass women!

"I'm sorry, babe," Mike said and kissed me on the cheek.

"Awww. Ain't that so sweet!" Cameron said sarcastically. "So are you gonna introduce us to your boo or what? He came all the way here to see yo ass, so don't try to act brand new! He just wanna see you and his baby! Ain't that right?" she said, waiting on Mike to respond.

"Girl, I'm not even about to fool with you today, Cameron. You just like to start shit. Anyway, Mike, as you probably already know, this is Cameron."

Mike walked over and shook Cameron's hand and told her he had heard a lot about her and it was nice to finally meet her. That was the absolute wrong thing to say.

"What you mean you then heard a lot about me? It better had all been good stuff. You been talking about me behind my back, Kel?"

Mike started laughing, not realizing that crazy girl was dead serious!

"Girl, ain't nobody been talking about you behind your back! I've just told him about all of you. Calm your ass down."

I went on to introduce Mike to Isis. She was one of our newer stylists. She came along after the other stylist, Sabrina, abandoned us and went to another shop. Isis was only twenty-one and had not too long before finished beauty school, so she didn't have much clientele. She spent most of her days in the shop doing her own hair, in the mirror putting on a ton of makeup, or shampooing clients for the rest of us. She was a nice addition to the shop because she was very different, or maybe I should say eccentric, and she didn't give a damn what people thought of her.

One day, she came into the shop with pink and turquoise eye shadow on, and small diamonds outlining the edges of her eyes. No one said a word to her, because with her, nothing surprised us. She wore her hair shaved on the left side and the rest long. We were just waiting on the day she would come in with her entire head shaved.

"Isis, this is my . . . man, Mike. Mike, this is Isis."

That was my first time ever introducing Mike as my man, and it felt a little strange. I was used to just referring to him as "Mike." I knew Mike could tell I felt a little weird about introducing him that way because he raised his eyebrows when I hesitated. No one ever said this was gonna be easy. It was definitely gonna take some getting used to.

Lastly, I introduced Mike to Rhonda. Rhonda was cool most of the time. Everyone just knew not to mess with her. Just because she was older did not mean she wouldn't whoop your ass. She had a motherly side to her, but the hood could and would come out!

"No wonder you've been trying to keep him a secret Kel!" He is fine! Gone with your bad self!" She ran over to give Cameron a high-five.

I could tell Mike was a little embarrassed and was probably regretting just popping up, but now he knew! He stood there looking uncomfortable, and I told him to have a seat at the empty station behind me while I finished my client. The whole time he sat there, I kept catching the girls staring his way. They couldn't keep their eyes off of him. They could look all they wanted, but they just better not had tried to touch. Mike kept whispering shit behind me making me laugh.

"Ooh girl, look at that fat ass. I can't wait to squeeze it! He whispered."

"Boy, you know you are crazy!"

I finally finished my client and told Mike to go outside with me so we could talk in private. He told everyone bye before we walked out and seemed relieved as soon as the door closed behind us.

"So, what really brought you over this way today?" I asked Mike as we held hands walking to his car.

"I just wanted to see you . . . And I must admit, I did feel like you were keeping me too much of a secret. Now that you're divorced, you shouldn't feel ashamed of anything. I don't have to be a secret anymore. Have you even told your mom about us?"

Truth was that I didn't feel comfortable going around broadcasting that Mike and I were an item. It seemed like everything was moving so fast. I was married one minute, having affairs with two other men the next, then I'm pregnant, divorced, and now seeing someone on a serious level. I just felt like real-life shouldn't move that fast. That shit only happened in the movies.

"No, I haven't told my mom yet. There just hasn't been a good time."

"When is it gonna be a good time? When we meet at the hospital when you go into labor?"

"That sounds good!" I said jokingly, but by the expression on Mike's face, he didn't find any humor in it. "I'm just messing with you. Soon, I promise."

I leaned up against Mike's Porsche and opened my arms for him to give me a hug, and he squeezed me tight like he always did. I wanted him to feel the same type of comfort and reassurance that he always gave me. I got the feeling that he felt like I was just gonna up and leave one day, but that wasn't my intention at all. My fear was staring me in my face. One of the main reasons I told Mike there could never be anything between us was because of the fact that he knew too much about my history with Terrance and the other men involved. I felt like Mike would never be able to trust me, and I didn't think he did at this point in our relationship.

After we sat in the car, I told Mike that Jada had called and wanted for all of us to go out to dinner tonight. He said he had a short meeting at six, but we should be able to make it. Maybe this would be the start of us doing real-couple things together, and help him to feel more secure in our relationship. I knew I needed to help him feel more comfortable before I lost a really good man over some bullshit.

"Girrrrrl!" Cameron said as soon as I left Mike and walked back into the shop.

"What?" I said frowning as if I didn't know what she was talking about.

"And I thought Terrance was fine! Where the hell you find all these beautiful ass men? I need to hang out with you!"

"Uh . . . No, you don't! And I can't help who I attract."

"Whatever, smart ass! But for real, good job. He seems nice. I'm not even gone lie."

What had gotten into Cameron? She didn't have a negative thing to say and that definitely wasn't like her. Maybe that man of hers had changed her a little bit. I was just waiting on her to tell me how he wasn't the right one for me, and how it was too soon for me to be serious with someone, and how he's gonna leave when the baby is born, blah, blah, blah. That's how it normally went with her. Just maybe, subconsciously, I was thinking those things.

I finally got around to calling Jada back to tell her tonight would be cool. She said good because she had already made eight o' clock reservations at a very high-end French restaurant called Everest. I told her she must've had a lot of confidence in me, and she replied by saying we're just alike, so she knew I could convince my man that tonight would be the perfect night to spend with other good people. After my call to her, I had a good rest of the day with my clients and co-workers. I was kinda happy that Mike had stopped by, so I could get a little taste of the response we would get from people as a couple, and it was all good.

When I got home from work, I saw Mike's car parked outside, then saw him rushing out the door. I looked at the time and noticed that he was running late for his evening appointment. I got out the car, and before grabbing all of my work equipment, I stepped in front of Mike to give him a quick kiss before he left. He told me he would see me in about an hour or so, and then we could head over to meet with Jada and Silas.

Once I got in the house with all my stuff, I relaxed in my recliner for a little while, thinking about my life. I did that often, but what was different this time was that I was content with it. Everything was falling in line and coming along the way that it needed to. I had not yet hit anymore bumps in the road and I prayed it remained that way. I had a good man, good job, good friends surrounding me, my family, and was soon gonna have the joy of my life. I couldn't ask for much more. I was feeling so good that I thought that maybe the next step I would take would be to introduce Mike to my momma. What could've possibly gone wrong? I think I had already seen it all and nothing could've been worse than everything I had already gone through. Right now, the good outweighed the bad, and I was happy with that. Life would never be perfect, no matter how hard I tried.

I got up from my brief resting period feeling more confident than I had felt in a long time, so I had to find something in my closet to put on to match my confidence level. I took my clothes off and stood in the middle of my closet, looking around wondering what in the hell I would put on. If I had known before today that we were gonna be going out, I could've already been prepared. While I was rummaging through the closet in my bra and panties, my baby girl was kicking and moving all around. It seemed like she knew what was going on and was excited to go out to dinner. I rubbed my stomach with one hand to calm her down and moved hangers back and forth trying to carefully choose something for the occasion. I couldn't let Jada outshine me. I didn't have to worry about that when I was with my other girls, but Jada was on a different level.

By the time I finished getting dressed, I heard the alarm chirp, which meant Mike was walking through the door.

"Kel. You ready?" Mike was yelling from downstairs.

"Almost, babe. Just got a few more things to do."

Mike came up the stairs and as he came around the corner, I was coming from out of my bedroom. Mike looked me up and down and whistled.

"Lookin' good! Maybe I should change clothes!"

"For what, silly? You look great as always," I said with a smile.

"I don't know, Kel. I might be a little underdressed."

I knew Mike was just messing with me now because he had on one of his best suits. There was no way he was underdressed. I wore a long spandex-filled, fitted dress, and some of my tallest heels, which kept it from dragging on the floor. Mike didn't really like me wearing heels anymore, with me getting further along. He was afraid of me falling and hurting myself and the baby. I told him he didn't know me very well, because I was queen of walking in heels. I had been doing it since I was about eight years old. I would put on my momma's shoes and walk around the house, pretending I was walking on a runway. Mike just never said anything else about it because he knew I was stubborn and I was gonna do what I wanted to do anyway. I was glad that he at least knew that much about me. My dress pushed up the bountiful set of titties that I had inherited since being pregnant, making them look irresistibly juicy. That was one asset that I was very proud of since I had never had it before, so I was going to flaunt it while I had it. I was sure that Mike would've had a problem with me exposing my goods, but surprisingly, he didn't mention it. It was all with class anyway. I would've never gone out looking trashy. All he did was give me a hug and put his head down in all that cleavage.

"Damn girl. You smell good. You think we have time to . . ."

I already knew what Mike was about to say, and no, we did not have time for a quickie. Then I would have to clean myself up all over again, and a quickie was never a quickie with us.

"No, Mike, but I got something else for you," I said as I popped a few Altoids in my mouth.

Mike stood there looking at me with his eyes squinted, not knowing what I meant. I unbuckled his belt, then unbuttoned his pants. He didn't try to stop me, and I didn't expect him to. His pants dropped to the floor after I unzipped them, and I could see his dick trying to escape beneath his boxer briefs. It was already hard and fully extended, past his navel. Before I could do it, Mike pulled them down and his dick quickly popped up from against his stomach and greeted me. While Mike was standing, I pulled my dress up over my knees, and knelt down. I licked my fingers, and rubbed them up and down over his shaft, then down underneath his balls. As I jacked his dick, I put the tip to my mouth and licked it slowly as I looked up at him to see the expression of pleasure on his face. That always made him go crazy. I could feel his legs shaking, so I pushed him towards the bed, while crawling on my knees, and dick still to my mouth.

Once Mike sat on the bed, I took all of him into my cold, minty mouth. Listening to him moan made we wanna get on top of him and ride the shit out of that big ass dick, but I had to remain composed, and satisfy my man, for now. We would have all night after dinner to do whatever we wanted to do. I sucked his dick harder and harder and I knew he was about to cum when he started saying my name and grabbed my hair, bobbing my head back and forth, faster and faster. I was so into what I was doing that I didn't even think about the fact that it had taken me forever to get my hair perfect and this negro had just fucked it up. I felt the cum pulsating through his dick and he was on his way. Mike let out a huge sigh of relief as he released his love potion in my mouth. I didn't swallow these days because I didn't feel comfortable doing that while I was pregnant, so I got up off the floor as Mike laid there out of breath. I went in the bathroom and everything he had just released, I spit out and flushed down the toilet.

While I was brushing my teeth, Mike came in the bathroom with only his dress shirt and tie on. No pants and no draws.

"Baby, baby, baby! Where did you learn to do that?" he asked, smiling like he had just experienced the best feeling of his life for the very first time.

I looked at him standing behind me through the mirror, and continued to brush my teeth. Mike reacted the same way each time I gave him a head. He just loved it. I just figured that maybe the women he used to mess around with didn't know what the hell they were doing. I never got any complaints.

I had a his and her vanity, which I didn't know why, because when I bought my condo, I didn't have a "him." Mike walked over to the other sink and washed up before he put his clothes back on. We both stared in the mirror and he looked at me and said, "I love you so much." By that time, I had finished brushing my teeth and was wiping my mouth.

"Oh, is that why you love me? Because of how good I suck your dick?"

"Kel, don't even say that! You know I'd still love you if you never sucked my dick."

I couldn't even hold in my laughter anymore because I had never seen anyone look so serious when they were talking about dick sucking! It was so hilarious, I spit all over the bathroom mirror. I hadn't laughed like that in a very long time.

"What's so funny?" Mike said, still looking very serious.

"You are! I was just joking with you and you made something very serious out of sucking a dick. How do you do that?" I asked, beginning to laugh again. "Loosen up a little bit!"

"I just don't want you to get the wrong idea. I learned the hard way about you and your hormones. I have to walk on eggshells around you because anything will set you off!"

"Awww. Have I been that bad?"

"Nothing that I can't handle."

I hadn't realized that I had been so rough on Mike, but to think about it I did go off about small stuff, then would think about it later and feel bad. Now that I knew Mike felt like he had to walk on eggshells around me, I was gonna try to contain my emotions a little better 'til the end of this pregnancy. How it was gonna work out was what I was unsure about, but I was gonna put forward some serious effort.

Mike and I were finally ready to go after I had to redo my hair, which I wasn't very happy about, and of course, it didn't look as good as it did the first time! We had just enough time to get to the restaurant on time as long as highway traffic wasn't bad. It usually wasn't during this time of the evening. While on our way, I had to loosen my seatbelt because baby girl was kicking the shit out of me.

"What's wrong?" Mike asked.

"Your daughter is full of energy tonight," I answered.

Mike grinned and looked back and forth at me and the road. I took his free hand and put it on my stomach so he could feel his princess moving all around. It seemed like she got even more excited when she felt Daddy Mike's hand. I looked up at him and he looked so happy. I would've never thought that things would've turn out like this. I never thought that Mike would've gotten used to the fact of me being pregnant with someone else's child, but it seemed like he was adapting very well and was already attached to the child he hadn't even met yet. It was like he was already connected to her and they shared a special bond. That was the first time I had ever felt like we were a real family and it was a wonderful feeling. I could tell that Mike felt the same way.

We were only a few minutes late and as soon as we were pulling into Everest's parking lot, my phone started ringing and I saw that it was Jada.

"Hey, Jada."

"Hey, girly. You're still coming, right?"

"Yeah, we just pulled up, looking for a park."

"Okay. Well, we're already sitting at the table. I told them we were waiting on you, so just tell them you're with Silas' party."

"Okay. See you in a minute."

I felt like something had been telling me that I needed to get some exercise because everywhere we went, I ended up having to walk a long distance to get to where I was going. I didn't know so many people were into French food. I was just glad that Jada had made reservations or we would've been in trouble.

When we walked inside, everything was so fancy, and it was decorated beautifully with pieces of expensive art and mirrors everywhere. The host, who did in fact have a French accent, greeted Mike and I, asking how he could help us. I told him we were with Silas, and he signaled for another man who looked quite a bit younger than himself to come over and take us where we needed to go.

"This nice couple is with Mr. Cooper. Can you please take them to the VIP section?"

I was tripping. I didn't know what was going on, and from the looks of it, Mike was even more confused than I was. We looked at each other in astonishment. It seemed like we walked forever. The restaurant didn't look as big on the outside as it was on the inside.

As we walked behind the gentleman leading us to the VIP section, Mike said, "I've been here before, and in order to be VIP, you have to be spending some major dough in here. Whoever this dude is must really got it going on."

We finally made it to the VIP section, which was sectioned off by stanchions, and a big sign that read in big, bold, black letters "VIP Only." I agreed with Mike. Silas must've been a very important man and I definitely couldn't wait to meet him now. Our host led us into the VIP area and he said, "Mr. Cooper, your guests are here."

I still couldn't see Jada or Silas because the host was still standing in the doorway in front of us, as if he was making sure it was okay with Silas for him to lead us in. The suspense was killing me. *Who the hell is this man?* I thought. The host finally moved out of the way so that we could enter. Mike walked closely behind me holding my waist. When I entered and looked over at the table my mouth about hit the floor, and my heart began pounding like I had just run a marathon. I could literally feel the blood racing through my veins. I could not believe this shit!

Chapter 11

"Hey, Kel!" Jada said as she stood up to give me a hug. I stood there in shock, unable to wrap my arms around Jada as she hugged me tightly, shaking me from side to side as if she hadn't seen me in years. As we hugged, Mike walked over to the table to introduce himself to the man who called himself Silas.

Jada finally released me and said, "Oh, I am so sorry! How rude of me not to introduce y'all to my baby! I am just too excited! It's so nice to be able to get together with another nice couple and have a good time!"

"No problem," Mike said, as he stood behind me to help take off my jacket. I still stood there, not saying a word. The host came by and grabbed my jacket from Mike, while Jada anxiously waited to introduce herself.

"I assume you're Mike," Jada said, holding her hand out for Mike to shake. "I'm Jada, and I've heard so much about you. Good things, of course. I see you and my Silas already got acquainted."

"Relax, baby," Jada's beau said, grinning, showing off his beautiful smile that was all too familiar.

He got up out of his seat, stood right in front of me still smiling, grabbed my freshly manicured hand with his soft warm hands, and kissed it, saying, "Very nice to meet you, Kel." At first I just stood there, but I knew I had to snap myself out of it before anyone noticed how strange I was acting.

"Nice to meet you too," I said, trying to fake a smile, which wasn't going too well.

I could feel myself visibly shaking, so I excused myself to go to the bathroom so I could try to get myself together.

"Are you okay?" Jada asked.

"Yeah, I'm good. The baby is sitting right on my bladder, and I'm running to the bathroom every five minutes these days. I'll be right back."

I left fast enough before anyone could ask any more questions because I felt as if I was in the middle of a nervous breakdown. I briskly walked around the restaurant in search of the restroom, almost knocking over three waiters who were carrying handfuls of plates. Finally, one of them stopped me and asked if I needed help. I had never had a panic attack before, and had no idea what one felt like but at that moment I was panicking. I was sweating like a pig and breathing heavily, struggling to get my words out.

"Where is the nearest restroom?" I said, looking at the waiter with desperation in my eyes.

He pointed in the direction of the restroom, which was only a few feet away, and luckily no one was in there, because as soon as I entered, I ran into the nearest stall and threw up. When I finished, I immediately burst into tears.

"Why God???? Why?" I cried.

If it wasn't one thing it was always another. It seemed like every time my life seemed to be getting back on track, something always had to happen to throw it off . . . Way off! The expression, when it rained, it poured, was most appropriate for that moment. After I finished letting my tears flow, and I finally caught my breath, I stood in front of the mirror staring at the mess I had made of my makeup. I knew I needed to hurry up before Jada or Mike came to check on me, so I grabbed some tissue out of my purse and tried to clean it up as much as possible. Even though I didn't really need to, I forced myself to pee because I knew if I hadn't, I would be running back in there very soon.

As soon as I stepped out of the bathroom with my head hanging down, my eyes caught a black, very expensive pair of men's Prada dress shoes.

The person that the pair of shoes belonged to asked, "You okay?" in a deep, seductive voice, which was also too familiar.

I slowly lifted my head, knowing I would be facing a beautiful man. Jada's Silas and I were face to face once again. His brown skin was without any imperfections. His beard and mustache, neatly trimmed. Hair, freshly cut, and those eyes . . . Oh my God. Those deep dark eyes, with the most beautiful eyelashes, that just grabbed you and took you to another place. Those eyes were the eyes of a man that I once would've done almost anything for. A man who was once a very special part of my life at the wrong time in my life. Silas was actually Ty.

"I'm fine," I said as I tried my hardest to look away from Ty, but my eyes wouldn't leave his. They were stuck. I could feel them welling up with tears, so I slightly tilted my head back to keep them from escaping. I could feel my body begin to shake again and I squeezed both fists tight to try to control it. Ty could see it, so he grabbed both of my hands and held them tight to try to calm me down. I had so many things on my mind that I wanted to say, but nothing would come out. I didn't even know where to begin. We stood there in front of the lady's room staring into each other's eyes, holding hands. The feelings that I used to have for Ty seemed like they instantaneously returned, and it felt like we were the only two people in the world.

When Ty felt that I had calmed down and was no longer shaking, he released my hands, looked down at my stomach, put one hand on each side, and gently caressed it. My baby girl immediately began to kick, and Ty smiled.

"How far along are you?" he asked, and at that exact moment, my cell phone rang. I looked at the number and it was Mike. I looked up at Ty, and he said, "Go ahead and answer it. I told them I'd check on you while I was going to the bathroom."

"Hey, babe," I said trying to sound like everything was all right.

"Is everything okay?"

Ty looked down my throat as I talked to Mike, watching my every movement and listening carefully to my every word.

"Everything's fine. I felt sick for a minute, but I'm okay now. I'll be there in a sec."

When I hung up, Ty was still staring, and I began walking.

"So, you just gonna ignore the fact that I asked you a question."

"It doesn't matter," I said, walking as fast as I could, without looking back.

After walking in circles a couple of times, and Ty still following behind trying to get an answer out of me, we finally made it back to the table. Jada and Mike were sitting there across from each other laughing. Ty and I both sat down, once again acting as if we were complete strangers. What Jada and Mike didn't know wouldn't hurt them. At least for now. I wasn't ready to lose a good friend and a good man all at once. What I did know was that telling Mike what was going on would probably be best because if my baby was Ty's, the truth was probably gonna come out anyway. Ty definitely wasn't the type to let another man take care of his baby while he sat back and watched. I also knew that Ty had a feeling that the baby was his. Especially by the way they bonded within just a few seconds.

"Kel, you feeling better, girl?"

"Yeah, I guess the baby got a little upset," I said with a slight, insincere laugh.

"Mike was just telling me about how he has to roll you out of the bed these days! That's what we were over here laughing about." Jada giggled as she tried to finish her sentence.

The seating arrangements were not good at all. I was sitting next to Mike, which was fine, but Jada and Ty were sitting across from us, and yes, Ty was sitting directly across from me. The look on Ty's face while we discussed the baby and my pregnancy wasn't the most inviting. I remembered him having that same look in his eyes when I would be spending time with him and Terrance would call. He was so jealous that he hated hearing me have conversations with my own husband. He literally begged me to leave Terrance, but I couldn't. Ty wanted to take care of me, and since I wouldn't let him, I guessed he had found someone who would.

Now I understood why Jada had so many nice, expensive things. When I was with Ty, he made sure I had everything I wanted and needed. What I wasn't happy about was how little time it took for him to find someone to take my place. Don't get me wrong, I had moved on too, but I still hadn't even told Mike that I loved him due to the fact that I wanted to know for myself that I really meant it when I said it. Mike hadn't even completely moved in yet. Ty had bought Jada a car, and they were living together. Shit, in my eyes, they may as well had been married! One thing I noticed was that Ty didn't stray away from his type in women. I definitely knew now that I was his type. He found someone who was a lot like me.

Jada was such a good friend and she and Mike seemed to be getting along fine. Everything would've probably been perfect if Ty really had been Silas, and not Ty. I didn't know how all of this would play out, but I knew I needed to think really hard about what I needed to do on my end to make the situation go as smoothly as possible. I didn't wanna mess up anybody's happy home, especially my own.

During our meal, Mike and Jada did most of the talking. I could barely eat because every time I looked up, Ty was staring at me. Every time Mike would kiss me or make any type of intimate gesture towards me, Ty would look down at his plate and begin stabbing at his steak. I completely understood the feeling. It was very hard sitting there listening to Jada call Ty, baby. It made me cringe each time. I just hoped how uncomfortable I was didn't show as much as Ty's anger. However, he did seem to loosen up when he decided to tell the story about how he professed his love to Jada. I knew he did it on purpose to try to get a reaction out of me, so I was trying to not take it personal.

Ty said that the day he realized he loved Jada was one day he said he had to go out of town on business, like always, and Jada got fed up and told him how she really felt. She told him she was sick of him putting his business before her, and she was tired of lying in bed alone at night. He said he had never let a woman get in between him and his money, but that day, he did. He told her he wouldn't go and he didn't. He sent someone in his place. After that, he bought her a promise ring. When Ty mentioned the ring, Jada pulled out her left hand and wiggled her fingers, showing off the beautiful, pink rock to me and Mike. Ty made sure to explain that it wasn't an engagement ring. It was just meant to reassure her that he would always be there for her. I was ecstatic when that story ended until Ty asked Mike how we met.

Mike seemed very uncomfortable answering the question because he knew how I was. He didn't wanna say the wrong thing and have to hear about it later. I guessed he couldn't think of a lie fast enough because before he knew it, he said,

"I was Kel and her ex-husband's neighbor."

Oh shit! Here we go! I thought.

"I had a crush on her sexy ass from the day they moved next door to me, but of course, I knew she belonged to someone else. Unfortunately, we lost touch for a while when she moved, but fate brought us back together, luckily for me."

"Wow. Ain't that a coincidence? You was her neighbor and you two ended up together, huh?" Ty asked, as he sipped on his fourth glass of Hennessy which was four too many.

"Yeah, man. Like I said, I believe in fate, and this is definitely fate," Mike said, sounding defensive.

I looked over at Jada, and she sat there with her elbows on the table, holding her head up with her fists, attentively listening to Mike and Ty's conversation. It was getting too deep, and the deeper it got, the worse off the night was gonna get, but Ty wasn't about to quit. Especially with that alcohol running through his veins.

"So how long have y'all been together?" Ty asked.

I answered before Mike had a chance to open his mouth. I could see his yellow skin turning red, so I felt it was best that he and Ty communicated as least as possible.

"A little over three months," I answered.

"So, I guess you're not the daddy, Mike."

Jada looked at Ty with her eyes big as saucers. She looked embarrassed that he would say something like that, but didn't say a word to him. It definitely struck a nerve with Mike, because I was about to respond, but before I could, he put his index finger up to my lips, basically telling me to shut the hell up and he got this. I just hoped what was about to come out of his mouth didn't upset Ty to the point that he told everybody what was really going on.

"Look man . . . I believe everything happens for a reason. Kel was put back into my life for a reason. The difference this time was that she was available. I love her, and everything that's a part of her, including this baby. I offered to accept the responsibility of being this child's father and I would never turn my back on her or her mother. I don't have any children of my own, but this little girl will be treated as my own, and whenever Kel is ready, I will make her my wife."

When Mike finished speaking his peace, he took a sip of his Vodka and slammed his glass down on the table. Ty was sitting there with a slick look on his face, and I could tell he was thinking of something else to say. He sat back in his seat, grinned, and said, "I guess time will tell."

What the fuck is that supposed to mean? I thought. I was reading way into that last statement and just didn't get it. Maybe he was just drunk and talking. The table was completely quiet and being around both Ty and Mike made me the most uncomfortable I had ever been. Ty had really offended Mike without him even knowing who Ty really was, so I could just imagine what things would be like if and when Mike found out the truth. The checks didn't come soon enough. Surprisingly after all of the emotions that had revealed themselves at the table, Ty grabbed our check and said, "After all the trouble, I got this."

"Naw man, it's cool," Mike said.

"I know I was a muthafucka. I apologize. I got this oil in me and actin' like I don't got no sense. It's on me. Next time it'll be on you," Ty said laughing.

I didn't know what Ty called himself doing, but I knew whatever it was, he was up to no good. First, he stirred stuff up, and then wanted to apologize. It just didn't make sense, but I have to admit, it did lighten the mood. After the check was paid, and the host brought over our jackets, we all stood up. Ty and Mike did a little manly handshake thing while Jada and I hugged, and she said that we had to do this again. We all agreed, but I definitely didn't mean it. I didn't know if I would've been able to make it through another one of those.

Once we got outside of the restaurant, Mike grabbed my hand, and as Ty watched, he grabbed Jada's. He seemed a little different. Besides now being clean-shaven, instead of having his rugged Eric Benet look that I always loved about him, he didn't seem as arrogant as he used to. He did still have the same swag, and some arrogance about him, but he never wanted to fully show his true feelings before. He certainly had shown them tonight, even though nobody else at the table understood it besides the two of us. We all said goodnight and went our separate ways. I couldn't wait to get home. I was mentally drained and desperately in need of some rest.

On the way home, Mike didn't say much. He turned on some old school music, which I loved, and I sat back and relaxed. After getting home and taking a nice hot shower with Mike, I laid in the bed butt-naked, with my head on Mike's chest. Butt-naked was how I felt most comfortable these days and Mike loved to stare at me and the baby, after oiling down my entire body. I always loved the feeling of being cuddled up under my boo, but tonight was different. I would normally drift right off to sleep, but every time I closed my eyes, I could see Ty's face.

There were so many questions that I had that I wish I had asked him when I had the chance. I wanted to know how in the hell he became Silas. I also wanted to know, since he obviously wasn't dead, why he hadn't tried to contact me. The whole situation was strange. I knew he cared about me, but when you care about a person the way I thought he cared about me, you just don't let them go that easily. The main reason I thought he had been killed was because I hadn't received a phone call, text, nothing from him. Maybe he didn't care about me as much as I thought he did, and the only reason he was acting as if he cared now was because he knew there was a chance I was carrying his baby. I didn't know what to think. I wished there was a way to completely avoid Jada so I didn't have to make up excuses as to why Mike and I couldn't go out with them when she asked the next time, because I was sure there would be a next time. I had a feeling Ty was gonna make it his business to make arrangements to be able to see me every chance he got. As every thought filled my head and I analyzed each and every one of them, I finally drifted off into a deep, sound sleep.

Chapter 12

"Hey, girl! Why you so quiet over there!" Cameron shouted from her station, which was right across from me. She was quickly slapping relaxer in her client's, hair. The little girl had to only be around nine or ten years old, and her scalp must've been burning like hell because she closed her eyes so tight, that she squeezed out a few tears.

As I finished putting the last few curls in my client's hair, I said, "Girl, just tired. I stayed up pretty late last night, and I know I should know better!"

I lied. I had an abundance of shit going on in my mind. I couldn't stop thinking about when would be the best time to tell Mike about Ty, and what was gonna happen next. Mike and I were already prepared to possibly have to deal with Terrance once the baby was born, but I truly didn't think we would've had to worry about Ty. As a matter of fact, I knew Ty would pose more of a problem for us than Terrance would. This was very unexpected. I was really afraid to tell Mike that Silas was really Ty because Mike knew how I used to feel about Ty and I didn't want him to feel threatened by him in any way.

Miss know-it-all Cameron continued by saying, "Girl, you betta get your rest now, cuz when that baby gets here, there ain't gonna be no more of that! No more nappin' when you feel like it, no more full nights of rest, no more goin' wherever you wanna go when you wanna go, no more just spending your money on you . . . Chile, it just goes on and on!"

"For you not to have any kids, you shole do act like you know everything about havin' one!" I said sarcastically.

Cameron never had any kids, but she loved them to death. Any time any of her friends had babies, she would go to Babies R Us and buy up the entire store, and baby-sat anytime they asked. If I couldn't say anything else good about Cameron, she was good with the kids. I never knew why she didn't have any of her own. She had been married three times within her thirty-eight years of life, but had no kids with any of her husbands.

Cameron started laughing hysterically as she led the little girl to the shampoo bowl to put the fire out in her head.

"I knew that would get your smart-ass to talkin'! But I was for real though. You need to get some rest. Maybe you should go on maternity leave a month before you're due."

"You sound crazy as hell! I need all the money I can get before this baby is born! You've been a stylist longer than I have, so you already know we don't have the luxury of getting paid while we're off on maternity leave, although that would be real nice! I'm workin' 'til this baby is about to climb out of my vajayjay!"

Rhonda couldn't help but to butt in on that note and said, "Well, make sure I ain't here cuz I ain't into looking at no other woman's vajayjay, let alone, delivering a damn baby!"

Isis smiled and said, "I don't have no problem whatsoever lookin' at a pussy, or doin' some other things with one, but I'm not trying to look at one while it's being stretched out by a big ass head!"

Cameron covered her client's ears, but it was a little too late for that. I could tell everyone in the shop was in shock by that comment just by looking at the uncomfortable expressions on everyone's faces: both, stylists and clients. My next client, who had just sat down in my chair looked back at me as if I was supposed to say something. We all knew Isis was different, but I never took her as being a lesbian. I wasn't homophobic at all. I had no problem at all with the lesbian or gay community. I was just shocked to hear Isis put her business out like that. I guess there was no better way to come out of the closet than to do it while the subject at hand was one of her favorite meals! Like I said once before, nothing would surprise me when it came to Isis.

The next half hour seemed like the longest thirty minutes ever. Isis sure knew how to silence a room full of women. Once the old women who were in the shop getting their hair done were done rolling their eyes at Isis, and we were all tired of sittin' up in there listening to just the clicks of curling irons, and the sound of hairspray, I broke the ice by asking everyone what they thought was better and more convenient: breastfeeding or bottle feeding. I knew that topic would get everyone involved: especially the older women who I was sure would say breastfeeding was best. I was just hoping Isis didn't start talking about suckin' on some damn titties!

As soon as I got everyone talking, or I should say debating, my cell phone rang. As I reached for it, I told my client to go to the shampoo bowl.

"Hello."

"Hey. You got a minute."

I took the phone away from my ear to look at the screen to see who I was talking to. I didn't recognize the number, and whoever it was didn't have the best phone signal, so the voice sounded very muffled.

"Who is this?"

"Oh, you forgot about me already?" the muffled voice on the other end said.

"Oh, Ty?" I said as I finally realized who it was.

"Oh, Ty?" His sarcastic ass said, mocking me. "What the fuck you mean, oh Ty? Ain't you glad to hear from me?" he asked, in his powerful tone that I was very much acquainted with.

Whenever he would use that tone with me, he ended up gettin' some pussy. That was the past and I knew I couldn't let him get in my head like he used to. I walked towards the back of the shop because I knew Cameron and whoever else were secretly trying to eavesdrop.

"I just wasn't expecting to hear from you," I said, trying to sound calm when in actuality, my heart was beating out of my chest.

"Then I guess you wasn't expectin' to see me either."

"No, I wasn't expecting to see you last night, ummm, Silas, or whatever the hell your name is! But I gotta go. I got a client waiting on me."

Ty laughed and said, "I see that smart ass mouth of yours ain't went nowhere, but I wasn't talkin' about last night. I'm talkin' about right now. I'm outside, so your client gone have to wait a little longer."

As soon as Ty said that, the palms of my hands became sweaty, and I felt a huge flutter in my stomach and it wasn't the baby.

"Ty, we're gonna have to do this another time. I'm busy right now and I'm not about to lose no money for nobody."

"Woman, I could pay you what you gone make for the whole goddamn month right now! Get your fine ass out here or I'm comin' in."

Shit! I thought. I definitely didn't want or need Ty coming in the shop so these nosey-ass women could get to asking me a million and one questions, and Ty's slick ass knew that. I had no choice but to ask Isis to shampoo and set my client and put her under the dryer for me. I told my client I had an emergency and I'd be back by the time her hair was dry so I could style it. She didn't seem very happy about it, but she was gonna have to deal with it today. She wasn't one of my regulars anyway, so it didn't really matter to me if she never came back. As I walked around in circles trying to grab my jacket and purse, I felt like I was being closely watched, and I knew that I was. I was sure the other stylists, especially Cameron, were trying to figure out what was going on with me. As I looked back, closing the door behind me, everyone commenced to what they were doing. I didn't know it would be so soon that I would be back in the presence of Ty Wesley.

Once I got outside, I looked around and saw nothing but cars flying by. I walked down the sidewalk, with my hands in my jacket pockets, holding my head down to protect my face from the strong, cool wind. My hair blew wildly. When I made it to the side of the shop where the parking lot was, I saw a parked blue Maserati, and

Ty was sitting inside. When he saw me approaching, he stepped out, wearing a rugby type black, gray, and white, V-neck sweater, with a gray button down shirt hanging out the bottom, a pair of nicely fitted jeans, and casual black shoes. His beautiful eyes hid behind his dark sunglasses. He walked around to the passenger side of the car, waiting on me to get there. I could smell his cologne floating through the air. Once we stood face to face, Ty looked me up and down, grinning and biting his bottom lip at the same time.

"Look at my two ladies! I'm glad you decided to oblige," he said conceitedly.

I looked at him, with my eyes squinting from the sun and said, "What do you want?"

"I'm just trying to find out the truth. Is that my baby?"

"Why? You dropped off the face of the earth and now you want to reappear, questioning me? On top of that, you're in, what seems to me to be a serious relationship. That one I don't quite understand when you claimed to be so in love with me at one time, which wasn't too long ago!"

"Don't none of that shit mean nothing if you carryin' around my blood. Family comes before everything. I don't have no family, so if this is my child, I need to know."

I thought about what Ty said about him not having any family, and I realized the time we were together, he never mentioned anything about any parents, siblings, cousins, nothin'. I never even thought to ask, which now that I thought about it, seemed a little selfish of me. I was still shivering from the wind, and really wasn't in the mood to be arguing with Ty.

"Look, Ty, we've both moved on and your girlfriend happens to be a very good friend of mine, and I'm not gonna let a man get in between that."

"So now I'm just any ole' man now, huh? Y'all wouldn't even be friends if it wasn't for me."

Looking confused as hell, I said, "What you mean by that?"

"Who do you think told her about your shop? She was looking for a new hairdresser and I told her I had heard good things about Hair Haven."

"You are sick! Why would you want your current girlfriend to meet up with your past girlfriend?"

"Aint nothin' sick about it. It seemed like a way to be close to you, but I didn't think y'all would become tight! Now I'm glad you did because I probably never would've known what was going on. Now, we all off the subject at hand, so are you gonna answer my question or not? Is—the—baby—mine?"

Just standing there looking at Ty brought back so many memories of how I used to feel about him. We had so much fun together, and I was sure he could be a great father, but I knew by the car he was driving that we was still involved in the drug life. I didn't want my daughter to be subjected to any of that.

"You look like you cold. Let's sit in the car. Maybe some heat will unfreeze your brain and help you answer my question," Ty said with sarcasm.

He opened the car door for me, but as I was about to put one leg in, he grabbed my arm, turned me around, and hugged me. I slowly wrapped my arms around him, and dug my face in his chest as I could feel tears about to fall. He kissed the top of my head and softly told me he loved me. As we stood there holding each other, I came to my senses and realized anyone could've been watching, so I let go of Ty and sat in the car as fast as I could. He looked down at me and closed the door. As he walked around to the driver's side, I looked around the inside of the car, and noticed that he had a picture of Jada taped to his dashboard. It wasn't any type of picture. She had on some very erotic, black lingerie, and had a "Playboy" pose going on. From that one picture I knew Jada had to be a freak. It also made me think that for Ty to have her picture out in the open like that, he must've really been in love.

It took Ty a while to get back in the car, so I looked out the window and saw him standing there smoking a black and mild. Too much hadn't changed about him, but he never had a problem smoking in the car. Maybe Jada didn't allow him to, but I just couldn't see Jada running Ty like that. He always did what the hell he wanted to do. We were two of a kind in that department. He finally opened the car door and sat down. Instead of looking over at me, continuing our conversation, he just sat there staring through the tinted windshield. The silence made me uncomfortable, but I also didn't want to finish the conversation we were previously having.

After two or three songs played on the radio, Ty finally decided to say something.

"I already know the answer to my question. So now what I wanna know is what you plan on doin' about it."

I took a deep breath and without looking his way, said, "There's a lot I'd like to know right now!"

"Like what? All you gotta do is ask. I don't got nothin' to hide."

"Not anymore, huh? You just decided to lie to me about your occupation before!" I said turning sideways in my seat so I could watch him as he tried to explain.

"Look. I told you then why I wasn't completely honest. I didn't wanna lose you. You were the first woman in a long time I felt was feelin' me for me and not my money. I didn't wanna mess that up. It backfired anyway, so can we just let that go?"

Now it had clicked why Ty was attracted to Jada. Not only did she look a lot like me, she also continued to work even though he was giving her the world. That showed him she wasn't just after his money. She wasn't a gold digger, which is what he also loved in me.

I folded my arms and rested them on top of my belly and said, "Well, I hope you have it in you to be honest now because like you, I need to know the truth."

Looking into my eyes, Ty said, "I'm willing to answer you honestly to the best of my ability cuz I know there's a lot of unanswered questions."

"You damn right!" I said feeling like I was now in control of the conversation.

As I was just about to ask my first question, Ty pulled the car out of park and pulled up to the parking lot entrance, and slowly exited into the traffic.

"Where are we going?" I asked.

"Just riding, like we used to. We have a lot to discuss, so let's ride and talk."

I shook my head, but went ahead with my first question that I had been waiting to ask since the night before.

"Where the hell did Silas come from?"

"I knew that was gonna be your first question. You remember the trouble I got into with that bad drug deal. Well, since we bein' completely honest, I had the niggas who put me in that situation, passing off bad product to my best clients, taken care of. That didn't take care of the problem of me owin' my clients for that shit. I got paid five million for that drop, and I sure as hell wasn't givin' it back and I didn't have the extra product that those stupid niggas took from me to give to my client. I did the best thing I could think of. I changed my identity. I legally changed my name. Moved to a different area, switched cars, new social security number, new clientele, and new people to work for me. The people who work for me now fear me so much that stealin' from me won't even cross their minds. That was the problem with those other dudes that worked for me. I didn't put enough fear in their hearts. I joked around with them too much, and in this business, there's no joking with the help. That's how I went from bein' Ty Wesley to Silas Cooper. Personally, I'm likin' Silas a little better than Ty," he said.

I sat there astonished as to how easy it was for a person to become someone else. Ty actually answered two questions in one. I was gonna ask him if he was still selling, and even though he had answered, I still wanted one more confirmation.

"So you're still selling drugs?"

"Yeah. I told you there's nothing else I can do. I love my lifestyle and it's not gonna change. I have enough money right now to retire, but I'm not ready yet. Call it greed or whateva you want, but I call it wanting the best. I had the best of everything until I lost you. That shit hurt like a muthafucka. I never felt the way that I felt when I knew I had lost you."

Listening to Ty talk, I had mixed emotions. At first I was feeling those same emotions that I felt when Ty and I first started dating, until he reminded me of why I said I could never be with him. He lived a life that I could never become accustomed to. It just wasn't in me. I didn't feel like I was the type that could be a ride or die chick, and quite frankly, I didn't see Jada being that chick either. She couldn't have had any idea what Ty really did for a living.

"So, let me get this right. You would prefer to live in fear than to get a regular nine to five like any normal person?"

"I'm not scared! You scared?" Ty asked jokingly. I didn't know how he could joke around about something so serious, but I guessed he had been doing this for so long, it was normal to him.

"Kel, this is my life. I been on my own since I was fifteen and this is all I know and will ever know. You and my baby will also be a part of my life and I will protect y'all with everything I got!"

Ty put his hand on top of mine, as he continued to drive. At that moment, it seemed as though he thought everything was gonna go back to the way they were, but he was sadly mistaken if that was the case.

"Ty, I have a new life. You are not part of it. The only involvement you will have will be with my child if she's yours! On top of that, you have Jada!" I exclaimed as I pointed to her picture that was staring me in my face. I have to admit, it hurt bad as hell seeing a picture of another chick in his car and Ty must've noticed it.

"Oh, that picture bothers you, huh?" he said, arrogantly snickering, which he knew I hated. It always made me feel so small when he did that. "Didn't you tell me we both moved on? So me and Jada bein' together don't bother you, right?"

"No, it doesn't bother me!!! What bothers me is that you never tried to contact me after I left you in Atlanta! I assumed your "clients" had killed you. Now you walk back into my life with a completely new identity. Did you think about me at all?"

I knew this conversation would have to end soon because I could feel myself getting so upset that I felt like crying, but I definitely didn't want Ty to see me crying over him. I was happy before he had suddenly reappeared, and I vowed to myself that I would not allow him to interfere with what Mike and I had going on.

"Hell yeah! I thought about yo ass constantly. I couldn't get you off my mind. Matter of fact, have you really looked at Jada? I mean really looked at her? She reminded me so much of you I had to snatch her up. It wasn't like I could have you. I knew in the back of my mind after you found out what I really did for a livin', there was no chance for us. I didn't feel like bein' rejected. That's why I didn't contact you. I sent you flowers though! Don't that count for somethin'?"

I sat there looking dumbfounded trying to figure out what Ty was talking about. I hadn't received any flowers from him. I thought, *Is he runnin' game to get in my head?*

"Quit playing with me, Ty! Take me back to the shop cuz I don't have time for your lies and I need to get back to finish my client."

"I don't got no reason to lie. Didn't I always outdo myself whenever I sent you somethin'?"

Ty wasn't lying there. I thought about the time when I was still married to Terrance, Ty didn't know what I'd like, so he sent me one of each thing the floral shop had. It wasn't fun trying to explain to Terrance who had sent me all that shit.

"I sent you roses of every color, and your favorite Belgium chocolates," Ty continued. "Like I said, I don't have any reason to lie about what I buy somebody."

I couldn't believe what I had just heard. I instantly became furious. Not because Ty had sent me the flowers and candy, but because Mike took the credit for it. I didn't think of Mike as the type of man who would do something like that, but he did!

"That lame ass nigga' took the credit for 'em, huh? I knew he would." Ty laughed. "Don't go in too hard on him. I know he probably wished he could've thought to do something so special for his sexy ass woman. He probably don't even know what to do with a woman like you."

"I can't believe this. Please take me back to work," I said despondently.

Ty didn't stop there. He had more to tell me than I could've ever imagined. Stuff that I never would've thought he had anything to do with.

"I also called you every couple of days just to hear your voice. I neva could get up the nerve to say anything, but as long as I heard your voice and you sounded okay, I was cool."

I turned to the side, staring out my window, and said under my breath, "That was you too?" The hang up calls that I had been getting on the regular, who I thought was Terrance playing on my phone, had been Ty all along. Now, I definitely couldn't say that I hadn't been on his mind. I watched the bare trees go by as we headed back in the direction of the shop. Ty suddenly pulled over in an empty parking lot.

"What now?!?!" I asked in frustration.

"I need to take a smoke. Is that okay with you?"

"Oh, so you suddenly don't smoke in the car?"

Ty looked at me with a serious look on his face and said, "Yeah, but not with my unborn child in the car."

He grabbed his pack of blacks and a lighter from the console and stepped out the car. As I waited for him to finish, I looked at the picture of Jada again imagining the pain she would feel if I had to tell her as her good friend, that I was pregnant by the man she adored. I started wishing that there was a possibility that the baby was Reggie's. Things had to be bad for me to feel that way! At least he didn't have a direct tie to anyone but me.

After about five minutes, Ty got back in the car and exhaled before putting the car in drive. The rest of the way back to the shop, we were quiet, but Ty couldn't keep his free hand to himself. When he wasn't rubbing me on my thigh, he was rubbing my belly, smiling each time he felt the baby kick or move. This baby wasn't even here yet, but already had captured the hearts of two men. We finally pulled up in the shop's parking lot and parked. I sat there, still not saying anything. I could feel Ty staring at me.

"You asked me to bring you back. Here you go."

I put my purse on my shoulder and got ready to get out. Ty grabbed my hand, but didn't say a word. I turned to look back at him and everything he wanted to say was all in his eyes. He wasn't ready to let go, and to be perfectly honest, I didn't know if I was. I was wishing I could continue to think he was dead. Life was a lot simpler that way. I knew I didn't want a drug dealer for a man. I needed a man who made his money honestly, therefore, Ty wasn't a candidate. I gently pulled my hand away from Ty, rubbed his face with the back of my hand, got out and closed the door. I stood there for a second, wondering if I was doing the right thing, and I came to the conclusion that I was. I walked into the shop without looking back.

Chapter 13

I had never felt so uncomfortable walking into the shop. I was trying my best not to draw attention to myself, but the nervousness must've shown on my face.

"What's the matter girly?" Cameron asked.

"Nothing girl. I'm cool. Why you ask?"

"You flew out of here without sayin' much. I thought maybe somethin' happened at home."

Cameron was trying to see what she could get out of me. I knew all about slick women. She knew something wasn't right, but she wasn't about to get shit out of me. I wasn't about to be the gossip of the shop. My client had a few more minutes under the dryer, so I sat in my chair and relaxed while I waited, watching the other stylists do their thing. My cell phone vibrated on the counter. It was a text message. I knew exactly who it was because it read: I still love you. I quickly deleted the message, hoping that at the same time, everything else about Ty would be deleted from my memory. Even though Ty and I had been away from each other, it seemed like we had never lost touch. It didn't feel strange being in his presence like it had the night before. Maybe it was because

Mike and Jada weren't around. Being alone with him had felt exactly like it had before, and he still had the same affect on me. Unfortunately, the magnetism between us hadn't changed a bit. Being in his presence made me feel like I could bask in that ambiance forever.

I didn't respond to Ty's text, only because I didn't know what to say back. Those three little words were very powerful and I knew that would've been the worst thing I could've said. The rest of the day, I was pretty much quiet, thinking about poor Jada. Ty had basically used her to feel close to me. She had no idea what she had gotten into. I really felt bad for her because she had just gotten out of a horrible relationship before Ty, and Ty was like her savior from that situation. He was the one who helped her realize her self-worth again. I didn't know what would happen to Jada if Ty wasn't there. I didn't plan on causing any distress in her and Ty's relationship, but I just didn't believe Ty was gonna let it end like that. In fact, if the baby was Ty's, which he strongly believed, there would definitely be no way of keeping it from Jada.

I didn't even wanna think about Mike's ass. I couldn't believe he had taken the credit for another man's work in pursuing me. I wondered why he just didn't tell me that it wasn't him who sent the candy and flowers. Maybe he just didn't wanna accept the fact that another man was sending me gifts, or maybe he thought if I knew another man was sending me gifts I would leave him for that other man. Just as men say about women, men are some confusing creatures and I was just tired of trying to figure them out. I tried to figure out a way to tell Mike that I knew he didn't send the flowers, but I couldn't come up with anything without telling him I had talked to the person who actually sent them. I guessed I was just gonna have to let him get away with this one.

I got home, planning to take a nice hot shower and going straight to bed. Having so much on my mind had mentally exhausted me. To my surprise, when I walked in the door, candles were lit everywhere, and there were red and white rose petals trailing from the front door all the way to my bedroom. There was a fabulous aroma of something in the oven, and the house was immaculate. I didn't see Mike anywhere, but I heard water running in the master bathroom. When I walked in the bathroom, he was standing next to the tub with just a pair of boxers on. The rest of his body was bare and beautiful. His six-pack was so defined and his biceps were huge. Mike worked hard to keep his body intact and it worked. Part of the reason he hadn't completely moved in with me yet was because he had a workout room in his house, with all of his workout equipment and I told him all that shit wasn't coming up in here.

When Mike looked up and saw me, he licked his luscious lips and smiled.

"Hey, babe. How was your day?"

"It was good," I said hesitantly. "What's all this for?"

"Because I love you and I missed you today. I was surprised not to hear from you. I figured you must've been extremely busy and you'd be tired when you got home, so I wanted to make sure you didn't have to do anything when you got here."

"Thank you so much sweetie," I said as I walked towards him with my arms spread wide and my lips puckered.

He grabbed me and twirled me around like he always did, no matter how big I had gotten. It never seemed to faze him. He always picked me up as if I was light as a feather. After everything Mike had done, I had forgotten all about why I should've been pissed off at him.

Mike had cooked filet mignon, broccoli with cheese, loaded mashed potatoes, and his famous homemade biscuits. I was living it up. Mike had it all and I couldn't even deny it. After everything I had done, God still had blessed me with this man who could've had any other woman in the world. He loved me unconditionally, and I knew I better had started showing him how much I truly appreciated him. If only my past would be just that . . . My past.

While the steaks were still cooking, I got in the bath water Mike had run for me. The temperature was perfect. I leaned back as Mike knelt on the floor behind me and began messaging my temples. He was the best masseuse. I told him he needed to go into business, but then I took that back because I thought about that. I didn't need my man's hands all over no other broads. I knew all about the way thirsty bitches thought. They would see a fine ass man working as a masseuse and would make sure to save enough money out of their welfare check just so they could see him on a regular basis. Each time, they would have a different trick up their sleeve leading up to finally snatching up your man. Men are so dumb, or try to act that way, that they fall for that shit all day every day.

I moaned as Mike massaged me from my temples all the way down to my titties, which were always sore these days. Then he went to the other end of the tub and lifted each leg one by one, massaging from my thighs, all the way down to my feet. When he finished, he sucked each toe one by one, while gazing into my eyes. Mike knew exactly what to do to get me to that point of no return. He was so determined to show me he could satisfy me sexually, that he bought a small safe that I didn't have the combination to and locked up all my sex toys. I shole wasn't about to let him throw them out! I had invested way too much money in my toys! He told me I wouldn't need them as long as he was around. So far, he hadn't let me down. After massaging me from head to toe, Mike gave me a gentle peck on the lips, and left me so that he could finish up dinner.

By the time I got downstairs to the kitchen, Mike had already fixed my plate, and of course a glass of sparkling grape juice for me, and red wine for him. He pulled out the chair for me, helped me sit, and pushed me up to the table. He sat across from me, and I looked at him with a hint of a smile. I realized that night that I really did love Mike. He would do anything for me and I knew I would do anything for him. He made me feel special all the time, and so far hadn't given me any reason not to trust him or made me feel insecure in any way. Him, being deceptive about the flowers and candy wasn't a good enough reason for me lose any trust in him. In his eyes, I was the most beautiful woman in the world. Well, at least that's what he always told me, and I chose to believe him. Once dinner was over, the night had just begun, and I was anxious to see what Mike had in store for me.

He picked me up, carried me up the stairs and gently laid me on the bed. He went in the bathroom and came back with nothing on except for butt ass naked. His long dick stood straight out looking for its master, who would be me. I stood up and raised both arm so Mike could raise my white lace gown above my head. Mike was so anxious, before he could get my gown all the way off, he bent down to put one of my titties in his mouth. I manipulated my arms and hands enough to get the gown off and threw it on the floor. All that was left was bare skin. I lifted Mike's head, and crawled up on the bed. I gestured for him to follow me. I continued to crawl on the bed until I got to the headboard. I stood up facing the headboard, grabbed it with both hands and squatted. Mike followed suite and slid underneath me, grabbing my thighs, losing his tongue in the wetness of my never-ending sultry abyss. As he licked my lips and sucked my clit, I teased him with the taste of my pussy by moving up and down, making him chase it. I then slid down his perfect body and positioned myself on top of that dick that I craved. As I sat on it, Mike let out a moan as he said my name. He tried to come up, but I pressed his chest down, telling him to stay right there. I rode that dick like the stallion that it was. I could feel my juices running out all over the place and I wanted a taste. I lifted up off Mike's dick, scooted down, and made it disappear before my eyes. I sucked all my juices off of it as I massaged his balls as good as he had massaged my entire body while I was in the tub. Then I gently licked them and moved down to his perineum, flicking my tongue over it back and forth. I could feel Mike's body shaking uncontrollably as he sat up a little and grabbed my hair. I pushed him back down and crawled back on top of him so we could climax together. Mike sat back up and tightly grabbed my ass. I wrapped my arms around his neck and my legs around his waist, and aggressively gyrated on top of him. My thighs began to have aftershocks as we both moaned wildly. As I screamed his name, Mike squeezed me tighter and tighter, letting out a huge growl.

Both of our bodies limp from the huge explosion we had caused, Mike plopped back on the bed, bringing me down with him. I had heard some pregnant women complain about not being able to comfortably have sex, but I had no problem getting mine in. Sex was better than it had ever been in my life. I didn't know whether it was due to the pregnancy or Mike, but the truth would be out soon. I was hoping it was Mike because I knew once I was back down to size, I wouldn't be limited to anything and sex with Mike would be even better. Mike and I didn't move the rest of the night. We marinated in our juices and it felt great.

The next morning I woke up to the sound of my phone vibrating on my nightstand. Mike didn't move. I didn't know how early it was, but by the way I felt I thought it had to be pretty damn early. I looked at the phone, squinting my eyes trying to make out what it said. It was Jada.

"What the hell does she want this early on a Sunday morning?" I said under my breath. I started to let it go to voicemail, but with it being so early, I thought it might've been an emergency.

"Hello."

"Hey, girl," Jada said so loud, it sounded like she was screaming in my ear. "You sound like you're still asleep."

"Yeah, I was."

"Oh, I'm sorry! Silas and I were about to get ready to go to breakfast in about an hour and he had such a good time the other night, he told me to ask y'all to join us."

"We had a good time too," I said lying, "but I don't think we can make it this morning. Mike is still asleep."

"I'm not asleep," Mike said with his face in the pillow. "Who is that and where can't we make it?"

I was so mad at Mike for opening his damn mouth. There was no way I was going anywhere with both Ty and Mike sitting at the same table with me.

"This is Jada, and she was asking if we wanted to go to breakfast with her and Ty, but I know you're tired. Especially after last night."

"Ewww. TMI!" Jada said.

I was so tired I had forgotten Jada was on the line. "I know, right! I'm sorry, girl. That slipped out, but we did have a good time last night, you know what I'm sayin'!" I said jokingly.

Mike interrupted our laugh and said, "We can go if you're up to it. I know lately you don't like to turn food down." This negro had jokes, even though it was the truth. Today I was turning it down though, for obvious reasons. I told Jada maybe another time, and told her to enjoy her time with her man. Ty thought he was so slick. I wondered how long this game would go on, and how long I would have to put up this façade. Since Mike had done so much for me the day before, I decided to get up and cook breakfast after I washed all the sex off of me from the night before.

Once I finished cooking breakfast, I called Mike downstairs to eat. When he came down, before he sat down, I wrapped my arms around him and gave him a peck on his lips. I then softly said, "I love you baby." When the words left my mouth, I exhaled, not believing I had finally said it. Evidently, Mike couldn't believe it either. He said, "What?"

"You heard me. I love you." The second time, it came out with more ease.

Mike, showing all thirty-twos, said, "I love you too, baby. Always will."

My heart fluttered, and I tried to hold in my smile, but I couldn't. We stood there holding each other, and both burst out laughing. It felt so good for me to tell Mike how I felt about him and know that I really meant it. I had felt like I loved him for a while, but I just wanted to be certain that I meant it before I said it. I believed that the worst thing you could do was tell a person you loved them and didn't mean it. I had another surprise planned for Mike later on that day. He had no idea!

Chapter 14

After breakfast, I sat in the middle of the bed Indian-style, watching TV, waiting on Mike to get out of the shower. He was getting ready to do what he did every Sunday morning: go to church. That was another plus for Mike. He was God-fearing. I needed a man like that in my life. He went to church faithfully. Some people may have called him a hypocrite because we were fornicating, but how could he have possibly resisted me?

Mike finally came out of the bathroom with a towel wrapped around his waist, with water still running down his clean-shaven chest.

"Why don't you go to church with me this morning, babe?" Mike asked.

He caught me off guard, and I stuttered over my words trying to think of an excuse as to why I couldn't go with him.

"Uh, maybe another Sunday, but not today. I . . . Um . . . I'm just really not prepared today."

Truth was, I had thought about going to church for a while now. Especially since I hadn't been since all my infidelities began.

I just felt like I wasn't worthy enough to be in the house of the lord. I was taught that when we repented, God forgave us for our sins, but I felt like I had done so much, I didn't deserve for Him to forgive me. I hadn't talked to God in so long He had probably forgotten my voice. I knew that wasn't true, but that's how I felt.

"Tell me, how do you prepare to go to church?" Mike asked inquisitively.

"Honestly, I don't know. I just don't feel comfortable. Look at me . . . Pregnant and not married."

"You're not the first, and certainly won't be the last. Who cares what people think anyway? You shouldn't, and if the people at church judge you, they are hypocrites. No one can judge you except God. Didn't you ever learn that?"

"Of course. I grew up in church. I just don't know . . ."

"Look, these people don't know you, and you're not going for them anyway. You would be going to be in the house of the lord with your man who you . . . What did you say? Love?" Mike said, as he smiled.

Mike was absolutely right. I was gonna have to face my fear of being judged sooner or later anyway because I definitely wanted my baby to grow up in church just like I did. I wasn't feeling completely confident about it, but I was trying to make some changes in my life, and this would be a good start. I got up, put on my Sunday's best, and headed to church with the man I loved.

Church service was very emotional for me, from the prayer and worship, to the choir, to the message, and the benediction. An older lady, who strongly resembled my grandma who had passed away a few years before, wearing the stereotypical big church hat kept handing me tissue every time she heard me sniffle. My grandma and I had always been very close and I told her almost everything, and knew none of it would ever be repeated. I even told her the first time I had sex, which was something I never told my momma. To this day, my momma probably still thought I was a virgin even though I had been married and was pregnant.

Mike kept his arm around me during the entire service, continuously looking over at me making sure I was okay. I felt like a lot was being lifted off of me. I was giving all my problems to God and I could literally feel them being lifted off my shoulders. I never understood that feeling when I heard people say it, but I had finally felt it for myself.

At the end service, the tissue lady, who was only about five feet tall, reached up and grabbed me and gave me the most loving hug. It was so warm and sincere. She gave me a kiss on the cheek and said, "You, your husband, and that baby be blessed my child. You already have a beautiful family, and when that baby girl is born, it will be even more beautiful and perfect."

I gently pulled away from her with more tears in my eyes, as I wondered how in the world she knew I was having a baby girl. She looked at me, smiling, and handed me one more tissue before she turned around to go greet and give out more loving hugs to the rest of her church family.

While I was still in a daze, Mike tapped me and said, "What was that all about?"

"Nothing. She was a very nice woman. She had a wonderful aura about herself."

"Oh, that was Sister Elnora, and you're right. She is a very nice woman."

I looked at Mike in astonishment because my grandma's name was also Elnora. I looked around for Sister Elnora, just to get one more look at her, and I felt the need to hug her one more time, but she was nowhere in sight. From the church to the parking lot, I continued to look around through the crowd of people standing around talking, for the woman with the most beautiful spirit I had ever encountered. I had no luck.

While on the way home, I told Mike I needed to stop somewhere. There was something that I needed to do and it couldn't wait any longer. He didn't ask any questions. He just told me to tell him where to go. I grabbed his free hand and held it tightly as he drove. As I gave him turn-by-turn directions, I still couldn't get Sister Elnora off of my mind. I had heard people say how their loved ones visited them in spirit using the body of someone else, but I hadn't completely bought into that theory. I knew anything was possible with God, but that was just unbelievable!

When we were finally arriving to our destination, I told Mike to pull up in front of the red brick house that was coming up on the right. When Mike stopped the car and put it in park, he looked over at me and said, "Okay. And where are we?"

At first I just sat there smiling, feeling good about my decision. Then I said, "At my momma's house."

Surprisingly, I didn't get the response I was expecting and hoping for from Mike. His entire expression changed. That was the first time I had seen panic on his face, and then I became unsure and worried.

"What's wrong, Mike? I thought this was what you wanted? I felt this was the time!"

"It is what I wanted, but today I'm not prepared!"

"How ironic that you said that! Didn't I say the same thing to you this morning about going to church? And what did you tell me? So what I'm gonna say is how do you prepare to meet your woman's momma?" Mike was at a loss for words. He didn't know what to do, so he cleared his throat, wiped the sweat from his forehead, and said, "Come one. Let's do this."

Mike got out of the car and walked to the other side, while I patiently awaited him to open my car door. When he made it around the car, he peeked at me through the passenger side window, and I smiled, batting my lashes at him. He smiled, but it wasn't one of those sincere smiles that I was always used to seeing. I couldn't believe the way he was acting. All of the shit he had given me about not introducing him to my momma, making me feel guilty, and now his ass had the nerve to be nervous.

He opened the car door and helped me out. He then straightened out his clothes and tugged at his tie while asking me did he look okay. I started to realize how important it was to Mike that my momma got a good first impression of him. As confident as he always was, I never imagined this ever being a problem for him.

Mike grabbed my hand and we slowly walked up the walkway as if it were judgment day. I caressed his sweaty hand to try to calm his nerves as we walked. When we finally reached the porch and I rang the doorbell, Mike stood there inhaling, then exhaling as if he were having a panic attack.

After we waited for about a minute after I rang the bell, Mike said, "Maybe she's not home."

"Oh, she's home! Her car is sitting right there," I said, as I pointed to my momma's silver Toyota Camry sitting in the driveway. "It takes her a while to get to the door if she's not downstairs."

Finally, from outside, I could hear footsteps coming down the stairs, and my momma's loud mouth saying, "Here I come! Don't go nowhere!" Mike began rubbing his hands together, then looked at me raising his eyebrows.

I saw the doorknob turn, and suddenly began to feel sorry for Mike. Obviously my momma hadn't looked out the window to see who it was because she slightly cracked the door enough to peek out. From where she was standing, she couldn't see me, so the first person in her view was Mike.

"What can I help you with? I'm gonna let you know right now I'm not buyin' nothin'! I'm on a fixed income."

I stayed where I was on the other side of the door with my hand over my mouth trying my best to hold in my laugh. Mike stood there not knowing what to say, so he stood there gesturing to me with the weirdest faces I had ever seen, trying to tell me to let my momma know what was going on.

I finally revealed myself and my momma wrinkled up her forehead, saying, "Kel, what are you doing out there with that salesman? Is he trying to get you to buy something too?"

"No, Ma," I said giggling. "Can we please come in?"

As my momma pushed the screen door open, Mike grabbed it, and held it until I was inside, and he followed.

My momma still looking confused, said, "Girl, you betta tell me what's goin' on!"

"I will! Let's just go and sit down."

Mike remained quiet the whole time, and just followed my lead. I walked towards the family room, and my momma followed, keeping her stern eyes on Mike. Once we were in the family room, all three of us stood, facing each other.

I began by saying, "Well, momma, as you probably know, someone's been making me happy these past few months . . ."

"I hadn't noticed!" My momma said sarcastically, folding her arms and rolling her eyes at Mike.

"Don't be like that! Can we just talk? Please?" I begged.

My momma sat down, with her arms still folded. I looked at Mike and nodded, giving him the cue to have a seat. Once they were both seated, not next to each other, of course, I sat next to Mike and grabbed his hand. Before I began, my momma thumped her fingers on the armrest of the sofa as she watched me stroke Mike's hand.

"Momma, we're sorry to intrude if you're busy, but I felt it was time that you met someone who has become a very important part of my life within the past few months."

My momma interrupted by saying, "Before you even feed me this ridiculousness, I need to ask a question. How in the world can someone be an important part of your life if you've only known him a few months? That's the dumbest thing I've ever heard you say! I thought I taught you better than that!"

"Momma, just listen for once!" I shouted.

My momma's mouth dropped in astonishment. I had never yelled at her like that, and I knew it was disrespectful, but I didn't know how else to get my point across and get her to listen. Mike sat there looking even more uncomfortable than he did before.

"Ma, I'm sorry, but I need for you to hear me. This is Mike. Like I said, he's very important to me. I know you've heard this before, but he treats me very well and we love each other."

My momma opened her mouth to say something, and I put my finger up to my lips to tell her to let me finish.

"I know what you're thinking. You're probably thinking I'm just vulnerable right now due to what I've gone through, but that's not it. I'm way past that and seeing very clearly. What I see is that this is an exceptional man and he wants nothing but the best for me."

I could tell that everything I was saying to my momma was making Mike a lot more comfortable. He sat up, gazing at my momma waiting for her reaction. The room was silent for a moment, and when my momma realized I wasn't about to say anything else, she said, "Well, can he speak for himself or do you have to do all the talkin'?"

Mike stood up and said, "Yes, Ms. Armstrong, I can speak for myself. I just didn't want to get in the middle of the discussion between a mother and daughter. I've been wanting to meet you for a while now, but Kel wanted to wait for the best time. She respects your feelings and opinions very much, and I love and respect her as much as I know she loves you. I can't think of being with anyone else. I set my eyes on her a long time ago, and deep down I knew she would one day be a part of my life."

My momma watched Mike intensely as he poured out his feelings for me to her. Once he finished, I knew it was her turn, and I wasn't anxious to hear what she had to say. Her eyes had already become double the normal size, and they only did that when she was furious.

"So Mike, you think you love my baby, huh?"

"No, ma'am. I know I love her."

"So what do you plan on doing when my granddaughter gets here?"

"I'll be here for Kel and the baby. I'll be there for her as if she were my own. I've already bonded with the baby, and no one can take that away."

"I don't think you quite understand what Kel has gone through. This is not a game. She's fragile and don't need a man like you around to confuse her. She's about to have a huge responsibility and needs to keep her priorities in order. I've seen men like you. The pretty ones who think they're God's gift to women, but find the vulnerable ones, who you think you can dog out and go on about your business."

"As you already know, your daughter is a grown woman, and you've raised her to be a very strong, intelligent, and independent woman. She's not naïve in any way. She knows how I feel about her. I know you're just meeting me, so I understand it's gonna take a while for you to understand, let alone trust me with your daughter. I give you my word that my intentions are not to harm Kel in any way. I'll keep her safe always and I stand by my word."

My momma listened, but I could tell she still wasn't trying to hear a thing Mike was saying. She just had that look on her face like she just wanted to blurt out "Bullshit" at any moment. She had already made up her mind that she wasn't gonna like him. She took her attention and focus off of Mike, turned towards me, and rudely said, "Anyway Kel, where you comin' from lookin' so nice?"

I was hoping my response broke the tension. "Mike and I just came from church."

My momma got extremely loud, laughing hysterically and said, "Church? Ha! Now he's a churchman, huh? That's the oldest trick in the book! Men always think a woman will always go for the "God Fearing" man! Kel, poor child! When are you gonna learn? My grandchild will not be subjected to such bullshit!"

I knew it was coming soon. Her favorite word when it came to men. Bullshit! I didn't know what was coming over me, but I felt like I was gonna explode, and I did!

"I can't control what you feel is bullshit or not, but I can control who can and can't see my baby! I don't like negative energy and you're giving off a lot of it!" I stood up as my mouth continued to run, and the more I said, the more my momma's eyes welled up with tears. I didn't mean to be so harsh, but it was like I couldn't control what I was saying. I think it was a buildup of everything I ever wanted to say to my momma, but I had learned to always bite my tongue just so I could keep the peace with her. I didn't like to argue with her, and I wished she would've just tried to give Mike a chance, so we could've avoided all of this. Tears streamed down her face as I continued to threaten her with not being able to see her first grandchild, and as hers flowed, mine began to flow.

Mike stood up and stood in front of me grabbing me and holding me. Still trying to talk, I could no longer make any sense out of anything I was trying to say. As Mike held me, I buried my face in his suit jacket, not wanting to look either of them in the eye. For the first time, I had shown the other part of me to the people in my life I loved most. I just wanted them to be able to love each other the way that I loved them.

Mike rocked me as we continued to stand. My momma was silent and I was wondering what was going through her mind. Mike led me back to the sofa and sat me down. I put my face in the palm of both of my hands, still not ready to face my momma. I heard Mike ask my momma where she kept the Kleenex. I didn't hear her say anything, but I figured she must've pointed where he needed to go because I heard his dress shoes moving across the hard wood floors.

"I never thought my child would be speaking to me the way you just did, after everything I've done for you. And how could you threaten me by saying you won't let me see the grandchild that I already love so much? That's just evil!" My momma said sounding disgusted. I was still confused about how I felt at that moment. Some of the things I had said, I meant, but I would've never kept my baby from my momma and I think she knew that. She was just hurt that I would even allow that to come out of my mouth.

I took my face out of my hands when Mike came back with the Kleenex. First he handed some to me, and then my momma.

He took center stage and said, "Look, I'm not here to come between the two of you, and I don't like the way this is going, so if you two need to work some things out, I can disappear for a while . . . not too long though, and when you straighten out your differences, Kel, you know I'll still be around. I just couldn't live with myself knowing I ruined a perfectly good relationship between you and your mom. That just wouldn't sit right with me."

With bloodshot eyes, I glanced over at my momma, and I could see the guilt in her eyes as she looked up at Mike. We were both wrong and I could admit that, but could she was the question. Being the bigger person, I stood up, walked over to my momma and stood her up. I gave her a long heartfelt hug as I told her I was sorry. Surprisingly, she apologized to me too. I didn't think it was really me that needed an apology. Mike was the one that was treated like shit, which he didn't deserve.

When we let go of each other, Mike was standing there with his hands in his pockets, admiring the love between me and my momma. She gave me a kiss on the cheek, looked at Mike and said in a low, shaky voice, "I'm sorry. I just worry about her. I just don't want her to get hurt again. I'm gonna trust her judgment, and hold you to your word. Don't make me come hunt you down 'cause I will."

She could've kept that last statement to herself, but I was just happy that we managed to get that far. I was even more willing to accept her apology to Mike after she walked over to him and gave him a hug. "Thank you, Ms. Armstrong. I appreciate that and I won't disappoint you."

I felt like that had been enough for one day, so I told my momma we'd stop by another day to talk. We had to get past the initial shock first and get our emotions in order. When Mike and I got in the car, my momma was still standing in the door. I waved bye to her as we headed back to our side of town. I knew Mike was definitely a keeper. Anyone who could withstand my momma's crazy antics and make her feel the need to apologize was all right with me.

Chapter 15

The next morning, I woke up in the mood to be pampered, so I called Jada and asked if she wanted to go to the spa during her lunch hour.

"What time you goin'?" Jada asked, trying to talk over the kids in the background. She was already at work. Fortunate for me, it was Monday, and still considered to be my weekend.

"I'm thinking around noon."

"Uh . . . I don't think I can join you today. I wish I could."

I was disappointed Jada couldn't go with me. I figured she and Ty had something already planned for lunch. I hadn't been to the spa alone since Jada and I had become cool. It was nice to have someone to talk to but I guessed I would have to get over it because I was really looking forward to getting pampered and I wasn't cancelling my plans for anyone. Mike did a great job at spoiling me, but it felt good to get away sometimes.

Still trying to get Jada to change her mind or get it out of her why she couldn't go, I said in my baby voice, "But we always go together." Sometimes getting stuff out of her was like pulling teeth, unless, of course, she had alcohol in her system.

"Girl, don't think I don't wanna come! I definitely need it after being around these kids all day every day, but the teacher has an afternoon doctor's appointment, so I'm in charge of the class for the second half of the day."

"Okay. Well, I guess I'll accept that excuse. Talk to you later, girly!"

"Enjoy!"

I kinda felt relieved when she told me she was stuck at school and not going to lunch with Ty. Every time she would bring him up, I would quickly change the subject before she gave me any information I didn't wish to hear.

I continued to lay in the bed for a little while longer. It felt strange having the entire bed to myself. Mike stayed at his house the night before. After dealing with my momma the previous day, I just needed some time alone to calm my nerves, and Mike, being the considerate man that he was, understood that. I didn't sleep well the whole night because I was used to Mike holding me from behind, and me backing my ass all up on him. It was so crazy how some things became so natural. I would be spending most of my day alone, but I was okay with that. Me time was a necessity in my life.

When I walked into the spa, a cute little Asian girl with straight, jet-black hair that reached her butt greeted me at the front door. She looked and sounded as though she couldn't have been any older than fifteen. She told me that her name was Jamie and she would be in charge of making sure I received excellent treatment. She asked me had I ever been there, which I had, several times, which is how I knew she must've been new because everyone else who worked there knew me by name. Before she could even ask, I told her I would be getting the Platinum Spa package. It consisted of everything, except for touching my hair. The only people who I let put their hands in my head were Cameron and myself.

I signed in and followed Jamie. On our way to the massage room for my aromatherapy massage, I advised Jamie that the only masseuse that I would accept was Leslie. Leslie always took care of me. She told me Leslie was with someone, but she would make sure that my request was granted. That was exactly why I loved going to the spa. The employees always made me feel like I was queen bee.

Jamie took me into the massage room for pregnant women. The only difference between that room and all the others was that it had a table with a deep, oval dip in the middle, so pregnant women could be comfortable laying on their stomachs. That was one of the best things ever invented. Jamie gave me a towel, told me to get undressed, and Leslie would be there soon.

After Jamie walked out, I took the scrunchie that I had wrapped around my wrist and pulled my hair up in a bun. I didn't want anything getting in the way of the fabulous massage I was about to receive. After stripping down, I wrapped the towel around myself, stepped onto the stepstool, and carefully climbed onto the table. As I laid there, waiting, with my hands folded under my chin, I looked around at the beautiful fountain that looked like a waterfall sitting in the middle of the room. Smooth jazz played in the background. The smell of the aromatherapy immediately comforted me. The entire atmosphere was just so calm and serene.

I heard a faint knock on the door, then the door cracked open.

"I'm descent," I said loud enough for Leslie to hear me.

Leslie walked in with a big smile on her face and said, "Kel! I am so happy to see you and the baby!" Leslie had the most beautiful slanted eyes I had ever seen. I had always envied Asian's eyes. The shape of them seemed to symbolized sexiness and eroticism. Leslie favored the young girl Jamie, except for the fact that she looked more mature.

As Leslie used her magic oils on me and knead each joint and muscle perfectly, from head to toe, I moaned like I always did during her massages. I wasn't even embarrassed to admit that she always made me feel like another woman should've never made me feel. It felt too good to be wrong in any type of way. I never desired to be with a woman, and I knew that was the closest I would ever get to being intimate with a woman. It was just a massage, but it felt like so much more, and Leslie always satisfied me. I always told her she had magic in her hands and I could tell she was always intrigued by how I reacted to them.

Once my erotic massage was over, Leslie left, and Jamie returned with a plush, white robe, and spa shoes for me to put on

so I could move on to my facial. There was no one in particular
who I preferred to do my facials, so I took the first person who was
available, which was actually a guy. I received a deep cleansing
and exfoliation, even though I really didn't need it. Since being
pregnant, my skin had been the clearest it had ever been. Once he
finished covering my face with an avocado mask, and put
cucumbers over my eyes, I could hear the sound of other voices in
the room. Those voices belonged to my manicurist and pedicurist. I
relaxed and dozed off as they finished serving me.

I felt a tap on the shoulder, and when I opened my eyes, Jamie
was standing over me. There was no one else in the room. I didn't
know how long I had been asleep, or when the cucumbers had
been removed from my eyes. I looked down at my hands and feet
and they were perfect. I rubbed my face, and my skin was even
softer.

"So, how were your services, Kel?"

"Everything was great! Thank you so much."

After going back to the massage room and putting on my
clothes, I walked towards the front to pay. It seemed like the place
was empty, but there were several rooms, where there were
probably several other people receiving massages. Just not as good
as the one I had received!

I was waiting for someone to get to the front desk so I could
pay, and Jamie came from the back looking surprised to see me.
Maybe they think I already paid. I thought.

Jamie walked behind the counter, stood in front of me and said,
"Is there something else I can help you with?"

At that moment, it was evident that Jamie did think that I had
already paid, and I started to go along with it, but I knew I would
be back for their services again. I knew they would figure out at
the end of the day that I didn't pay, and I wanted to make sure that
I was welcome to come back.

"I would like to pay you, but if this is on the house, I'll accept
that too," I said with a smile.

"But it's already taken care of," Jamie said in a soft innocent
tone.

I squinched up my face, saying "Huh?" with my expression. I
followed Jamie's eyes with my own, which led me to believe

something or someone behind me was grabbing her attention. I turned around so quickly, my face ran straight into the jacket of the person standing behind me, causing me to inhale the scent of fresh leather. Embarrassed, I looked up, and it was Ty, wearing a brown, leather jacket, lookin' like a million dollars, like always. His swag was at one hundred, which was a bad thing for me. How long he had been standing there, I couldn't tell you.

"I thought I would treat you to some much needed pampering," he said smiling and biting his bottom lip.

I turned around, and looking at Jamie, I said, "Thank you." Jamie nodded and headed back to the back of the spa.

Once she was gone, I turned back towards Ty and said, "I had the money to pay."

"I didn't say you didn't have it! Can you just let people treat you sometimes without opening your mouth? All you gotta say is 'thank you'!"

"I don't have to say thank you! I didn't ask you to do shit!"

"Ugh! Here you go!" Ty said, sounding frustrated. "You're welcome," he said, and walked towards the exit.

At first, I just stood there watching him walk away, but then guilt set in thinking about the disappointment I had just seen on Ty's face.

"Ty."

Ty stopped, but didn't turn around to look my way, so I said his name again.

"Kel, I don't have time for your games. I tried to do something nice for you and you wanna beat me up."

"Just turn around." Still nothing. "Please," I said.

He hesitantly turned around, and looking in his eyes, I said, "Thank you."

"No problem. Anything for my baby momma," he said as he turned around to continue walking out the door.

"Wait!" I exclaimed. "So that's it? You just come to pay for my spa day and leave?"

"What else do you expect?"

I was so disturbed by the fact Ty had paid for my spa services that it hadn't even crossed my mind 'til that moment as to how he even knew where I was.

"Wait . . . How did you even find me? Did you follow me?"

"Girl, I ain't gotta follow you! Jada called and told me you had asked her to go to the spa with you and she was upset she couldn't make. I went to every spa in the area 'til I found you."

"Ty, there's like thirty spas around here!"

Ty stood there looking at me with nothing but seriousness on his face. "And your point is?" he asked.

"I'm just sayin' that was unnecessary hard work."

"It was very necessary for what I'm workin' on."

There Ty went with that slick-talkin' shit. That's the kind of shit that got my panties wet.

"I did what I came to do, and I'm tired of standin' around in the spa, so you ready to get out of here?"

Ty reached out his hand waiting for me to grab it, but I just walked right past him grinning. As I walked past he smacked me on the ass. I stayed ahead of him as I walked towards my car. I saw his car parked a few spaces down from me and hoped that he would keep walking, but I knew that he wouldn't.

"So you headin' home to yo man?"

"You know it."

"You keepin' him as happy as you kept me?"

"Happier."

"Is that right? I don't think that's even possible."

"Well, it is. You wanna ask him how happy I keep him?"

Ty laughed, but I could tell I was starting to piss him off. All I could say to that was people need to stay out the kitchen if they can't take the heat. He always started shit, and then wanted to get pissed and act shitty. *Same 'ole Ty.* I thought.

"Come on girl. Let's go for a ride."

As soon as I was about to tell him no, he quickly stuck both hands under my shirt and rubbed my belly. He then looked at me and brought his face closer and closer to mine until our lips were a centimeter apart. I watched as his lips parted, and I turned my head.

"Oh, it's like that, Kel? Why you actin' brand new?"

"You know what it is! You're the one that's acting like you don't know we're both in serious relationships, so you quit actin' brand new!"

"I know you still love me. You just can't turn that shit off. I know I still love you. As a matter of fact, I'm still in love with you. I don't think that ever left."

"Well, I can tell you that I don't love you and I'm not in love with you. Now if you ask me if I care about you, then I would say yes. Definitely."

"You have to love the father of your baby."

"You are not the father of my baby!" I said angrily.

"How you know?"

Sad part was, I couldn't answer that question, because I didn't know. I just felt like getting in the car and driving off without having any more words with Ty. The conversation had already gotten too deep when he said the "L" word. *Maybe if I just take a ride with him, he'll leave me alone.* I thought naively. Ty could tell I was giving in, so he grabbed my hand and led me to his car.

When I got in, the first thing I noticed was that the picture of Jada was gone. Ty got in, and I nosily asked, "What happened to the picture?"

"I took it down. I thought it would be disrespectful to have that up while you're around. I knew you would be ridin' with me today," his arrogant ass said.

"So, where we goin'?"

"Just enjoy the ride."

As we rode, we ended up in parts of Chicago I had never seen in all the years of living there. He asked me questions, trying to get a little insight as to how serious Mike and I were. The way Ty talked, it sounded as if all I had to do was say I wanted him, and he would drop Jada, but I was confused by that. I was confused because they seemed even more serious than me and Mike. I didn't understand how someone could be so serious about a person, and drop them for someone else so easily.

Since Ty asked all the questions he wanted, I chose to ask Ty if he really loved Jada. Whether or not his answer would be honest, I didn't know. I just wanted to hear what he had to say. His answer wasn't clear, but surprisingly sounded sincere.

"I don't know how I feel about her. I felt like I might've before I saw you again, but after I saw how clear my feelings are for you,

I feel like my feelings for her should've been that clear too. I shouldn't have to question it. I should just know."

After burning gas for about an hour, I saw the outskirts of what looked to be a beautiful subdivision in the distance.

"While we're out sightseeing, and you're showing me parts of the city I didn't know existed, let's drive down there to that subdivision," I said, pointing straight ahead.

"You in the market for a new house?"

"Maybe . . . Just take me! I just wanna see what else I've been missing."

"Oh, I can tell you what you've been missing . . ."

The more Ty smiled and talked slick to me, the more his eyes captivated me, making me feel like Calgon was taking me away. We pulled up to the entrance of the subdivision and it was a gated community. I figured we wouldn't get past the guard. Ty rolled down his window and said, "My beautiful lady friend is in the market for a house, so we just wanna look around."

The guard nodded, and Ty smiled. I didn't know what it was about Ty, but it seemed like he always got his way. The guard lifted the gate and we proceeded slowly.

"Wow! Now this is what I'm talkin' about!" I said amazed by what I saw.

There was not one mediocre house in sight! I understood why they were gated, but I didn't know how safe it was when the guard let strangers in just because we said we wanted to buy a house.

"See, if we were together, I would put you in one of these houses."

"I'm sure you got money, but not this kind of money! These houses are like triple the size your old house was!"

"Don't be countin' my money."

As we continued down each street, I guessed how much each house was. None of my guesses were less than two million. The subdivision had to have been a newer one because there were still several vacant lots. I thought we had seen every house and was about to tell Ty to head back to the spa so I could get my car until we came to a house that stood out from them all.

"This is it. This is the house that I will strive to have!"

Ty slowly pulled up in front of the house that I was in awe of and put the car in park.

"You look like you wanna get out and look at it."

"We better go. We don't need anybody callin' the police on us. Let me quit teasin' myself."

"You don't wanna at least go to the door and ask the owner if you can look around?"

"Boy, you are crazy!"

"Come on girl!"

Ty got out the car and started walking towards what looked to be a marble walkway. I didn't know if it was actually marble, but it sure did look like it. I jumped out and started after Ty. This was what I loved about Ty. He was so fun and full of spontaneity. Ty looked back at me and waited for me to catch up.

As we approached the huge, solid oak door, I said, "This house has to be at least fifteen million."

I waited for Ty to ring the doorbell since he wanted to act like a badass. He looked at me and said, "You gonna ring it or what?" I exhaled and lifted my index finger to press it, thinking to myself, *All they can do is say no.* I quickly pressed it and stood there fidgeting. Ty laughed, put his hands in his jacket pocket and pulled out his keys, then said, "Try twenty million." He put his key in, turned the knob to my dream house, and opened the door.

"I guess I do got that kind of money, huh?" Ty said, staring at me as if he was waiting on me to bend down and pick up my face. "Come on in so I can show you around." I could tell he was getting off on this and I felt so stupid!

As I stood there, with my mouth close to hitting the ground, Ty grabbed my hand and said, "Come on girl." I slowly began to follow him until I suddenly came to my senses.

"Boy, I am not going in your house!" I said as I snatched my hand away from him and folded my arms.

"Now, not even five minutes ago you said you wanted to see this house, and now you got the opportunity and don't want to! Bring yo stubborn ass on!"

"Ty, you and Jada share this house and Jada is my friend."

Ty looked at me as if nothing that I had just said meant anything to him.

"Okay? What is your point? This is my house. I own it, not Jada. As a matter of fact, I paid cash for it. I can have any muthafuckin' body in here I choose. Anyway, who gone tell? You?"

Ty did have a point there. I wasn't gonna tell, and I was curious about what it looked like on the inside. I left my arms folded and began walking towards the entrance, trying to still act as if I wasn't very happy about it. As I walked in front of Ty, I heard a snicker behind me. I already knew he was thinking he had me exactly where he wanted me, but he could think all he wanted. Wasn't nothin' happenin'!

Ty's house was the most magnificent thing I'd ever seen! It was like a work of art. Nothing in the entire house was inexpensive, from the marble flooring, granite countertops, custom cherry oak cabinets, gorgeous chandeliers hanging from every room, to the most simplest things, such as the beautiful, porcelain vase in the shape of two lovers kissing. The kitchen was huge enough for at least five chefs to cook their own full course meals simultaneously without getting in the way of one another. As we walked around the main floor, in addition to the kitchen, I saw three out of eight of the bedrooms, four huge bathrooms, a family room, gym, and basketball court! I couldn't believe my eyes, and I still couldn't make myself believe that this all belonged to Ty.

There was a golden dual staircase that led upstairs to the rest of Ty's gorgeous mansion. Ty held his arm out in front of me, granting me permission to head on up. As I walked, choosing the staircase to the left, Ty followed behind with his hands on my hips. Once we reached the top, I waited for Ty to take the lead. I could tell he was proud of what he had, but he was never the type to boast. We headed towards what I would consider the east wing of the house, passing up several closed doors. The last door we came to, had a set of double glass doors, which were frosted so you couldn't see on the other side of them.

"You wanna see what's inside?" Ty asked.

I tried peeking through the glass, but I couldn't see a thing.

"You wanna see or not? You not gone see nothin' from out here."

Before I could answer, Ty opened the door. That one room was probably bigger than my entire condo. The only reason I knew it was a bedroom was because there was a bed! There was also a minibar, microwave, fridge, a master bath, and a closed off area that looked like an office. The entire ceiling was covered with mirror, except for the skylight. I already knew what the mirrors were about. Ty liked to watch himself as he made love. It was kinda strange when I first found that out about him, but when I was involved in the pleasure that it gave him, it was very sensual. I opened another door, which was mirrored, and walked in, leaving Ty, as he walked over to the stereo to turn on some music. I entered a walk-in closet that was bigger than my living room. I stood in the middle of it, staring at all the clothes and shoes. In particular, Jada's. I also noticed a tall safe on the far end that I imagined had enough money and valuables in it to take care of Ty and whoever else he wanted to take care of for the rest of their lives. I just didn't understand why Ty continued to do what he did if he already had everything he needed.

While still staring at the safe, daydreaming, Ty snuck up behind me, wrapping his arms around my waist as he kissed my neck and rocked me from side to side. I closed my eyes, enjoying his touch, rocking with him to the sound of Robin Thicke singing "The Sweetest Love." Ty held my arm up and twirled me around towards him, put his face so close to mine, our noses touched, and looked at me as if he was waiting for permission to kiss me. As his face moved closer and closer, I tilted my head back further and further. He grabbed the back of my head, trying to move it towards his, but still trying to be strong, I stiffened my neck.

"Relax, Kel. Can I just have one kiss? It don't gotta go no further than that."

I figured one kiss wouldn't hurt, so I loosened up. Ty held my face in his hands and all I could see were his beautiful lips coming close to mine. I closed my eyes as my lips parted and I soon felt Ty's lips pressed gently up against mine, and I felt an explosion within my entire body. My heart was pumping double time and I could feel all the blood rush to head. His long, thick tongue intermingled with mine, and explored every part of my mouth.

Without allowing our lips to part, Ty picked me up and walked me over to the bed and laid me down. I watched him as he pulled his shirt off, and being careful not to lie on my stomach, straddled me, kissing me more aggressively this time. How we used to kiss before we had rough sex. As I laid there, saying a whole lot of no's in my head, but not a word out loud, Ty raised both of my arms over my head and pulled my shirt off in one motion. He looked into my eyes, then down at my stomach, shaking his head.

"This is my family right here," Ty said, low enough to be talking to himself, but loud enough for me to hear.

He slid down to my stomach and kissed it over and over and over again. Then he just laid there, with his ear pressed up against it. After a few minutes, without even looking at me, Ty said, "I love y'all, man. You just don't know, but I'm 'bout to show you." He proceeded with slipping off my shoes, then sliding my pants off.

"You still wearin' thongs huh?" Ty said, grinning.

I rolled my eyes, but really couldn't have an attitude because this man had already gotten in my head and he knew it. He especially knew it when he was able to pull my thong off without any resistance from me. I had gone into this strong and had every intention on just having a mature, innocent conversation with a man I used to be in love with.

He spread my legs pushing them way over my head, looking amazed that I was still capable of doing that. As soon as he spread them, I could hear the sound of the lips of my wet pussy parting, and the cool breeze from the ceiling fan caused my clit to throb more than it already was. First he put his nose close, and inhaled my womanly scent.

"She always did smell good. Now let me see if she still tastes good since you been lettin' another nigga' get it," Ty said.

He licked me from the front of my pussy to the back, then stuck his tongue in deep, collecting all my juices. I turned my head to the side moaning as if Ty was killing me. I was hoping that when he started, I wouldn't feel anything between us and tell him to stop. The complete opposite happened. It felt better than it had ever felt before and I couldn't tell him to stop if I wanted to. I knew it felt good when I looked over and saw Jada's picture on the nightstand staring right at me, but I just stared back at her and continued to moan as her man ate the shit out of my pussy. As he continued pleasuring me, he took my entire swollen clit in his mouth and sucked it hard, tickling it with his tongue at the same time. My whole body shook as if I was having a seizure and tears ran out the corners of my eyes onto the red satin comforter as I let out a scream. Ty released my numb legs and came back up, wiped the tears from my eyes, and gave me a peck on the lips.

As soon as Ty stood up to pull off his pants, he said, "Did you hear that?" I was so out of it, I didn't know what he was talking about. Then I started to listen, and heard the sound of keys coming down the hall. We then both heard the sound of Jada's voice calling Silas' name.

"What the fuck?!?! She ain't supposed to get off 'til four!"

We both looked at the clock and it said four-thirty. "Shit!" Ty said, as we both frantically started moving around, grabbing clothes off the floor. Ty opened the closet door motioning for me to go inside. As soon as he closed the door, I heard Jada walk in room.

"Hey, baby!" she said in her normal excited tone.

Being nosey, I wanted to see what was going on, so I went over to the door to see if I could crack it open, but to my surprise, I didn't have to. The mirrored closet door happened to be a one-way mirror. I could see everything that was going on, on the other side. The first thing I saw, which I wish I hadn't, was Jada and Ty kissing. I was sure she could taste and smell my pussy all over him and the thought kinda made me excited all over again.

Jada walked towards the bathroom and I could no longer see her. Ty looked at the closet door, obviously knowing it was a one-way, putting his finger up to his mouth, telling me to be quiet. Jada came back in view with only a black bra and black lace panties on, hugging all over her man, telling him all about how rough her day was with the teacher being out, and how much she missed him. Surprisingly, Ty was able to act as if he was really engaged in the conversation after what had just happened and what was about to happen between us.

I began to feel guilty after Jada told Ty she wished she could've gone to the spa with me today because she definitely needed it. That wasn't the part that made me feel guilty. She expressed how it felt good to have a good friend to be able to hang out with, and how real I was. After I heard that, I was ready to go. I desperately needed to get out of there. I finished putting my clothes back on that Ty had taken off, thankful that we hadn't left anything lying around.

Even if and when I do get out, where will I go? I don't even have my car! I thought. I thought about calling Tasha to have her pick me up somewhere on a corner, but I knew that would cause too many questions to arise. Just then, I thought about the fact that my cell phone was in my purse, and I had laid my purse on the couch in the family room downstairs! Jada went back in the bathroom, and I cracked the door, whispering, telling Ty where my purse was. He sprinted out of the room to get it.

I could hear Jada talking, obviously thinking Ty was listening. When she realized he wasn't responding, she came out of the bathroom looking around, brushing her teeth. She then walked up close to the mirror on the closet door staring at herself, flipping her hair from side to side, with her hand on her hip and toothbrush sticking out of her mouth. Nervous as shit and sweating, I tiptoed to the back of the closet and hid behind the safe, hoping she didn't come inside. I peeked from behind the safe, and I just saw an empty room through the mirror. Suddenly, the door cracked open, and I stuck my head back behind the safe. I heard a loud thump, and it was my purse hitting the floor. If I hadn't been trapped in this negro's closet, he would've gotten cussed the fuck out for throwing my damn Louis Vuitton purse!

After a minute of too much quietness, I went back to the mirror, and I could faintly hear Ty and Jada laughing. All of a sudden, they came out of nowhere, butt ass naked. He was carrying her, with her legs wrapped tightly around his waist, and arms around his neck. Ty went towards the window, and sat Jada on the windowsill. He kissed her rough and hard, and I could tell that she liked it. She put her feet up, balanced them on the sill, and squatted, preparing herself to take all the dick Ty was about to give her. I couldn't believe I was watching this, but for some reason I couldn't stop. Ty lifted one of his legs and plunged his long black dick into Jada's pussy. Under the circumstances, I was shocked that Ty's dick was even able to get hard! I watched his ass muscles tighten, with each thrust, and Jada's face full of elation. My clit began to throb more and more as I began to cry from the hurt I was feeling of seeing Ty fuck another woman.

When I finally couldn't take anymore, I went back and hid in my little corner. I looked at my phone to see what time it was and to see if I had missed any calls. It was going on six, meaning I had been stuck in that damn closet for almost two hours and I was hungry. Mike had called me several times, which didn't surprise me and didn't make me nervous. I wasn't married, so I didn't feel like I owed him any explanation. I knew that was wrong of me to say, especially after everything Mike had done for me, and how much he loved me, but I was upset at the moment and Mike's feelings weren't even close to being important to me. My feelings were what was important, and they were badly hurt.

The closet door opened once more. I didn't peek out, not knowing whether it was Ty or Jada.

"Kel," Ty whispered.

I peeked around the safe.

"Come on. She in the shower. Let me take you somewhere else."

Not wanting to do a damn thing he told me, I moved slowly. I didn't have much of a choice in the matter. He took me into one of the guest rooms and said, "She never come in here. She about to leave so just stay here and I'll be here to get you when she gone." I didn't say a word. Just listened. This whole situation was not making any sense to me.

About twenty minutes later, Ty came back to find me staring at the wall.

"Okay, Kel. The coast is clear. Come on."

I didn't move. I just continued to stare at the wall, then Ty did something he shouldn't have at that moment. Touched me.

"You okay?" he said nudging me.

"Motherfucka! Don't you touch me! How dare you disrespect me the way you just did. How the hell did I get back to this same place with you? I should've known better!"

Ty tried to grab me, and I started swinging on him. He finally got a hold of both of my arms and held them down, trying to talk to me at the same time. I couldn't stop crying, thinking about everything that had just happened. It was all so wrong in so many ways and it had just complicated things even more.

"Kel, this can't be good for the baby. Just calm down so we can talk."

"Talking is what we were supposed to be doing! How the hell did I end up in your bedroom? There is nothing between us, Ty! It's over! Been over for a while now! I have someone who loves me and only me, and not confused about it."

Ty grabbed me, hugging me and said, "It's not over. We're not finished. We have a family and I'm not lettin' it go. I love you and only you."

"Bullshit, Ty! I just saw how you fucked that girl! You wouldn't have done that in front of someone you love!"

"Look, what was I supposed to do? I don't say this often, but I'm sorry if that hurt you."

On that note, I jumped up and said, "Let's go. Just take me to get my car so I can go home to the person who really cares about me."

Ty punched the wall, and if that had've been a cheap wall, there would've been a hole there, as hard as he hit it. I jumped, but tried to act like it didn't scare me. Ty had fire in his eyes. I guessed I had struck a nerve with that last comment, but I didn't care. He was foul and he knew it!

"Kel, I don't know what I gotta say for you to know I'm bein' real with you. I never thought we would be back at this point again. I'm kickin' myself now for startin' a relationship with somebody else. Especially somebody who was vulnerable when I got with her. I'm the world to her. I don't know how to just let her go without hurtin' her too bad. I don't feel the same way about her as I feel about you. I want you and my baby to live in this house with me. I wanna come home to y'all every day. Since we been back in contact, I've even considered retirin' if that's what it's gonna take to have my family. We'll have plenty to live off of."

I had never heard Ty be so vocal and express his feelings the way he just had. Although beautifully said, I didn't understand how Ty could think it would be so easy for me to leave Mike for him. He was only thinking about himself, and how he would leave

Jada, so I had to make him realize that Jada wasn't the only other person in the equation.

"I know Jada loves you. It's quite evident. Mike loves me too. Has been loving me for a long time. Even when I was married. He even knew I was messing around with you, and still didn't judge me or think any differently of me. He has earned my heart and I can't leave him like that."

"Oh, so he knows about me?"

"Not exactly. He knows I messed around with 'Ty,' not 'Silas,' so he thinks you're two different people, and I prefer it stays that way."

"Well, I'm gonna tell you one thing. These feelings you call yourself havin' for him are gonna leave. I don't want you givin' my pussy away to him either."

"Oh my god! It's really time to go. Come on," I said giggling and shaking my head.

"I'm serious. It has to stop today."

"Okay," I said, trying to get him to shut up so he could take me to my car.

Finally making it to the spa, where I left my car, Ty pulled up next to my car, and parked. As I opened the door, about to get out, Ty grabbed the back of my jacket and said, "I meant what I said. We belong together, and I enjoyed today, even though it was interrupted. Give me a kiss." I looked at him and rolled my eyes, amazed that he had the audacity to tell me to give him a kiss after all I had seen today. He noticed I wasn't budging, so he reached over, pulling me close enough to him to get his much-desired kiss. He even managed to force his tongue through my tightly sealed lips, leaving me with the taste of my own pussy in my mouth. I was sure if I could taste it, Jada could too. Maybe she was one of those women who knew her man was cheating on her, but was in denial. Ty rubbed my stomach one more time and said he'd talk to me later. When I got in my car, I sat there looking straight ahead in a daze until Ty blew his horn. I hadn't even noticed that he hadn't pulled off. I looked over and he motioned for me to roll my window down, as he did the same.

"What's on yo mind?" he asked.

"Nothing. Why?"

"Cuz you just sittin' here in the parking lot lookin' like a lost puppy. You thinkin' about goin' back in to get another massage?"

"Shit, I need one! You stressin' me out!"

"Naw. I just gave you some shit to think about. I'm not here to stress you out. I'm just tryin' to make your life a lot easier. Stick with me and you won't have to worry about shit. You won't have to deal with not one more nappy headed client! That's a promise."

I had heard enough from Ty for one day, so without warning, I rolled up my window, and pulled off. I turned left, leaving out of the spa's parking lot, and noticed through my rearview mirror, Ty turned right. I then pulled out my phone to call my man.

"Hey, babe," Mike said with love in his voice. "I been missin' you."

"I missed you too. Sorry I'm just now calling you back. I left my phone in the car."

"No explanation needed. I trust you," Mike said, making me feel guilty.

If only he knew what I had really been doing.

"So have you had enough alone time? I mean . . . Is it okay to come home tonight?"

"Home?"

"I mean, to your house. You know what I meant, but maybe one day, I can call your home or my home, our home."

Now Mike wanted to start this serious talk. I felt like I was being pulled every which a way, and soon I was gonna break. On that note, I changed the subject, telling Mike about how much I enjoyed my day at the spa, especially the massage. He asked me if it was better than the ones he gave me, and of course I had to stroke his ego, telling him no one could massage me better than he did. Talking to Mike was like a breath of fresh air. He cleared my head and made me remember what was important.

Chapter 16

The next few weeks were miserable for me. I was constantly in Jada's presence while she helped to get ready for my baby shower. She always had such a sweet smile on her face, and every time I tried to smile back, I felt like a phony. I felt like she was a real friend to me, and I would've liked to consider myself a real friend to her, but I knew I had betrayed her in a way that could never be forgiven. Ty began calling, almost on a daily basis, trying to act as though he was checking on me, but he knew exactly what he was doing. He and I both knew that mental attraction was even more powerful than physical attraction. From past experiences, I learned when a man actually had in depth conversations with a woman, that lead to an emotional connection that's hard to break. On the other hand, when it was just physical, meaning, all about sex, more than likely there were no emotions involved. With me and Ty, even though we weren't currently having sex, we were still both physically and emotionally connected. It seemed like Ty was stalking me, because he always knew the right time to call. Coincidentally, Mike was never around.

Being around Jada was even more uncomfortable, due to the fact that every time I saw her, I visualized her on that windowsill, enjoying what was once mine. I envied her and didn't know why. I knew that I could have Ty if I wanted him. Problem was, I didn't know if I really didn't want to be with him, or if I was trying to convince myself that I didn't want him. The only thing I didn't like about him was his occupation, but he was willing to give that up for me. He was willing to do a lot for me, so he said, but I always thought, *What If I gave up what I had with Mike to be with Ty, and everything he promised me ended up being lies?* I let Mike get away once, and I wasn't about to let it happen again. I believed Mike was right when he said it was fate that brought us back together.

The day of my baby shower had finally arrived, and I couldn't wait 'til it was over. Tasha, Jada, and my momma were supposed to be handling everything, but the weeks leading up to the date, every time I looked around, they were calling me, frantic about something. It was important to all of them that everything turned out perfect. I was so flattered that I had people who cared so much about me and my happiness, but this was almost as bad as planning a wedding.

Pulling up to the banquet hall that the ladies in my life had rented for the day, there were cars galore, and all I could think was, *I didn't know I was cool with so many people!* Mike helped my huge eight-month-pregnant body out of the Porsche. I knew that traditionally, men didn't come to baby showers, but I begged Mike to stay with me. He really didn't want to go. I don't think it was because other men weren't gonna be there, but because he felt uncomfortable knowing he wasn't the biological father. I had decided to wear a pink sleeveless dress, with a sheer, pink shawl that I had specifically bought for the shower a few days prior. I didn't realize I was gonna look like a super-sized bottle of Pepto-Bismol! To top it off, I wore my pink eye shadow, speckled with gold, and a light pink gloss.

Tasha greeted us as we got to the door, wearing the cutest pink pantsuit. Since I was having a girl, I had chosen light pink, white, and lavender as my colors for the event.

"Y'all late! Where y'all been?" Tasha asked with her hands on her hips as if I was her child and owed her an explanation.

"Girl, move out my way!" I said extending my arm, pushing her out of my way.

"Wait! I gotta introduce y'all!"

"Oh, lawd! This must be my momma's idea! Can't we just walk in?"

"No, you can't! And no, it wasn't Momma Armstrong's idea! It was Jada's!"

"Ugh! Come on then," I said, looking up at Mike, rolling my eyes and shaking my head.

I grabbed Mike's sweaty hand and followed behind Tasha 'til we reached the door to the entrance of the room where the shower was obviously being held.

"Wait right here!" Tasha said, as she excitedly attempted to run in her pink iridescent heels.

Mike and I could both hear her loud mouth on the microphone telling everybody we had finally arrived.

"Let's give a warm welcome to the parents of the most precious little girl who still remains nameless!" Tasha said, sounding like a real-live talk show host.

Mike and I walked in to a large crowd of people standing and clapping for us. I had never cheesed so hard in my life. I looked up at Mike, and his smile was bigger than mine. My momma came out of nowhere and grabbed me, giving me one of her famously painful hugs. She wore a lavender pantsuit, with a pink and lavender silk scarf tied around her neck. She even got extra jazzy and put on just enough lavender eye shadow.

"Gone Ma! You look gorgeous!"

"Thanks baby! You too." She looked at Mike, smiled, and said, "Both of you look nice." She winked at Mike and he nodded at her. They had been getting along very well. I was glad my momma had decided to trust me with my judgment, but Mike only had one time to mess up and that would be all over. I didn't see that happening.

Everyone walked up to me, giving out hugs. I saw family and friends, who I hadn't seen in years, but I was happy to see every last one of them. I had printed out a list of my contacts and given them to Jada, but it was evident that my momma had her own guest list! Jada was beautiful as always. It was the first time I had ever seen her with her hair pinned up, and that brought out her stunning features even more. I couldn't blame Ty for choosing her. She patiently waited on everyone to get their turn to chitchat with me a bit, so she could get her hug in. When she hugged me, I could smell Ty all over her. I knew they must've made love before she left, and that caused my mood to turn sour.

I interrupted Mike as he held conversation with one of my cousins from Alabama, to tell him I'd be right back. I had to go to the bathroom to try to get myself together. I knew me and Jada's friendship wouldn't last if I reacted this way each time I was around her. Luckily the bathroom was empty, just in case I needed to let out a good cry. I sat in the stall for a few minutes trying to catch the tears before they fell so they wouldn't ruin my makeup. When I came out, surprisingly, there was a very curvaceous woman in a very tight dress, who I hadn't even heard come in, standing at the sink washing her hands. Even though she was standing in front of the mirror, I couldn't see her face because she had her head down.

I stood at the sink next to her, and she lifted her head. I glanced over at her, and it was my worst nightmare. My rival and I stood face to face. I always dreaded the day that I would run into Tiffany, and it had finally happened at my damn baby shower! She looked the same besides she had cut her hair in a sassy, short cut. Why she was at my baby shower was what I wanted to know.

"What the hell are you doing here?" I said, folding my arms across my belly.

"I was invited, but you don't seem happy to see me. Awww! Are you still salty?"

"Bitch, if I wasn't pregnant, I would whoop your ass!"

Tiffany laughed, and said, "Girl, please! You had the opportunity to kick my ass when you found your husband fuckin' the shit out of me, and you didn't do nothin' but look like a fool! When I got the invite, I just had to come and see if it was true. If the hoe was really pregnant!"

At first I couldn't figure out why she kept saying she was invited, and then I realized her name must've been on the contact list that I gave Jada when she was trying to send out the invites. I had forgotten to delete her name.

"Who the hell you calling a hoe!" I exclaimed as I unfolded my arms and balled up my fists.

"Oh, how classy you are! Ready to fight! I'm a lover, not a fighter, hun!"

"While you're talkin' all this shit, I bet Terrance didn't tell you he took me through hell contesting our divorce."

"Bullshit! He don't want your skanky ass! He got all he need right here!" Tif said, running her hands down both sides of her perfect body and placed them on her hips. That's when I noticed Terrance's name tattooed in cursive above her left breast. I guess she noticed me staring at it because she laughed and said, "Oh, you like? He's gonna get his with my name next week." I swallowed hard to try and get the lump out of my throat from the hurt.

"I'm glad you got pregnant by somebody else, so we don't have to deal with your dumb ass. I don't do baby-momma drama!" she continued.

I laughed and said, "Oh. I guess he didn't tell you that I'm pregnant by him!" I knew that I was lying, and didn't know for a fact if Terrance was the daddy, but Tif didn't have to know that. I was determined to not let her get the last laugh. She had been a thorn in my side for way too long, and I needed closure. She and Terrance got the last laugh before, but that wasn't gonna fly tonight.

"Bitch, how the fuck would you know whose baby it is?"

"We had a prenatal DNA test, so unfortunately, I'm stuck with your man being a part of my life for the rest of my life!"

Tif's entire expression changed. She didn't look so confident anymore, which was exactly what I wanted. I knew exactly what she was feeling. She wasn't sure what the truth was and while I had her where I wanted her, I decided to add more pain on top of pain.

"Has he told you about Stacy yet?" I asked and before she could answer, I continued. "I'm sure he hasn't. She's pregnant too . . . By him! Imagine that! You sure are gonna have a lot of people to share Terrance with. Now who's the fool?"

By Tif's face, I could tell she didn't wanna believe me, but deep down she did. At that moment of silence, my momma walked in.

"Kel, what is takin' you so long in here? Your man out there looking for you!"

I didn't even look in my momma's direction or say a word. I kept my eyes focused on Tif and that dumb look on her face. My momma finally glanced over to see who or what I was staring at.

"Girl, if you don't get the hell up outta here! Ain't nobody invite your butt to my baby's event. You got a whole lotta nerve walkin' up in here like somebody in here like you!" My momma said, all up in Tif's face with her finger so close to her face, I thought she was gonna poke the girl in the eye. I wouldn't have been mad!

Tif snickered as she walked past the both of us, pushing the door open so hard, it hit the concrete wall on the other side. My momma, still with her stern look on, grabbed me, hugging me as I cried on her shoulder.

"Girl, this supposed to be a happy day, so don't let that heifa mess it up."

"It's too late! She already messed it up! I can't go back out there like this!"

Just then, Tasha came running in the bathroom, briskly shaking her hand, and talking to herself. I always thought she was bi-polar, and thought that maybe it was finally coming out entirely.

"Girl, what's the matter with you?" My momma asked.

"Excuse my language, Momma Armstrong, but that bitch got a smart ass mouth. I been waitin' to get her ass since she messed with my girl. I punched her ass in her mouth!"

"Who?" I asked curiously.

"Who you think? Tif's ass! She didn't see it comin' either! I got a splash of her blood on my pretty pink, but that's okay. It was worth it!" Tasha said, sounding out of breath as she pointed down at the bright, red spot on her pink jacket.

"Well, I don't condone violence, but this time it was okay! I would've got her if I was back in my younger days!" My momma said and laughed, patting Tasha on the back.

When we got back to the shower, it had turned into a party! Jada was on the dance floor leading the Cupid Shuffle, and so many people were up there they looked like they were about to knock each other over. Cameron was up there and her ass was taking up enough space for five people! Tasha ran up there, like I knew she would. She never turned down a chance to show off her moves. I had forgotten all about poor Mike. My cousin was still in his ear, and he was looking at me like he wanted me to come save him. I walked over to the table where they were sitting and told my cousin that my momma wanted her.

"Thanks for the save, babe."

"No problem! You know those down south folk can talk!"

The rest of the evening, we ate, and I opened up the millions of gifts that I didn't know how I was gonna get back to the house. They sure weren't gonna fit in the Porsche or anybody else's car for that matter.

"You want me to call Silas and have him bring the Escalade up here to help take some of this stuff to your house?" Jada asked.

"Um . . . No, that's okay," I said, looking around as if I had another solution.

"That's a good idea, Kel. We can't get it home by ourselves," Mike, said, needing to learn when to shut his mouth!

Before I could say another word, Jada was on the phone talking to Ty.

Mike looked at me and said, "See. Everything worked out!"

"Yeah, it sure did!" I said sarcastically.

While my momma, Tasha, and Jada cleaned up and got all the gifts together, I thanked everyone for coming as they left. Mike was busy carrying some of the larger gifts to the front door so they were ready once Ty got there.

I heard Mike say that Ty was out front. He grabbed a big box and headed out the door, which made me nervous. I tried to hurry and follow after Mike. I did not want Ty and Mike alone in the same room. That was just asking for trouble. There was no telling what either one of them might've said to press each other's buttons. I knew Ty's would be intentional, but Mike might've said something completely innocent that would've pissed Ty off.

When I walked outside, only a few steps behind Mike, Ty jumped out of the truck looking delicious. He was dressed to do some physical labor. It was still cool outside, but he still only had on a wife-beater and gray sweats that hung loosely off his waist. It reminded me of the way he was dressed the first time I ever snuck off to his house after we had first met. It shocked me because I was expecting him to try and impress me that night and he did the complete opposite. He always just wanted me to love him for him.

While Mike was loading the box he was holding into the back of Ty's truck, Ty looked at me and snuck in a wink. I tried to hold in my smile, but my dimples always gave it away. Ty and Mike had to make several trips, in and out of the building, until they finally had everything loaded up and they actually worked well together. Everything didn't even fit in the Escalade. Jada ended up having to put some of the stuff in her trunk. That night, I decided Mike and I would definitely have to invest in an SUV.

I kissed my momma goodnight, and hugged Tasha as they headed home. Then, Jada, Ty, Mike and I got in our cars to head over to my place. Mike talked about all the gifts we had received the whole way home. I loved seeing him so excited, which was most of the time. The closer it got to my due date, the more excited he was. Him talking about the shower and the gifts kind of kept my mind off the fact that Ty would know where I lived, and I wasn't happy about that at all. That would just add to his stalking capabilities. Then I thought about it. As slick as his ass was, he probably already knew where I lived. I contemplated on whether or not I should tell Mike about Tif showing up at the shower, because he had no idea what had gone on. I ended up telling him during the ride home and he got a little upset that no one had gone to get him when it happened. He said if anything would've happened to me, it would've been trouble. I told him I could handle my own, but he wasn't trying to hear that. He thought Terrance had something to do with her showing up and was ready to turn around and head over to his house. I told him I didn't believe Terrance knew anything about it. Tif's name was written all over that bitch move.

Once we pulled up at my place, Ty jumped out of his truck and opened the car door for me before Mike was able to get around to the passenger side of the car.

"Thanks, man. I can take it from here," Mike said, as he grabbed my hand and helped me out.

"Ty rubbed his hands together and blew in them, as if he was trying to warm up."

"You wouldn't be cold if you would learn to put some clothes!" Jada said sounding like his mother, walking over with bags in her hand.

"I'm not cold. How could I be cold with such beautiful women in my presence?"

Jada blushed and giggled like a little teeny-bopper with her first crush. I rolled my eyes and walked towards the door so I could get Ty in and out. I didn't need him to be at my house any longer than necessary.

"You got a nice crib, Kel," Ty said, looking around for a place to put the two boxes he was carrying.

Mike instructed him to put them down in the middle of the living room floor. I had a feeling Mike didn't want him to go any further than where he was. Jada came in with the bags she was carrying and sat on the couch next to me.

"This seems really cozy! It must feel good to have something so nice that belongs to you! I've never lived on my own."

I giggled at the term "cozy." I was sure Jada did feel as though my condo was "cozy" compared to the huge mansion she lived in. Out of all the conversations Jada and I had had, she had never gone into detail about where she and Ty lived or how well they lived. She was either a private person when it came to that, or Ty told her to keep her mouth shut since he probably did need to keep a low profile.

"You've never had your own apartment or anything?"

"Noooo. I've always ended up with men who wanted to take care of me and didn't even want me to work. At least Silas does let me work."

"All I can say is must be nice!"

Ty and Mike came in with the last of the boxes and Mike thanked him for letting us use the truck and for helping bring all that shit in. He even offered Ty gas money, but he turned it down, of course. Jada stood up, and walked over to Ty putting her hand on his back and sliding it under his wife beater, rubbing up and down.

"You ready, babe?" she asked him.

"Yeah. Mike, you want us to wait on you so we can walk out together?" Ty asked.

The room got quiet. Mike and Jada both looked at me, and Ty looked at Mike, waiting for an answer. I had never really discussed me and Mike's living situation with Jada. I didn't feel a need to.

I broke the silence by saying, "No, he's spending the night tonight. As a matter of fact, he's in the process of moving in."

"All right, all right. Sounds good." Ty said, still smirking.

After closing the door behind Ty and Jada, I sighed and fell right into Mike's arms. It had been a long day and I was physically and mentally exhausted. We both agreed that we would take care of the mess in the middle of the living room floor in the morning. Mike carried me up the stairs to the bedroom, helped me get out of my clothes, and cuddled with me until I fell asleep. The next morning when I woke up, the living room floor was clear of everything and all the baby stuff I had gotten at the shower was in its place in the baby's nursery. Mike had gotten back up some time during the night and got everything in order. I didn't know what I had done to deserve him, but I was thankful for him.

Chapter 17

L ater on that day, my phone rang, and it was a number I didn't recognize. As I answered, I left from out of the room with Mike, just in case it was Ty calling from a different number.

"Hello," I said in a low voice.

"Why are you tryin' to fuck up what I have over here?"

"Terrance?"

"Yeah. It's me. Tif told me all the shit you told her last night."

"First of all, she shouldn't have shown her face at my event, and secondly, she needed to know the truth! You did contest the divorce and you may be the father of this baby, and as far as I know, you're the father of Stacy's baby too!"

"What's going on between me and Stacy don't have nothing to do with you, so you had no right even bringing that up to Tif. You told her you was sure that your baby is mine, and you know that's a lie. On top of all of your lies and insinuations, I was in the emergency room all night because Tasha's ghetto ass broke Tif's nose!"

"Her nose? I thought Tasha hit her in her mouth?" I said as I laughed. Tasha must've just swung, not knowing where she hit the girl!

"See, you think it's funny. That ain't cute. You need to watch who you hang with! I always told you that."

That comment really pissed me off due to the fact I should've been watching Tiffany's ass when she was supposedly my friend, but fucking my husband.

"Oh, so I guess Tiffany wasn't one that needed to be watched, even though she was fucking you!" I said so loudly that Mike came running in the room like somebody was chasing him.

"Who is that?" Mike asked

"Who the hell is that in the background? Mike's shady ass? Tell him this is between me and you. This don't have shit to do with him. Tif told me y'all introduced him as the baby's father. Believe me, he won't be allowed anywhere near my child."

Mike was standing there impatiently, still waiting on me to answer his question as I was trying to hear what Terrance's dumb ass was saying. He was definitely not the same man I had fallen in love with. Tiffany had changed him so much, and it wasn't for the better. He used to be so loving that I could've never imagined him talking to me the way he was. It almost seemed like Tif had brainwashed him so much, he couldn't see clearly. Either that or she had put some voodoo on him. I couldn't help but to think maybe Tif wasn't who changed him. Maybe he hated me so much for cheating on him, that he was a man scorned. That didn't make much sense either, since he had been cheating on me with Stacy the whole damn time.

"This is Terrance, Mike," I said after Terrance shut up for a second.

Mike tried to grab the phone from me, but I told him it was cool because he wasn't talkin' about nothin'. That pissed Terrance off big time and he ended up hanging up on me. When I sat my phone down on the table, Mike asked me why I didn't let him talk to Terrance. I told him Terrance wasn't worth it, and he just called trying to defend his girl. I left out the comment about Mike not being allowed around his baby. I had never seen Mike lose his temper, but I could tell he had it in him, especially if someone was trying to get in the way of him and his family.

The very next day, I received a very unexpected phone call from Stacy, even though, I guess I should've been expecting it. I just didn't think after all that she told me she would actually have the nerve to call me.

"Kel, can we meet up somewhere? I really need to talk to you."

"About what Stacy? What could you possibly have to talk to me about?"

Stacy started crying to the extent of where I could barely understand what she was saying.

"Terrance came to my house with the girl Tiffany you were telling me about and he had the audacity to tell me he didn't wanna have anything to do with me and that he wasn't the father of my baby!" she said sniffling.

I was still trying to figure out what she wanted me to do or say.

"How could he treat me, the mother of his child like that? He said he loved me, and sat there and brought the bitch to my house looking like she had just gotten a nose job! I don't know what to do."

I sat there silent for a moment, first laughing to myself from the thought of Tif standing at Stacy's door with the cast on her broken nose. Then trying to digest the fact that this scandalous hoe had just asked me for advice on how to get my ex-husband back. I felt sorry for her for a quick second until I thought about the fact that she was Terrance's mistress while we were still married, and I probably had sucked his dick after he had just got done fuckin' her! The thought of it made me cringe! I knew they obviously weren't using condoms due to the fact that her ass was pregnant, which she had also thrown in my face on a couple of occasions. So many things were going through my mind at that moment, so I said the first thing that came to mind.

"Fuck you, Stacy," I said sounding like I had no interest in anything she was saying.

"Kel, I know I was wrong, but please don't do me like this. I'm sorry."

"Karma is a bitch, ain't it? I'll tell you what to do. Take his ass to court for child support and figure out the rest! Didn't I tell your dumb ass you got pregnant by the wrong negro? Your ass thought you really had something! Now deal with the repercussions!"

I had nothing else to say to Stacy, so I hung up on her whining ass, laughing at what I couldn't believe just happened. Stacy was a good one because I wished Tif would come to my house with Terrance talking shit. They wouldn't live to talk about it. As far as I was concerned, Stacy got what she had coming to her, and Terrance and Tif would be next.

So much was going on all at once, it was draining me. First was the baby shower, then my co-workers threw a very nice shower for me at the salon, which turned out great. It wasn't like I needed anymore onesies, booties, baby powder, baby lotion, etc., after all the stuff I had gotten at the big shower my momma and girls threw, but I was told I could never have too much of that stuff. Cameron bought so much stuff, it filled both my car and hers, but I wasn't surprised. I was just glad that Mike had talked me into going on maternity leave. I couldn't even imagine walking and standing on my feet all day. Now, the biggest day of the year was coming up in a few days, which was my birthday. I normally did it big my entire birthday week, but I felt too big to do anything. My stomach was tight and shiny, and itched like crazy. I felt like I was gonna pop any day! The doctor said it wasn't looking like I would deliver early, but I was hoping she was wrong. I was ready to meet the person I had been carrying around all this time, and couldn't wait to get back in my wardrobe that had been sitting in my closet for months being useless.

I hadn't mentioned anything about my birthday to Mike, since I really wasn't feeling up to doing anything, but it surprised me that he hadn't mentioned it either. I was just waiting to see how long it would take for him to at least ask what I'd like to do for my birthday. He was normally so thoughtful when it came to holidays or other special occasions. One thing I knew for sure was that he better not had forgotten my big day.

Mike had been acting strange lately, but I thought it might have had something to do with his nerves. I knew he was nervous about the baby being here soon, even though he wouldn't admit it. The last couple of weeks, he had spent more time than usual at his own house, and he wasn't calling, checking on me as much as he normally would. I kept asking him if everything was okay, and he assured me that it was. He said he was just working on some things from the firm, and since most of his client's files were at his house in his office, it was easier for him to work from there. At first, I started thinking someone else might've been in the picture, but I just couldn't make myself believe that. I didn't wanna believe Mike would abandon me so close to my delivery date. I couldn't even blame him if he was having second thoughts about taking on the responsibility that he so easily offered to take on.

The night before my birthday, Mike didn't call or come over, so I started becoming extremely worried. I watched the clock all night, waiting to hear the door open. Finally, at two in the morning, I decided to call him.

"Hello," Mike answered sounding groggily.

"What the hell is going on? I need to know right now! Are you backing out?"

"Calm down, baby! What do you mean backing out?"

"I mean changing your mind about being here for me and the baby! I've introduced you to my momma, all of my friends, told you that I love you . . . I've done all I can!"

"Look, I told you, the firm has been unusually busy, which is a good thing for us. I'm still here and I don't love you any less. Now get some sleep. I'll talk you in the morning . . . Well, later on."

After I hung up the phone, I still wasn't sure about how I felt. What I felt like doing was riding over to Mike's house to make sure he wasn't layin' up with some hoe, but I was beyond that phase of my life. I had been there done that, and I refused to regress for anybody. What bothered me most was that he still hadn't even mentioned my birthday. Normally when I was worried about something, Mike would always make me feel like everything was okay. He had failed me for the first time.

I knew it was late, or early for that matter, and I fought with myself about the decision that I made in that instance. I picked my phone back up, and not thinking about anyone or anything else, except for myself and my own feelings, I called Ty. Not expecting him to answer, I prepared to hang up after the third ring, when suddenly I heard his voice.

"What's wrong? You in labor?" he said immediately upon answering the phone.

I could hear noises in the background like he was outside somewhere.

"Naw boy! Where are you?"

"Out workin'. What you callin' for if that's not the reason? You don't call me any other time. I have to call you."

"I was just thinkin' about you."

"At two a.m.? Where's your boy?"

"He's not here."

"Oh, so that's what this is about. He den showed his true colors, huh? Got caught up?"

"No. He just stayed at his house tonight, and I can't sleep," I said, trying to sound like everything between me and Mike was okay.

"So, what you want me to do?"

I knew what I felt like I needed at that moment, and that was companionship and intimacy. Something I felt like I had been missing the past couple of weeks. I just didn't know if I wanted to give Ty permission to come and quench my needs. As I was in deep thought about how I wanted to answer Ty's question, he interrupted.

"Kel, you still there? You want me to come by?"

"I thought you were working?"

"I am, but never too busy for you."

I got quiet again, still fighting my feelings. I tried to make it right in my mind, but my heart knew it was wrong. I tried to make myself believe it would be Mike's fault since he hadn't been giving me the attention that I needed.

"You bullshittin'. I'm on my way," Ty said, and hung up.

I laid there, trying to make myself dial his number back and tell him not to come, but that was obviously not what I wanted. I got up and washed my face and checked my hair. By the time I finished, the doorbell rang.

"Damn that was fast!" I said to myself.

I went and hit the buzzer to buzz Ty up. To my surprise, when I opened the door, it was Mike. I felt my eyes buck and mouth hit the floor.

"I'm sorry. I forgot my key at my house. The way our conversation ended just didn't feel right, so I decided to come over."

I stood in the doorway, not budging, trying to think of something to say to get rid of Mike quick, fast, and in a hurry.

"So can I come in or are you gonna leave me standing out here all night?"

"You know what. I'm really not feeling this right now. Something hasn't been right the past couple of weeks. I think we may need to talk, but not now. I'm tired . . . Tired from trying to figure out what's been going on with us."

"So are you sayin' you want me to leave? I'll sleep on the couch if you want me to."

"No. I just wanna be alone tonight."

"You sure?" Mike asked, sounding disappointed.

I stood there looking down at the floor, without saying a word. Mike finally got the hint and said he'd talk to me later, and walked away from the awkward situation. I went and found my phone to see that I had ten missed calls that fast and I already knew who it was, so I dialed Ty's number. Before I could say a word, Ty started going off.

"You interrupted my work to come see yo ass, and that nigga' over there? I seen his Porsche sittin' outside. I started to still come to the door."

"I had no idea he was comin'! He just showed up, but he's gone now."

"Well, I'm not far. I'll see you in a few minutes."

"Maybe we should just cancel. I don't know if it's a good idea now. Mike might still be in the area."

"Well, if he is, that's his bad. I'm on my way."

Ty hung up in my face again. He always had to have his way, and the majority of the time, he got it. Ty wasn't lying when he said he wasn't far. He was at my door in a matter of a couple of minutes. This time before buzzing him in, I hit the intercom to make sure it was him.

I opened the door and welcomed him in. As soon as he saw me, he embraced me, and I returned the affection. He closed the door behind him. We hadn't been alone together since I was trapped in his closet, and I hadn't had any desire to be alone with him since. How things changed once Mike started making feel insignificant. He had promised me that would never happen.

Ty and I sat in the living room, hugged up, watching TV for a couple of hours until I fell asleep in his arms. I woke up on the couch, sweating from the sun beaming directly on me, and the blanket Ty must've thrown on me before he left. I got up, and headed upstairs, not knowing what time it was. When I got up the stairs, I heard noise coming from the nursery. I opened the door and Ty almost made me have a heart attack. He was standing there, holding one of the baby's teddy bears.

"I thought you were gone."

"You think I'd leave without telling you?"

"I don't know. Isn't Jada probably worried about you?" I said yawning and rubbing my eyes. "What time is it anyway?"

Ty looked at his Rolex and said, "Going on ten, and no, Jada doesn't get worried. She know I'm a very busy man, so she don't question me."

"Must be nice. So you could be out fuckin' around with everybody and their momma, and she wouldn't know."

"Yep, but I'm not fuckin' around with everybody and they momma. Just you. And I'm not officially fuckin' you!"

I felt the need to end that conversation, so I said, "Anyway, What are you doing in here?"

"Just lookin' around, thinkin' to myself how this room is too damn small for my baby. I have a huge room ready for her."

"You are really trying to speak into existence this baby being yours, huh?"

"She is mine. I can feel it."

Ty told me to follow him downstairs. He had to show me something. When we got downstairs, he told me to have a seat and grabbed his jacket off the coat hanger. He came and sat next to me, still digging in his jacket pocket. Ty finally found what he was looking for, and pulled out a small black cardboard box. I sat there not knowing what to expect. I had been given small boxes before, but I just knew Ty wasn't about to do what would've normally been obvious to a woman when a man pulled out a small, black box.

He took the lid off of the box, and pulled out what looked like a ring box. As my anxiety started kicking in, Ty turned directly towards me and flipped the ring box open, and a huge diamond blinded me. I covered my mouth with my hand, feeling like I was screaming, but it was silent.

"Happy birthday, Kel."

Tears began to fall because I couldn't believe that Ty had remembered my birthday, and Mike had forgotten. Ty telling me happy birthday still didn't explain the ring. That rock was too fat for it to be a birthday gift. I still sat there in astonishment, unable to say a word. I slowly took my hands down from my mouth and looked at Ty as he began to pull the ring out. He grabbed my left hand and extended my now bare married finger, and slid the ring on. The round brilliant cut diamond platinum ring was a perfect fit.

"You gone say somethin'?"

My mouth moved, but no words came out. I finally took a deep breath, and tried again.

"Ty, now you know I can't marry you. We have to accept reality, baby! We both belong to someone else, and we don't wanna hurt those people."

"Before you finish, that ain't no engagement ring. It's a promise ring, promising you we will be together and be a family. Trust, your engagement ring will be much bigger. That's only five carats. I got bigger and better in mind. What have I always told you? This is only the beginning."

"I can't accept this," I said as I started sliding the beautiful ring off of my finger.

He stopped me from taking it off and told me he wanted me to have it and to do him the honor of wearing it.

"What am I supposed to tell Mike when he sees me walking around with this rock on my finger. It is kinda hard to miss!" I said as I held out my finger, admiring the beauty of it. Ty really had excellent taste.

"I'm really not worried about him. All I know is I better see it when I'm in your presence."

I heard my phone vibrating, and told Ty I had to take it.

"Good morning," Mike said on the other end.

"Mornin'," I replied, sounding uninterested, still holding my finger out in front of me.

"Happy birthday babe. I love you."

Hesistantly, I said, "Thank you. I love you too."

Ty cleared his throat, and I put my finger up to my lips to tell him to be quiet. He sat there looking pissed as I continued my conversation with Mike. After a few minutes of not being patient, Ty grabbed his jacket, walked over to me and laid a loud, wet kiss on me. He put up the peace sign and walked out the door.

"What was that noise?" Mike asked, referring the loud sound of the kiss Ty and I had just shared.

"Oh, I was just slurpin' down some orange juice. Sorry if I was loud. Now what were you saying?"

"I'd be honored if you'd spend your special day with me. I've already made reservations. I'm hoping I can also make the last couple of weeks up to you. I didn't mean to make you feel neglected. I put work before you and I promised I would never do that. I'm sorry."

It was so nice to hear Mike sounding and acting himself. I was so happy that he hadn't forgotten my birthday and had actually made plans. Deep down I knew that he wouldn't do me like that, but the ugly part of me tried to convince me otherwise. I told Mike however he planned on making it up to me better had been good. He told me reservations were at seven and he'd see me later.

Chapter 18

Six o' clock rolled around, and I was still in my room putting on my final accessories when I heard Mike walk in the house. After putting on my favorite, diamond hoop earrings, which, unfortunately, Terrance had bought for me during happier days, I went to the staircase, to find Mike at the bottom with a bouquet of beautiful multi-colored flowers in his hand. With one foot on the step, he stopped in his tracks when he saw me, and an expression of admiration came over his face. I slowly walked down the stairs, and upon reaching the bottom, Mike grabbed my hand and gave me a kiss, handing me the bouquet.

"You might think I'm just telling you this, but you look more beautiful than I've ever seen you look. You have this sparkle in your eyes today that's just jaw dropping. I'm a lucky man."

I could feel myself blushing, and hoped it wasn't showing. I could tell I wasn't doing a good job of hiding it by the grin Mike had on his face. I couldn't even lie. He was looking quite scrumptious himself, wearing an olive green button down shirt that brought out the gorgeous olive undertone in his complexion. It was funny how he matched my olive–green-and-tan mini- dress perfectly, when we hadn't even discussed what we were gonna wear. Even though my stomach was huge, I was still in good enough shape to wear a mini-dress and had no shame in it. It was my birthday, which meant I could get away with anything. Mike and I were completely in sync with one another. I was really starting to think he might've actually been my soul mate, but my past was just getting in the way of me having complete confidence in it.

Mike didn't say where we were going and I didn't ask. I knew if he had arranged everything, it would be perfect. It was a beautiful evening. So beautiful, I was able to roll my window down on the way to wherever we were headed. I held my stomach and breathed heavily on a couple of occasions during our ride. Mike asked me if I was okay. I told him I was having Braxton Hicks, but it was completely normal. I knew one thing for sure. This little girl had better stayed put. She could have anything, except my birthday. Not to sound selfish, but this day belonged to me.

We finally pulled up to our destination. I had no idea where we were. Wherever we were looked very extravagant, and it was so far in the boonies I would've never found it on my own. There wasn't even a sign on the building, but several cars were parked in the parking lot. Mike got out and opened the door for me. Before I could stand up, I began questioning him, asking where the hell we were. He just shushed me and told me to trust him. As we walked to the door, arm in arm, Mike lectured me AGAIN about wearing heels. He probably wouldn't have even noticed if I hadn't almost been taller than him. What he was saying went in one ear and out the other. My confidence level was on ten. I was the hottest pregnant chick around!

"Reservations for Travis," Mike said to the blonde, chubby hostess that met us at the door.

"Right this way," she replied as she led us to our table.

We came to a door that had reserved on it. As soon as she pushed it open, I saw the room was dark. I looked at her and she told me that there was a motion light, so when I walk in the light would turn on. Not trusting what the hostess said, I told Mike to go first. He laughed at me and told me to just go, and he wouldn't let anything happen to me. This whole thing just seemed like some freaky shit to me. A restaurant out in the middle of nowhere, with no sign on it, then they wanted me to go into a dark room. I started thinking, *Did Mike get a life insurance policy on me I didn't know about?* Trusting my man, I stepped one foot in the door, and as soon as I did, the lights came on and I was startled by everyone jumping up screaming, "Happy Birthday!" Mike had outdone himself. He had gotten all my friends and family together to celebrate my day with us. I was so happy to see my momma and daddy, and Tasha and Lem. Then my expression briefly changed when I saw Jada hugged up with Ty.

I turned around towards Mike, and tongued him down in front of everyone, showing how much I appreciated what he had done for me.

"I guess that was a thank you!" he said showing all thirty-two of his sparkling white teeth.

Ty's expression let me know he wasn't very thrilled about what was going on, and throughout our entire meal, it didn't change very much. He had to have known about the celebration when he came by earlier that morning, and he could've easily declined the invitation when Mike invited him and Jada. I knew he only came to be nosey. I just tried to ignore him and carry on conversation with everyone else. I was especially trying to converse with Lem to see where his head was with my girl. Last I had heard they were doing great and I could tell she was in love. I just hoped he felt the same way.

After everyone was finished eating, and the itis had kicked in, the waitress had the nerve to ask if anyone was ready for dessert. No one had to say a word. I guess she could tell how everyone was slouched over in their seats that we were through so she smiled and walked away. A few minutes later, she came back with a silver platter with a lid on top and placed it in front of me.

"I'm sorry, I didn't ask for anything else," I said, trying to lift the platter to hand it back to her.

"I know, but since it's your birthday, this one is on the house. We do this for all of our guests on their birthday."

"Oh, that's so nice!" My momma said. "Open it Kel. See what you got. I might want some!"

As I opened the lid, everyone started sitting straight up, waiting in suspense. When I took the lid off, to my surprise, on the platter, there were chocolate covered strawberries in the shape of a heart. In the middle of the heart, there was a beautiful, marquis shaped diamond ring. I had been so intrigued with everything in front of me, I hadn't even noticed that Mike had gotten out of his chair and was beside me on one knee.

"Kel, as you should already know, I love you, and I know you're the person I should be with for the rest of my life. You are my life. Will you please marry me?"

I looked around at everyone thinking everyone kept this secret from me, including Tasha, with her big ass mouth, but by the expression on everyone's face, I concluded that no one knew this was gonna happen. I was so caught off guard I didn't know what to say. I had just gotten a divorce, and now I was being proposed to. Receiving two rings within a twenty-four-hour period couldn't have been good. During the moment while my man was proposing to me, Ty popped in my head. I had forgotten he was sitting there, so I looked over and saw that his chair was empty and Jada was looking at me smiling, and like everyone else, waiting on me to answer. Ty must've walked out when he saw what Mike was about to do.

Mike continued, "I know you just got out of a marriage, and I'm not saying we have to get married tomorrow. I just want to show you how committed I am, and when you're ready, I'm ready."

I looked at my momma for confirmation, and she gave me nothing. I think she was just giving me the opportunity to make decisions on my own. She was finally beginning to trust my judgment, but at that moment, I didn't know how I felt about that. Then, I looked at my daddy, and he smiled and nodded his head. My daddy had met Mike and they hit it off pretty well. They actually got along a whole lot better than Terrance and my daddy ever did. My daddy even took Mike along on a few of his golf outings with his boys.

I looked down at Mike, and saw the sincerity in his face. I looked at those perfect, dark eyebrows, his sexy go-tee, wavy hair, and beautiful smile that began to look unsure. His entire expression began to look unsure, as if he might've made a mistake. I then thought about the fact that this man was willing to accept me for me, and all of my flaws. Despite everything he knew about me, he treated me with all the respect in the world. What else could I had possibly asked for?

I smiled as tears welled up in my eyes, thinking about how happy I was gonna be being Mrs. Michael Travis, and I looked Mike directly in his eyes and said, "Yes. I love you, and I don't wanna live without you." Everyone in the room clapped, including my momma. I didn't know why I cared so much about what she thought, but her approval was very important to me. Maybe one day in the future, I wouldn't look to her so much, but during times like this, a mother's support was important.

Mike was finally able to wipe the sweat from his forehead and relax. He then took the ring from the platter, and placed it on the same finger Ty had just placed a ring on earlier that morning. Ty still hadn't returned to his seat, but when I glanced up he was glaring through the rectangular window of the closed door to where we were sitting. I took a deep breath and grabbed a napkin to wipe the tears from my eyes. Ignoring Ty once more, I began laughing and once again enjoying the great company surrounding me.

Ty was sure to call me bright and early the next morning making sure I was very clear about how he felt about the entire situation. He told me that Mike was never gonna marry me because he was not about to let that happen. He also said that I was not about to be sittin' up playin' house with another nigga' while his daughter was in the house. Ty was really lettin' this baby thing get to his head. It made him feel like he had some kind of power and control over me that didn't exist.

"How do you plan on resolving this, Kel?"

"Resolving what?" I asked Ty, trying to make him understand that there was nothing to resolve.

"You know where you supposed to be. Don't try to play me. You know what we had, and as far as I'm concerned, we still got it. This baby just gone be the missing link. I've always wanted a real family, and I finally got it."

"Sorry to disappoint you, but I'm gonna have to give your ring back. I'm not gonna sit here and lie. I do still have feelings for you, but that's not enough. As much as you don't wanna believe it, I am in love with Mike. He's the one, and I promise, if this is your child, she will be well taken care of."

"Yeah, by me!" Ty said sternly.

I knew this conversation wasn't gonna get anywhere, so I asked Ty where he wanted to meet up, so I could give his ring back. He refused to cooperate with me, and told me to keep it because he was gonna keep his promise, no matter what. Ty was determined to make us work, and I admired his persistence, but I knew what I wanted and where I wanted to be. It was crystal clear to me as long as I wasn't around him, but when I got around him, my entire perspective on things changed. I would begin to think maybe it could work between us, and just maybe I could even adapt to his lifestyle. I knew he was my weakness that I needed to try to avoid as much as possible.

After that conversation with Ty, a couple of weeks went by without me talking to him. He would call, but I wouldn't answer. He left a million voice messages, threatening to come to my job, or even to my home. I was tired of giving in to Ty's threats all the time. He was used to getting his way all the time by throwing out threats, but I wasn't thinking about him anymore. I knew he was mostly talk anyway. He said he loved me, so I figured if he really loved me, he wouldn't try to hurt me in any way. He hadn't given me any reason to think that he would try to do anything that would cause me any emotional or physical pain.

My due date was a week away, but the doctor said by the way my stomach had dropped and the positioning of the baby, it was possible any day. Mike packed my overnight hospital bag, making sure I would have everything I needed during my stay there. He was so protective, he wouldn't even let me go anywhere alone, so when I did go anywhere, he, Jada, or Tasha would be with me.

Summer break had just begun for Jada, so with her mornings being empty, especially with Ty out "working," she would come over and take me to breakfast almost every morning. I told her ass I was already fat enough, and she was just making it worse. It seemed like each day that went by, I gained another pound, which made me extremely anxious to deliver because I was getting worried about all the time it was gonna take to get all the extra weight off.

I was taking each day, one day at a time, and it seemed like they were moving extremely slow. Apparently, the doctor had been wrong about the baby coming a little early. I could tell this little girl was already stubborn just like her momma.

I woke up a day after my due date, not feeling well at all. I felt groggy, nauseous, and my feet, legs, and arms were about three times their normal size. I had slept till ten-thirty, which was late for me, so Mike had already left to run some errands. I looked at my phone and saw Jada had called a few times, probably in regards to our breakfast date. When I tried to get up, my entire body felt tight. I called Jada, hoping she answered. I didn't wanna call my momma and get her worked up over what was probably nothing.

"Hey, girl! I know you're not just waking up!" Jada said.

"Girl, yes I am, and I feel and look like shit!"

"Oh no! What's wrong?"

I told Jada all of my symptoms, and she said that didn't sound good, and told me to call the doctor and she'd be on her way over. I called the doctor and she immediately told me to meet her at the hospital. I didn't wanna keep Mike in the dark. I knew he should've probably been the first person I called, so when I called him, I acted as though he was.

"Hey, babe. How you feeling?" Mike asked. I could tell from the bad reception that he was in his car talking through his Bluetooth.

"I'm not doing too good. I'm all swollen and I feel horrible! The doctor wants me to meet her at the hospital ASAP."

"Shit!"

I knew something must've been wrong because Mike rarely ever cursed.

"What?"

"I'm stuck on the damn Dan Ryan. I should've known not get on this expressway knowing you could go any minute! It's probably gonna be at least an hour before I'm out of this mess!"

"Don't worry, babe. I'll have Jada take me, and I'll make sure the baby waits for you!"

I was kind of glad that Mike was stuck since Jada was already on her way. I stood all the way up out the bed, having to hold on to the footboard because I felt so dizzy. I went in the bathroom to drink a glass of water, hoping I would feel better, and quickly jumped in and out the shower. I felt so uncomfortable, I didn't even want to put any clothes on, so I found something that I would be as comfortable as possible in. The struggle was finding some shoes my fat feet could slide in to. I lost that battle, so I went looking through Mike's shoes to see if maybe I could just throw on a pair of his gym shoes. That actually worked. As soon as I finished putting my shoes on, I heard the doorbell and knew it was Jada.

I grabbed the handrail, and slowly wobbled down the steps. By the time I got to the bottom, Jada had rang the bell about ten more times. When I finally buzzed her in, and I opened the door, I felt and heard a loud pop. It sounded like the pop of a rubber band, and then I felt water gushing out of me. Jada made it to the door and stared at me looking just as scared as I did.

"Oh my God! What happened? You're soaked . . . and you're bleeding!"

When I heard Jada mention blood, which I hadn't noticed, I became extremely nervous.

"Bleeding?" I said hysterically. I looked down and both water and blood was running down my legs.

Jada began pacing the floor and said, "Maybe we should have the ambulance come and get you!"

"No, we have to go now! Can you please just run upstairs to my room and get me something dry, with elastic to put on out of my top drawer?"

Jada sprinted up the stairs in her purple, wedged heels, and was back within a matter of seconds. I pulled my wet clothes off right there in the living room, and put on the bottoms that Jada brought me. I wasn't in any pain, but still very uncomfortable. I didn't know if any of this was normal, but it scared me. I just wanted my baby to be okay.

While on the way to the hospital, Jada called Ty, feeling the need to share with him what was going on with me. She had the phone up to her ear, but obviously, Ty got nervous too because I could hear him shouting through the phone telling Jada to hurry up and get me to the hospital. She hurried up and hung up the phone and became even more frantic after that. I told her to dial Mike for me to see where he was. She gave him details on the situation as she stuttered throughout the conversation in a shaky tone. He told her it would be about another half hour before he would be there.

When we finally got to the hospital, Jada pulled up next to the curb, and jumped out the car and ran into the emergency room entrance. A few minutes later, she came running back out with what looked like a nurse pushing out a wheelchair. Jada helped the woman get me out the car, put me in the wheelchair, and wheeled me in.

It seemed like everything else moved so fast. It seemed like nurses and doctors were everywhere. They quickly got me into a room, which was new for me. I had remembered having to go to the emergency room on a few occasions and having to sit there for hours and hours, but I guessed this was different. I was quickly hooked up to all types of monitors and machines and the first thing I thought was, *I want my momma!* All of the nurses were small and petite, besides one of them. She was a very large woman. I became even more concerned when I saw her walking towards me putting on a pair of extra large latex gloves. *What the hell does she think she about to do?* I thought.

"Um, excuse me, but what are you about to do?" I asked fearful of how she would answer.

"I have to see how far you're dilated."

I had no idea what that meant, and she must've could tell that by the way I looked at her, so she verbally painted a picture for me of what happens when a woman goes into labor. After that session was over, she gently spread my legs, and I immediately felt the worst feeling I had every felt in my life when she plunged her entire hand inside of my pussy. I didn't think it would ever be the same again after that.

In the middle of all of the commotion, the nurses had kicked Jada out. I was hoping she called my momma for me because she would've killed Jada if anything had happened and she wasn't with me. I heard the doctors and nurses talking about my cervix, uterus, and water breaking, amongst a million other things. Out of width:1123px; height:1649px;

everything they were saying, the only thing I understood was that my water had broken, which was quite apparent.

After they had finished poking me a million times, and hooking IVs and everything else up to me, I saw my actual obstetrician, and I was happy to see her.

"Hi, Kelicia. How are you feeling?"

"Not great."

"Well, we've run some tests, that haven't come back yet, but it looks like you developed a severe case of toxemia very fast. That's why you're so swollen."

She explained to me that toxemia was basically high blood pressure during pregnancy and she was glad that I got here when I did because it could've resulted in death for both me and the baby if it hadn't been treated right away.

Seconds later, I heard a lot of ruckus, and following that, I heard my momma's voice, which didn't surprise me. She came storming in the room, out of breath, with a tissue in her hand. Every time anyone saw her she would have tissue in her hand to wipe her sweat from the hot flashes she would frequently have. I knew for sure she was definitely having one at that very moment.

"Dr. Spencer! Why the hell I gotta act a fool to get back here with my baby?" she asked sounding extremely frustrated.

My momma was very familiar with Dr. Spencer, being that she was her doctor too, so Dr. Spencer knew exactly how my momma was and how to handle her.

"Well, Ms. Armstrong, your baby wasn't doing too well, so we needed everyone out of the way while we tended to her and your grandbaby."

"Well, are they okay now?"

I felt a sharp pain, and made a loud moaning sound. They both stopped talking and looked over at me.

"Well, sounds like the contractions have finally started," Dr. Spencer said, as she looked at the paper that was printing out of the machine next to my bed. She told me that it was keeping track of my contractions, and how big and small they were.

"Well then that must've been a big one!" I said.

"Actually, that was a small one," the doctor replied.

Dr. Spencer left the room, reassuring me and my momma that everything would be okay. Nurses continuously checked on me, and after a while, one of them came in and said there was a man in the lobby who said he was the father, wanting to come back.

"Hell naw!" my momma said. "Terrance is not bringing his butt in here!"

"Ma, I don't think it's Terrance. It's probably Mike."

The nurse looked back and forth at me and my momma, probably making a spectacle of my life in her mind. I imagined her thinking, *Here goes another one, not knowing who her baby daddy is!*

"Oh. Well go ask him his name. If it's a high yellow one, and his name is Mike, tell him to come on, but if he blue-black and not as nice lookin' as Mike, and his name is Terrance, leave him right on out there! You hear?" My momma said.

The nurse sucked her lips in, looking like she was trying to hold in her laughter, and walked out the room. My momma and I could hear a whole lot of commotion, so my momma went to see what was going on. I couldn't imagine what the problem could've been, unless it was Terrance out there and not Mike. I knew Terrance probably would've gone off if that nurse came out there and told him he couldn't come in.

When my momma came back to the room, Mike was right behind her.

"What's going on out there?" I asked, while in the middle of one of the most painful contractions I had felt since they had begun.

Mike ran over to me, seeing I was in pain and grabbed my hand and started rubbing it.

"Don't touch me!" I shouted. Mike immediately dropped my hand and stepped back.

"Chile, don't be hollerin' at this man! He ain't the one who did this to you, even though I wish he had!" My momma said rolling her eyes at the thought of Terrance being the daddy.

Once the contraction passed, I apologized to Mike, and asked them both again what was going on out in the hall.

"Jada and that well-dressed thug of hers were trying their best to get back here! They told them only two people and he seemed to get more upset than she did! I got them straightened out though!"

I should've known. Ty was already startin' shit and the baby wasn't even out of my coochie yet! He wanted to be able to say he was in the room when I had the baby, and that just wasn't about to happen. Mike was not about to let no other man sit up in the room and watch his woman have "his" baby.

The big nurse with the big hands came back in the room, putting on another pair of gloves. *Ugh! Here we go again!* I thought. As Mike watched, he cringed as though he could feel my pain. He didn't know the half of it.

"This baby is about ready to come! You're eight and a half centimeters dilated. I'll go let the doctor know, so she can get prepared," the nurse said.

I was so glad this was almost over. I would soon be looking into the eyes of the most gorgeous baby girl in the world. Mike sat in a chair right by my side. The contractions became so bad that I was screaming and shaking the bed. One of the nurses, I don't even remember which one because I was so delirious from pain, finally came and gave me some Demerol for the pain and from that point on, I was high as a kite.

It seemed like within a matter of minutes, I could hear Dr. Spencer's voice telling me to push. My eyes were low, and my vision was doubled. After about five pushes, I heard my angel's first cry. As soon as I heard it, my eyes widened so I could see the little person that I had spent every waking and sleeping moment with for the past nine months. She didn't look the way I expected her to. She was all slimy and bloody. I guess I was expecting her to come out looking like the princess that she was.

The doctor told Mike to do the honors of cutting the umbilical cord. He looked at me to make sure it okay. I nodded my head and said, "Go for it daddy." As soon as he cut it, I watched the nurse as she grabbed my baby and took her to get her weight. Mikayla Celeste Armstrong was born on June 15 at three forty-two in the afternoon, weighing eight pounds even.

After Mikayla was cleaned up, the nurse brought her back to me to be reacquainted. She was beautiful. Coincidentally, she was the same high-yellow complexion as Mike, and had thick jet-black hair that was so straight, it looked like Indian hair. Her eyes were dark and mysterious. She was very aware and looked at me as though she already knew who I was. I knew for a fact that she was mine because she had the same dimple in her chin as me.

I didn't have her for long before my momma snatched her from me saying, "Give me my grandbaby! Ain't she precious?" Mike couldn't take his eyes off of her. He didn't have to say a word. I knew exactly how he was feeling because I was feeling the same way.

We all heard a soft knock on the door. Before I could tell the person on the other side to come in, the door began to open. Jada peeked in, looking a lot better than she did when she was panicking, trying to get me to the hospital. As she walked in, Ty followed right behind her.

"How you feeling girly?" Jada asked, trying to speak softly, but couldn't with all the excitement in her voice.

"I'm good, now that she's here. I should ask how you're doing! You weren't doing too good last time I saw you!" I said, trying to laugh, without causing too much pain.

I watched Ty, standing by the door, staring at my mother hold and speak baby talk to what may have been his daughter. Jada walked over to my momma and asked if she could hold her. My momma carefully handed Mikayla over, not really wanting to, but she knew she would have plenty of time with her. Jada held her like a natural. She stood with her, rocking her. "Silas! Come here! Look at her. She's gorgeous!"

Ty slowly walked over towards Jada to see Mikayla up close and personal. He stood right next to Jada, and they looked like a perfect little family. Ty slid Mikayla's hat off and gently rubbed her silky hair.

"Oh my God, Kel. She has so much hair, and she looks just like you! Look at those eyes! She's a heartbreaker already! What's her name?" Jada asked.

"Mikayla."

"Awww! After Daddy Mike, huh?"

At the sound of Mikayla's name, Ty gave me the ultimate look of resentment. I knew he wouldn't be happy, but I didn't care.

Mike had been there for me so much, and he deserved it. No one knew what I was going to name the baby. I had planned it, but wanted it to be a surprise, and Mike was very surprised.

After staring at the baby a little longer, Ty whispered something in Jada's ear, then walked out the room.

"Is something wrong?" I asked Jada curiously. I was actually trying to see what Ty was up to.

"No. He just hasn't eaten all day. He's going to the cafeteria to get something."

I had several more visitors before the day was over, including Tasha and Lem. Everyone finally got the hint and left after I fell asleep on them, and the nurse took the baby back to the nursery. I was getting my rest while I could because I knew the next day I would be going home and I wouldn't have nurses around to help me. I knew I was in for a lot of sleepless nights, but that's was a sacrifice I would just have to make. I preferred to get Terrance's paternity test out of the way while we were already at the hospital, instead of having to take Mikayla back out to get it done after I got her home, so I reluctantly called Terrance and told him which hospital I was at. He told me he would be there within the hour. I didn't even know which result to wish for any longer. Either way, I would be screwed. I was wishing miraculously that the baby was Mike's, which I knew was beyond impossible unless it happened through eye contact.

Chapter 19

The first couple of days at home were rough, waking up throughout the night for feedings, changes, and singing, and Ty wasn't making it any easier. He constantly called my cell phone, and I got sick and tired of lying to Mike, telling him it was telemarketers. Every time I picked up the phone, the only thing he would say was that he wanted to see his baby. I hadn't even set anything up with him yet to get his paternity test done. I wanted to wait to get Terrance's results back first. If his came back positive, then there would've been no need in Ty getting one.

Mike wasn't looking forward to getting the results back because he knew that if Mikayla was Terrance's, he was gonna have to share her, and he didn't want that. He just wanted it to be the three of us with no extra baggage, and I understood exactly where he was coming from, and felt the same way.

On the third day of being back at home, my cell phone rang, and I noticed it was Terrance's number.

"Yes, Terrance?" I asked sounding annoyed.

Mike, holding Mikayla, turned around and looked at me with worry in his eyes as soon as he heard me say Terrance's name.

"Well, I guess we can be completely out of each other's lives now, huh?"

"What are you talkin' about?" I asked inquisitively.

"Oh. I guess you haven't gotten the call yet. I'm not your baby's daddy!"

I heard what he said, and I didn't know whether to believe him or not. Then, I knew he was telling the truth when I heard Tif in the background laughing and talking shit.

"Yo ass don't know who your baby's daddy is! That's what happens when you hoe around!" Tif said.

I didn't say another word. I didn't know what to say, or even how to feel. I just hung up. I sat there staring at the wall, dreading making that call to Ty, the father of my baby. I knew Mikayla's eyes were just like Ty's, but I was still in denial. I thought about not calling Ty to tell him anything, but I knew he would continue to harass me, or even try to go to Mike with the truth. When Mike found out the truth, it would be from me.

I sent Mike to the store on a mission, with a list of baby stuff, so I could prepare myself and make time to call and have a serious conversation with Ty. I had finally gotten the baby to sleep, so I slowly dialed Ty's number, hoping he was able to talk because I didn't know when I would have another opportunity.

"I was just about to call you," Ty said as soon as he picked up.

"What did you want this time?" I asked.

"Don't act like you ain't happy to talk to me. I was calling to ask you when can I come see my baby."

I didn't know whether or not Ty was just talking, or he had gotten some information from somewhere about Terrance not being the father, so I played dumb.

"What do you mean by 'your baby'?"

"She's mine. I just got the results back."

"Results? You haven't even taken a test!" I said nervously.

"Do you think I'm stupid? I knew you would procrastinate gettin' the test done, so remember at the hospital when I went to the cafeteria?"

As soon as Ty said that, I knew what he had done. I remained quiet, not telling him if I remembered or not.

"Oh, so you do remember, huh? Yeah, I got it done myself. You can't keep her from me. The first thing we need to do is get her name changed."

"You want her to have your last name?" I asked as though I was surprised.

"Not only that. I want her first name changed. How the hell you gone name her after a man that ain't her daddy? You know you was wrong for that, but I still love you."

My mind was all over the place. Reality had finally caught up with me. I could no longer pretend that this whole ordeal wasn't happening. I had to fess up to Mike and I didn't know how in the world I was gonna do it. I was at risk of losing two people who were very special to me. Mike and Jada.

"Slow down, Ty. We need to really sit down and think about how we're gonna handle this. Remember, there are other people involved who are gonna be really hurt by this."

"Kel, I den already told you I'm ready to make that move to be with just you and share all of what I have with you and my baby. You need to get yourself together so you'll be ready to make that move with me. I'll give you some time to sort things out to figure out how you gone let yo dude down, but not too long. In the meantime, you gone have to set aside some time for me to see her."

At that moment, what Ty said sounded fair. At least that would give me some time to think up a plan. I told Ty it was too soon to have the baby out, but we could work something out within the next couple of weeks. He seemed to be ok with that and I was relieved, but was still hoping he didn't have something else up his sleeve.

The next couple of weeks I began adapting to motherhood. Cameron had told me it wasn't gonna be easy, and she was right. Mike helped out a lot by taking turns with me, getting up in the night. He didn't mind it. He was in love all over again, and was completely at ease, thinking he would be able to adopt Mikayla and be a real family. It hurt me to think about the fact that all of that would come crashing down. I kept Ty satisfied by texting him random pictures of Mikayla whenever possible, and he always replied by saying something like "beautiful just like her momma," or "lookin' just like her daddy."

We had finally set up our first visitation, and today was the day. We decided to first meet for lunch at a secluded restaurant, where we wouldn't accidentally run into anyone we knew. When I got there, I saw Ty's car parked outside. Before I got out of the car, I looked in the mirror to make sure I looked ok, and fingered through my curls. As I got out the car, I straightened out my thigh length dress, pushed up the little cleavage that I had left since my milk dried up, and licked my finger to wipe off a spot of dirt that was on one my sandals. I felt the need to look perfect for Ty, and now I could since I was back down to my regular size. When I walked in, before anyone could greet me, I called Ty and he led me to the back of the restaurant where he was sitting. As I approached the table with the baby carrier on my arm, he stood up to grab the carrier from me so I could set, what I called "my luggage" down. Carrying a diaper bag made me feel like I was carrying luggage everywhere I went.

The waitress brought over a high chair to sit the carrier in, and smiled at Mikayla as she left us alone.

As I got ready to sit, Ty said, "Can I at least have a hug? I haven't seen you in a while. I haven't seen you that size in a long while." He looked me up and down. He then put both arms around me, and from his scent, I could tell he had already had a shot or two of Hennessey before meeting up with me.

"Is that what I make you do? Drink?"

He looked at me frowning, and said, "What do you mean?"

"I can smell the Hennessey on you."

"Naw. I was just excited. I needed to calm my nerves."

He felt so warm as he held me, and his familiar scent just kept bringing back memories.

As we embraced, he kept looking over at Mikayla, 'til finally I said, "You wanna hold her?"

"If that's all right with you."

"She's yours," I said, extending my hand towards her, telling him it was okay.

Before he picked her up, he grabbed my hand, looking at the ring Mike had given me and said, "We gone have to do somethin' about that."

"Just pick up your baby before I change my mind!" I said playfully.

Ty was so gentle, as if he had held plenty of babies. I just knew he wasn't gonna properly hold her head, but he surprised the hell out of me when he did. As he held her, he looked at her as if he couldn't believe she was his. He suddenly turned away from me and I saw his hand go up to his face. I asked him was he crying, and of course he denied it, but his eyes were glassy when he faced me again. It was a very touching moment. During the whole meal, Ty either had his eyes on Mikayla, or was picking her back up. It was a wonderful feeling seeing my baby in the arms of her father, and seeing how happy they both were. She smiled the entire time, even the couple of times she fell asleep.

"See Kel. This is just so right. Can't you feel it? I told you, if it's the lifestyle, I'll trade it in for you and my little girl."

I noticed Ty refused to call Mikayla by her name. I guessed he was dead serious when he was talking about changing her name. I couldn't even lie. Everything did feel right at that moment, but again, things always did feel right when I was alone with Ty.

"I'm engaged, Ty."

"Why is it that every time I'm tryin' to talk to you about us, you bring him up? He don't have nothin' to do with me! This is about me and you."

I could tell Ty was getting irritated, so I tried changing the subject, but every time we talked about anything else, it led right back to us getting back together.

As we walked out of the restaurant, I assumed our little meeting was over, so I walked towards my car.

"Where you goin'?" Ty asked.

"Home."

"We're not done. I got more reservations."

"Okay. Well, I'll follow you."

"No, I don't trust you," he said with a smirk on his face. "Get in the car with me."

I hesitated, but Ty didn't allow me to for too long. He grabbed the baby carrier from me and strapped it in his backseat.

"Now get in. I know you ain't leavin' without her."

I shook my head and got in. The first thing I did was look at the dashboard, and the picture of Jada still hadn't returned. I wondered if he only took it down when we were together, and put it back up when I wasn't around. As soon as Ty got in the car, he reached over and gave me the most endearing kiss on the lips. It was full of emotion. Whatever emotion that was, I had never it felt come from Ty before.

We made it to our destination, and it was the Hilton. I raised my eyebrows, wondering what we were doing at a hotel, but with Ty, nothing should've surprised me. Ty got a key from the front desk, and we headed up to the top floor to our suite.

"Why in the world would you do this? You know I can't stay here all night!"

"I just wanna spend some quality time with y'all. I don't care how long. Some time is better than none."

Mikayla was knocked out, so we laid her in the center of the bed on her pink teddy bear blanket that my momma had knitted for her. Ty went to the bar and poured us some wine, which was much needed. As I took a few sips, he turned on the radio to my girl Aaliyah singing "At Your Best." He came and grabbed my wine glass from me, setting it down on the table. He took his shirt off and wore only a wife beater, exposing his sexy biceps. He grabbed both of my arms and put them around his neck, then put his arms around me. He looked into my eyes with those same beautiful dark eyes that our daughter also had.

We danced like we did the first time we met. It felt like no one else existed as I swayed my hips back and forth up against his body. He rubbed his hands up against the small of my back 'til there was nothing but heat between our skin. He moved his hands down to my ass, and held them there squeezing gently. As the song went on, he put his lips close to my ear, and began whispering.

"Baby, I know you think he's the one, but I promise you won't be as happy with him as you'll be with me. Just go pack your shit and I'll be ready for you."

I would've been lying if I didn't think Ty loved me, and I would've also been lying if I said I didn't think I would be happy with him. After Ty was done whispering not sweet nothings, but a lot of sweet somethings for me to think about, he started sucking on my ear, and tried unzipping my backless dress. I had to stop and remind him that I had just had a baby and I still had a couple of weeks before I could do any of that. We finished drinking our wine and enjoyed each other's company without being interrupted. We then ~~laid~~ lay in the bed with Mikayla. I laid on one side of her, and Ty laid on the other. We faced each other and gazed into each other's eyes trying to read each other's thoughts.

By the time I got home that evening, Mike was laying in bed in his boxers, watching some movie he didn't seem very entertained by. When I walked in the room after putting Mikayla in her crib, the tension could've been cut with a knife. He watched every move I made, as if that would tell him where I had been all day. I tried to hurry up and go in the bathroom, so I could get rid of Ty's scent and the smell of alcohol on my breath, but before I could get there, Mike jumped up out the bed, grabbing me and lifting me up off the floor.

"Where you been? I missed you," he said, glaring at me like he was just waiting on me to lie.

He hadn't called not one time. He had learned from making that mistake one too many times. I told him I didn't need anyone keeping tabs on me, and I meant it. I knew it had been eating him up all day to not be able to call me. I didn't tell him he could never call me while I was out. I just made it very clear that I don't wanna be checked up on like a kid. Before I attempted to answer his question, I held my head down before I spoke for obvious reasons.

"Nowhere really. Just went around town, showing off Mikayla."

Mike lifted my head with his finger and gave me a peck on the lips and commenced licking off every smidgen of pomegranate lip gloss that I had remaining on my lips. He moved all the way down to my neck, and said, "What kind of perfume are you wearing?"

"I can't remember which one I put on this morning. You know I got so many."

Mike stopped what he was doing and looked up at me.

"Are you really gonna sit up here and lie to me, Kel? Don't I at least deserve the truth, as much as I've tried to love and be there for you?"

"What are you talking about?"

"What are you talking about?" Mike said, mocking me. "What I'm talking about is I know a man's cologne when I smell it, and I don't wear that kind."

"So what are you insinuating?"

"I'm not insinuating anything. I'm just letting you know I'm not a fool. I may be for being in love with you, but I know when somebody is lying to me."

I stood there, fidgeting and looking helpless, but I stuck to my lie. I was not about to go out like this. Mike had no proof. He wasn't sure if what he was saying was true. He was just trying to make me crack under the pressure.

"Well, I haven't been around any other man, so I don't know what you could possibly be smelling! Maybe my perfume don't mix well with my body chemistry."

Mike folded his arms and said, "So you gonna sit there and continue to lie, huh?"

"You know what, I did run into an old guy friend today, and I did give him a hug. Maybe that's what it is," I said, hoping that would lead to the end of this very unnerving discussion."

He shook his head and said, "Unbelievable! Unfuckin' believable! I should've known you can't turn a hoe into a housewife! I don't even know why you would be any different. So where was our baby while you were out cheating on me? Oh, before you answer that, please think before you speak."

My heart began pounding out of my chest. I couldn't believe Mike had just called me a hoe. He was showing his true colors and they weren't so pretty. I knew he had said it out of anger, but I was a true believer that you say how you really feel when you're angry.

"Oh, so that's what you think of me, huh? A hoe? Well, you wanted to marry this hoe, so I had to have been more than that to you!" I really wanted to strike a nerve with Mike at that moment so I said, "And since I'm a hoe, Mikayla is not your baby. She's mine!"

"That's all you got to say, huh? The truth ain't in you. That's a shame. I thought we could work out, but I guess I was wrong. Trust me when I say you'll never find another man like me."

Mike turned his back to me, and walked towards the closet. As he disappeared inside, I tilted my head back, trying to stop myself from crying. I sat on the edge of the bed, trying to think of something to say to make this all go away, but I was at a loss for words. Almost ten minutes had passed and I still heard Mike moving around in the closet. He finally came out with a couple of his suitcases, which looked like they were completely full, and he had thrown on some clothes.

"What are you doing, Mike?" I asked, sounding miserable.

"I'm doing what you obviously want me to do. You can't be happy with just me, and I'm not willing to share. As a matter of fact, I don't have to share!"

He walked out the room, carrying his suitcases, and I followed not far behind. He made a stop to Mikayla's room, set his suitcases down on the floor, and stood there staring at her asleep in the crib. I watched him from the doorway as he leaned over the rails and gave her a kiss.

"I love you princess," he said with hurt in his voice.

It hurt me so bad to watch, I leaned on the wall on the other side of the doorway, looking up to the ceiling, hoping God would perform a miracle. When Mike stepped out of the room, he jumped, not realizing I was standing there. He continued on down the stairs, and as he got to the front door, he stopped to take the keys to my house off of his key ring. As he did that, he asked, "So who is he Kel? Who is the man that helped ruin your happy home?"

"I already told you, there is no one!" I grabbed his hand and he snatched it back as I said, "Mike, please rethink this. Don't go. Please," I said with tears in the corners of my eyes, ready to fall any second.

"Is that the same no one who sent you those flowers to the shop?" Mike asked.

I stood there, not having anything to say, once again. Mike stood there, waiting on an explanation that I didn't have for him.

He looked at me, disappointedly, turned and walked out my door . . . Again!

"Bastard!" I yelled, and snatched off my engagement ring, throwing it, as Mike slammed the door.

I leaned up against the door and slid all the way down to the floor and cried the rest of the evening. When Mikayla woke up, it almost seemed as if she could sense that Daddy Mike was gone because all she would do was cry. She wasn't her happy self, just like I wasn't. We cried together all night long.

Chapter 20

The next couple of weeks were very rough for me. Not having someone around to help me with the baby made a big difference. I missed Mike so much, and I felt like calling him, but there was nothing I could say to him to change his mind. I was surprised that he would be able to stay away so long without seeing Mikayla. I knew it had to be hard for him too. To keep my mind off of Mike as much as possible, I had started letting Ty come around more often. He was ecstatic when he found out Mike and I had broken up. I really didn't want him to know but he ended up finding out on accident.

One day when I agreed to meet him again to spend time with Mikayla, he noticed that I didn't have my engagement ring on. We had gone to the beach, and as we were sitting on a blanket in the sand, he kept staring at my hand, making a strange face, so I finally asked him what was wrong.

"I just noticed you don't have your ring on. You forget to put it on today?"

"No," I said, looking out at the waves of Lake Michigan, not wanting to talk about it, but I knew that wasn't gonna fly with Ty.

"You gone tell me what happened or what?"

"We just disagreed on some things, so we felt it was best that we parted ways."

I definitely didn't want Ty to know he was the cause of my break up. I didn't wanna give him that much credit.

"I guess that's all I'm gone get out of you, so I'll take it. I guess you can wear my ring now."

I didn't respond to that last statement. I was just enjoying the moment. From the corner of my eye, I kept seeing Ty look over at me, smiling. I could tell he was happy right at that moment. I knew right then and there that he was gonna really feel like he had a chance with me and it was going to be extremely hard keeping him away. What I predicted was absolutely right. From that day on, he expected to be able to see us at least every other day.

I had also been talking to Jada more than usual lately. She didn't seem her usual lively self, so I suggested that we have a girl's day out. She agreed, and my momma never turned down babysitting, so I knew that wouldn't be a problem. I think if I had asked her if Mikayla could move in she would've said yes!

Jada and I decided to start our day off with lunch, and Jada said she needed a drink, so we went to Cooper's Hawk winery so we could have some good, quality wine with our meals. When Jada picked me up, she didn't even look like herself. She was still beautiful, as always. She just didn't have that glow about her that she normally did. As I got in the car, she looked over at me and seemed like she was forcing a smile.

"Hey, girl," she said dryly.

"What's up girl? You don't seem like yourself. I'm worried about you."

"There's just a lot going on in my mind. I'd rather wait to talk about it once I get some wine in me."

"Okay," I said, sounding unsure, wondering what could possibly be bothering her.

As far as I could see, Jada had everything she needed and more. She didn't have anything to complain about. Once we got to the restaurant and were seated, Jada kept her head in the menu. The only time she looked up was when the waitress brought us different wines to try. After we tasted around twenty different wines, out of the huge selection, we finally chose our favorites that we would have for the afternoon.

Jada wasn't just sippin' on her wine at all. She was gulping them down like Kool-Aid! Finally, after her forth glass, while I was still on my first, I interrupted the party she was having all by herself.

"What's goin' on girl? Talk to me."

Jada just looked at me at first, like she wanted to talk, but didn't know where to start. She then inhaled deeply and exhaled. What I didn't know was that I wasn't prepared for what she was about to say.

"Silas is cheating on me."

I began gulping down my wine the same way Jada did with her last four glasses. Once my glass was empty, I sat the glass down, wishing I had another.

"Cheating? How do you know? Did you catch him?"

"No. I can just tell. He just acts completely different. He used to be way more affectionate towards me, always excited to make love, but now he acts like it's no big deal to him."

"Maybe it's stress from work. You know work can have a big effect on your stress levels, which can affect your libido," I said, trying to comfort my friend.

"That's another thing. I know he used to be away a lot for work, but now he's gone even more often, and I don't believe he's at work all the time."

"Jada, you just can't jump to conclusions without having sufficient evidence. What you've told me does not make me believe that that man is cheating on you. Look at you. You're smart, beautiful, great personality . . . Why would he cheat on you?"

Why wouldn't he cheat on you if he found an enhanced replica? Is what I said in my mind, which I knew was mean, but it was the truth.

"That's not all. Don't laugh, but he used to have this picture of me taped to his dashboard in his car . . ."

I knew exactly what picture Jada was talking about. I remembered it very well from the hurt it made me feel when I had to look at it.

"It was a picture of me in lingerie. He always loved it and swore he wouldn't take it down. It suddenly disappeared about a month ago. When I asked him about it, he said it must've fallen down when he got his car detailed, which I feel is some bullshit. If it fell, it would still be in the car somewhere! I searched that car up and down. Nothing came up!"

Jada's eyes were starting to turn red, and I was hoping she didn't start crying on me because that would've made me feel awful.

"You're just paranoid. Ty loves you."

"Who?"

Oh shit! I thought. *Think, think, think!*

"Girl, I meant to say Silas. Ty is one of my other girl's men. She's having problems with him you would never believe, so that's been on my mind. But yeah, like I was saying, he loves you."

Jada looked me directly in my lying eyes and asked, "So you don't think a person can cheat if they love the person they're with?"

I knew it was possible because I had personally experienced loving someone and cheating on them. I did it with Terrance, and now I had done it with Mike, but I was there to make her feel better, so that's what I attempted to do.

"Loving someone and being in love with them are two different things. If I just thought Silas loved you, then I might tell you, yeah, it's possible he could cheat, but that's not the case. Silas is in love with you, and when you're in love with a person, you just don't do that."

Jada looked at me like she was actually eatin' up all the bullshit I was feeding her. Maybe we weren't so much alike, cuz I could smell bullshit from a mile away.

"Maybe I am just overreacting. I just don't know what I would do if I lost him. He means everything to me. I know I probably shouldn't allow a man to be my life, but that's how I feel. I only have you and him."

Jada almost brought me to tears, but I stayed strong. This was supposed to be a day of enjoyment and that was exactly what it was gonna be. While I had a few more glasses of wine, trying to catch up with Jada, we had great conversation and laughs. I talked mostly about Mikayla. There wasn't much more to talk about. Jada didn't know that Mike and I were no longer together, and I wasn't trying to share that information. I was hoping Mike would come back around like he had before, but I honestly didn't think he would. I knew trust would eventually become an issue with him. It just happened sooner than I thought. He saw straight through bullshit just like I did most of the time, so there was no getting away with shit with him.

After lunch, Jada and I caught a movie. We went to see Tyler Perry do his thing in "Alex Cross" and he did not disappoint! Throughout the entire movie, Ty texted me, telling me he wanted to see his daughter. I didn't know what I was gonna do with him. Jada looked over at me during the movie every time I looked at my phone. Not once did I see her pull her phone out to look at it, so that just told me that Ty wasn't concerned about where she was or what she was doing.

After the movie, Jada said, "Mike missing you already?"

"Huh?"

"He was checking on you through the entire movie."

"Oh, girl, yeah. He can't get enough of me."

The lies just wouldn't stop! It seemed like I had to lie to everyone these days. I had even been still puttin' on a front for my momma, acting like everything was still cool with me and Mike. It would only be so long before she figured out the truth. After everything it took to get my momma to give Mike a chance, I just didn't want it all to be in vain.

Since the theater was right by the mall, to finish our day off, Jada and I did a little shopping, and got our nails done. Jada seemed in better spirits than what she was in at the beginning of our day, but I could still tell she was a little worried. I was trying to decide whether or not I should tell Ty about what was going on in Jada's mind. He was so arrogant, that information would've probably just stroked his ego. I decided I would just wait to see what happened and if I felt the need to tell him, then I would.

When Jada dropped me off at home, I saw a note taped to the entrance door of the building with my name on it. I grabbed it, waved good-bye to my girl, and headed inside. Once in the house, I dropped my purse and shopping bags on the couch and opened

the note. I was surprised to see it was from Mike. He had come by
to see Mikayla and wanted me to call him to let him know when it
would be a good time. I knew he wouldn't be able to take not
seeing her too much longer. The ball was now in my court. I
could've made him suffer even longer for calling me a hoe, but I
didn't know if I could be that cruel. Especially to him. I decided I
would just wait 'til the next day to call him because I knew I had to
mentally prepare myself to talk to him, as well as see him.

Before I could take my shoes off, I got another text from Ty,
asking me what I was doing. Before I could respond, he started
calling.

"Yes, Ty."

"You up there?"

"If you're askin' me if I'm home, yes I am."

"Okay. I'm outside."

"Mikayla's not here. She's spending the night at my
momma's."

"Well, can I come in to see you for a minute?"

I hesitated, thinking about Jada, and how she would feel, but at
the same time said, "Yeah. That's cool."

Without even saying bye, Ty hung up and I was sure he was
probably already standing at the door, so I hit the buzzer to let him
up. I opened the door, and it sounded like a herd of horses were
running up the stairs. Apparently, Ty was in a hurry. He ran
straight in, took his holster that was holding his gun off of his belt,
and threw it on the table. He picked me up and put me up against
the wall. I tightly wrapped my legs and arms around him, kissing
him like it would be our last. Ty pulled his lips away from mine
long enough to ask where my bedroom was. I pointed in the
direction and roughly grabbed his face, biting his bottom lip. As he
carried me up the staircase, I could feel my body temperature
rising. When we made it to my room, which felt like forever, we
quickly started snatching off clothes. There was no taking our time
about it. As soon as we were both completely naked, the first thing
I noticed was Ty's very impressive piece that I hadn't seen up
close and personal in a very long time. In fact, after seeing it, I felt
it had been way too long.

I laid back and extended my arms and spread my legs, telling Ty to give me what I wanted. He grabbed my inner thighs, and pushed his abdomen close to mine and I could feel his dick searching for my already wet pussy. He finally found it and from there it was all over. I released all my emotions with that first thrust, and each one that came after that felt better and better. He made himself right at home inside of me. I don't think Ty and I had ever made love involving so much love and emotion. It was like a build-up that had finally been released. At the moment, it felt like it was something much needed, but I knew that was far from the truth, especially when I had to tightly squeeze my eyes shut to try to keep Jada and our discussion from crossing my mind while I was fuckin' the shit out of her man.

Ty flipped me over on my stomach, and I got on my knees while he was on his knees behind me. He slid his hard, slippery dick back inside of me, as he grabbed my titties and hit me with long, hard thrusts from behind. We both moaned loudly and I was sure the neighbors would know both of our names before the end of the night.

After my very enjoyable night, I was awakened by the sound of my phone ringing. I looked and saw that it was Jada, so I answered.

"Hello," I said, still sounding half asleep.

"Hey, girl. Sorry for waking you."

"What time is it?" I asked.

"It's only seven-thirty. I'm just worried about Silas. He hasn't come home or called.

Right then, I completely woke up. I slowly turned around, and there was her Silas, right next to me, knocked out in my bed.

"Hello?" Jada said.

"I'm here. Did you try calling him?"

"Yeah, but it keeps going straight to voicemail. I know he works overnight sometimes, but he always calls me at least a couple of times."

"I'm sure he's fine," I said.

"Can you just pray and agree with me for his safety?"

I didn't know how I felt about that, but I couldn't say no, so I sat on the phone with Jada as she prayed for the safety of her man who I stared at as he slept so comfortably while she worried. Once she finished praying, she thanked me. I told her to call me once she heard from him.

After I hung up, I moved close to Ty and kissed him on the shoulder.

Without opening his eyes and barely moving his mouth, he asked, "Who was that?"

"Oh, you are awake! That was your woman. She's very worried about you and I had to sit there and listen to her pray for you when I know exactly where you are."

"My woman right here," he said slowly opening his eyes and rubbing my arm.

"Ty, you can't be doing this to her!"

"She knows my job consists of me gone overnight sometimes, so she shouldn't be checkin' up on me. She know I don't play that."

"Does she know exactly what you do for a living yet?"

"No, and she won't. That ain't none of her business."

When I realized that conversation wasn't gonna get anywhere, I told him about the conversation I had with Jada the day before at lunch. I needed for him to understand the seriousness of all that was happening. I also needed for him to understand how Jada was feeling, and that definitely wasn't healthy. Ty just looked at me like he wasn't trying to hear nothin' I was saying. After I finished, all he had the nerve to say was, "Gimme a kiss."

Everything about Ty was still so attractive to me, except for the way he had started treating Jada, and that was partially my fault. Ty and I showered, and made love one more time before he went back home to his real life. Before he left, he asked where the ring was that he bought me, and asked me to wear it so that I'd be used to wearing his ring by the time it was time for him to propose to me. I had it in the same place that I had put my engagement ring from Mike. I took it out, and he placed it on my finger once again. I kissed Ty goodbye after I walked him to the door. After I watched him walk down the hall, I closed the door, and plopped down on my couch, listening to the quietness of my home and trying to fathom what had just happened and what I was feeling.

Chapter 21

After having my moment, and making my way back to reality, I remembered I needed to call Mike so we could schedule a time for him to see Mikayla.

"Hello," Mike answered in his smooth and sexy voice.

"Hey, Mike."

"Hey, Kel. How you been?"

"Good, and yourself?" I asked, trying to keep the conversation on a friendly level.

"I'm great, but I'll be better once I see my baby. So when is good for you?"

"She's at my momma's house now. I had some things to do last night, so she spent the night there," I said trying to make Mike wonder what I had been up to since he had been out of my life.

"Well, I can go pick her up . . . If that's okay with you, of course."

I knew that would save me a long trip to the other side of town, so I agreed to let Mike pick up Mikayla. I still hadn't spilled the beans to my momma that we weren't together anymore, and I knew that Mike wouldn't say a word about it, so him picking her up would allow me to carry on that lie a little longer.

While waiting on Mike to get to my house, Jada texted me to let me know that "Silas" had made it home and thanked me for praying with her. A few hours had passed and Mike still hadn't made it to my house with my baby and I started worrying. I called my momma first, just in case he hadn't even made it there to pick her up. She said he had picked her up almost three hours ago, but that I shouldn't worry because they probably just stopped somewhere.

I couldn't do anything but worry. I trusted Mike, but then again, I knew he wasn't very fond of me at the moment, no matter how hard he tried to act like everything was cool when I had talked to him earlier. I knew people really liked to show their ass when they were given the opportunity after someone had pissed them off. I didn't believe there were any exceptions to that. There was truly a thin line between love and hate, and with me and Mike, that line was very, very fine.

After I got off the phone with my momma, I called Mike and didn't get an answer. After about the tenth call, I decided to leave a message, snapping on his ass, telling him he better had been on his way to my house or there was gonna be a problem. Another hour went by and I still hadn't heard anything. I sat on the couch trying to watch TV and keep my mind off of it, and trying to convince myself that everything was okay.

I finally heard my doorbell ring and I jumped up quickly hitting the button to buzz Mike up. When I opened the door, I heard Mike coming down the hall, talking to Mikayla. When he was finally in view. He carried Mikayla's carrier on one arm, and had shopping bags galore hanging on his other arm. I stood in the doorway with my arms folded, muggin' him as he continued walking my way.

"What the hell, Mike! I've called you a million times! You couldn't return my call to let me know everything was okay?"

"Can I please come in and set everything down before you get to cussin' at me?" he asked as if he hadn't done a damn thing wrong.

I followed Mike over to the sofa, still waiting for an explanation. He continued to talk to Mikayla and she looked at him smiling as if she knew exactly what he was talking about. He took her out of her baby carrier, then looked up at me while I stood over him.

"Now what were you saying?" he asked.

I unfolded my arms and calmed my tone a little bit and said, "Why didn't you call? I was worried."

"As you see, I took my little girl shopping, and I accidentally left my phone in the car. I apologize."

The tension immediately left the room. I couldn't even be mad at Mike, no matter how hard I tried. He didn't have to do the things he was still doing, and I was grateful.

"What did you do? Buy up the whole store?" I asked, digging through the bags.

"No. Just the things I wanted her to have. She's a special little girl."

"Yes, she is," I agreed.

I sat down next to Mike and there was silence between us. The only sound were the noises that Mikayla was making as she blew spit bubbles. I had never felt so uncomfortable around him. We were friends before we were lovers, but it didn't even feel like we were friends. We felt more like strangers.

"You want something to drink?" I asked, trying to break the ice.

"Yeah, thanks."

"Let me guess . . . Apple juice?" I asked.

I had to keep lots of apple juice in the house when Mike lived with me because he went through so much of it.

"You got some vodka?"

"Vodka? Yeah . . ." I slowly got up, and constantly looked back at Mike, waiting on him to change his answer as I walked to the kitchen.

The only time Mike used to drink was when it was a special occasion. It was very odd for him to randomly drink something hard as vodka. All I could think was maybe I had driven him to drinking. I knew I was good, but damn, I didn't wanna turn nobody into an alchy.

When I got back with Mike's vodka, I handed him his glass and said, "So, you drinkin' like that now?"

He looked down at my hand as he grabbed the glass from me, cleared his throat, then said, "No, I just do when I feel I need one. By the way, nice ring."

Shit! I thought to myself as I went into panic mode. I didn't intentionally leave my ring on for Mike to see. It completely slipped my mind that I still had on Ty's ring. I didn't know what to say, so I just started playing with Mikayla as Mike gulped down his vodka. When he finished, which was within a matter of seconds, he gave Mikayla a kiss and stood up, shaking his head at me.

"I guess I'll be seeing you," I said, as I followed him towards the door.

"Yep. Have a good one," he replied as he walked out the door.

That didn't go well at all, and the rest of the day I felt bad for Mike and what he was going through, but he didn't trust me, and I knew I had to move on. Once I got Mikayla to sleep I went in my room to change the linen on my bed that Ty and I had made a mess of. As soon as I lifted the pillows off the bed, underneath the pillow Ty slept on, there was a roll of money. I was surprised at first, but then after thinking about it, I wasn't. Ty was known to do stuff like that, and I knew he was trying his hardest to get all the way back in with me, so I would probably see a lot more of that kind of thing.

I texted Ty and told him thank you. He replied by texting no problem, and he'd call me, but he was at home, and Jada was all in his face. Jada wasn't completely dumb. Naïve yes, but she knew something was going on. She just couldn't put her finger on it. My thoughts on it was that if he didn't wanna be with her, he needed to tell her, but not let it be because of me. If it was that easy for him to cheat on her with me and straight up tell me all I had to do was say the word and he would leave her alone, then the love wasn't that deep anyway. At least not on his end. Obviously, he wasn't reciprocating the same kind of love Jada was giving him.

The next week, I finally went back to work, which was a sad occasion for me. I didn't mind working, but I didn't enjoy dropping Mikayla off at daycare. I was stressed out every day for the first couple of weeks. Mike had started coming by every few days to see Mikayla, and didn't say another word about the ring. As a matter of fact, he didn't say much to me at all. It was all about the baby. He did offer to keep Mikayla when he wasn't at work, but it was already uncomfortable enough being around him so I didn't wanna have to see him any more than I had to, so I declined.

Ty and I had started spending lunches together, and some evenings while he was working he would come through. Mikayla started looking more and more like him every day, and he threw it in my face every time he saw her. What he didn't know was that I didn't mind that she looked liked his fine ass! We enjoyed our time together, and everything just felt so right. Problem was, I had felt that way before with a few other people in my life, and if anybody knew, I knew that everything that felt right, wasn't always right. I tried my best not to put all my feelings on the table, and just tried to take it day by day.

In some ways I wanted Ty to leave Jada and be with me, but I also didn't wanna lose Jada as a friend. She had done nothing to me for me to wish anything bad on her. I wanted her to be happy, and I felt like I was keeping her from the happiness that she deserved, but what about my happiness? I deserved to be happy too. I was punished for my wrongdoings, and now it was my time to be happy again. I just had to figure out how to make that happen, and make it permanent this time.

I tried not to be around Jada too often, because I thought maybe she would begin to be able to see right through me, but she made that impossible. She was always inviting me somewhere or always wanting to do something together and she was the type of person who was hard to say no to. This particular night, she just wanted to go bowling.

"Bowling girl? You sure you don't wanna go shopping?" I asked, laughing as I was talking to Jada on the phone and curling my client's hair. "I don't even know if I know how to bowl anymore!"

"Come on! It's just for fun! You'll have a good time!"

Once again, I gave in to Jada, and told her I'd see her later. Of course, I had to find somewhere for Mikayla to go. I loved being her mother, but when people say your whole life changes with a baby, they are not lyin'. I couldn't just get up and go whenever I felt like it, which sometimes drove me crazy, but I was learning to get over it.

I called Mike first because I knew he loved spending time with his little girl. I was unpleasantly surprised when he told me he wouldn't be able to tonight. I just knew before I even called him that I wouldn't have to call and bug anyone else. It wasn't very often when Mike told me no, but I guess he told my ass this time and it did not feel good at all! I felt like asking his ass what the hell he had to do that was more important than her, but I thought before I spoke. I told him okay and moved on to the next person on the list.

"Maaaa! Can you do me a favor?" I asked in my little girl voice.

"Bring my baby on over here girl! What time you gone be here?"

I loved my momma so much. She was always there for me. It wasn't like I asked her to keep the baby all the time, and she knew that I needed some time to myself sometimes.

As I resumed with my day, I didn't do much talking to the other stylists or my clients. I was thinking up all the scenarios possible as to why Mike would decline on seeing Mikayla. It just didn't make a whole lot of sense to me. I even thought that maybe he was attempting to wean himself away from her so he didn't have to see me.

The bowling alley that Jada and I were going to was on my side of town, so after I dropped the baby off, Jada met me at my house so that I could jump in the car with her. The bowling alley was kinda quiet with a small crowd, which was cool with me. It was a very nice environment and a good way to relieve some stress. Maybe that was why Jada picked bowling. I knew damn well she had some stress to relieve.

We bowled a couple of games, while sippin' on Tequila Sunrises. After that, the crowd started flowing in. We took a break in between games and chatted a bit. We were sitting there talking and laughing one minute, then Jada just started crying on me. I didn't know if it was just the alcohol, or if she was just hurting that bad inside.

I scooted my chair next to hers, and wrapped my arms around her, saying, "What's wrong? Please don't cry." I looked around to make sure no one was looking.

She sniffled a few times before she could get any words out. I grabbed a napkin off of the table and wiped the corners of her eyes.

"It's the same thing we talked about before. Silas is cheating. I know he is and don't try to tell me otherwise. Yes, he does work a lot and I knew that before, but I kind of got to the point where I knew his routine. Now, from day to day, it switches up all the time. I'm gonna start following him!"

"No! Don't do that!" I exclaimed. "I mean, you don't want to stoop to that! You are sooo much better than that. Don't even start actin' like these insecure bitches out here," I said, as I moved my chair back across from Jada.

"I don't want to, but I gotta see it for myself to give me enough reason to just walk away."

"If you truly believe he's cheating, that's enough reason to walk away right there. Female intuition doesn't normally lie."

Jada was quiet for a minute, then said, "Has your intuition been talking to you lately?" as she pointed behind me.

I quickly turned around and started fuming at what I saw. Mike was at the bowling lane right next to ours and he wasn't alone. He was with some light-skinned chick with long blonde weave almost down to her ass. She had on some blue jean leggings that fit her hourglass body perfectly, and a simple white tank. They smiled at each other like they had been together forever. I couldn't do anything but stare with fire in my eyes.

"Um, Kel . . . Are you gonna do something?"

I had forgotten Jada was even sitting there. I was too preoccupied trying to see what Mike and his rebound bitch were gonna do next. I still hadn't told Jada or anyone else, besides Ty, that Mike and I were no longer an item, so what was actually going on was something totally different in Jada's eyes.

I turned around looking Jada directly in the eyes and said, "I don't know what I can do," in the calmest tone I could find.

"What the hell do you mean? You need to confront his ass!"

I had never seen Jada get so angry. She looked liked she was ready to get up and say something herself, so I knew I had to tell her the truth.

"Calm down, Jada. I have to be honest with you. I haven't told anyone, but Mike and I aren't together. We haven't been together for about a month now."

Jada looked back and forth at me, and Mike and the bitch, with her eyes as big as quarters.

"Kel, why didn't you tell me?"

"Like I said, I didn't tell anyone. I thought we would be able to iron things out before anybody noticed, but it doesn't look like that's gonna happen."

"I'm so sorry. And look at me, sittin' here telling you about my problems when you have you own."

I felt a huge lump forming in my throat as I looked back and saw Mike with his hands on the nameless woman's hips, showing her the correct bowling form. My emotions were raging, so I told Jada I'd be right back. As soon I made it to the bathroom, I made it into one of the stalls, and I broke down. Jada knew me as a strong woman, and I didn't want her perception of me to change, so I refused to break down in front of her and everyone else in the bowling alley.

Once I regained my composure, and felt like I could handle what I was about to face when I stepped out of the bathroom, I looked in the mirror to make sure my face was intact, and headed back into the heat. Jada was still at the table staring at the couple when I sat back down.

"You okay?" she asked.

"Yes, are you okay?" I asked sarcastically.

"I'm sorry. Just worried about you."

"I'm sorry too. You ready to bowl?"

"Yeah. Fuck him!"

I looked at Jada, now with my eyes big as quarters. Jada didn't curse much, and when she did, she didn't use words like "fuck"! I definitely knew I couldn't lose Jada as a friend then. She was a real ride or die chick! She looked at me and smiled as we headed back over to our lane. I grabbed my bowling ball and headed towards the lane. I threw that ball with more power and force than I had used all night, and ended up getting a strike. I turned around smiling and Jada ran up to me giving me a high five.

"Gone girl! I knew you had it in you!" she said.

Walking back towards the bench to sit down, while Jada went for her turn, me and Mike's eyes met, and I quickly removed the smile from my face.

"Nice strike," he said, trying to smile, as his little girlfriend looked at me grinning like she knew me.

"Thanks," I said, thinking Mike would go on about his business and act like he didn't know me personally.

"Oh, I'm sorry. Kel, this is Melody. Melody, Kel."

Melody stuck her hand out for me to shake, but I stood there with one hand on my hip, and said, "Hi." By that time, Jada had made it back, and was standing there looking confused.

"Hey, Jada," Mike said. "This is my friend, Melody."

Jada reluctantly shook Melody's hand, then the bitch said, "Nice to meet you both! Kel, I've heard so many things about you, and you have the most beautiful little girl. She's sweet as she wanna to be."

I pushed Jada out the way, folded my arms and said, "Wait a minute! You've seen my baby?"

Melody looked at Mike as if she was unsure if she should answer that question.

"I'm not talking to Mike. I asked you a simple question."

She hesitated, then said, "Yeah, Mikey and I took her shopping one day."

I could feel the heat rising, and could see Jada in my peripheral vision shaking her head. I felt like slapping the shit out of that hoe, but I learned a long time ago that I couldn't put all the blame on the other woman. Mike or "Mikey" had to have known that I would be upset if he took my baby around another woman. That was just common as sense could get!

"Oh. Okay," I said, still trying to stay calm. "Your hair is pretty. Where'd you buy it?"

Looking shocked that I would ask her that question, Melody said, "Oh no, it's all mine." Flippin' all that fake shit to the back.

Mike must've never disclosed to her that I was a stylist and could point out even the best weave job from a mile away, but I was done with her, so I told Mike I needed to speak with him privately. He told the Beverly Johnson weave and Maybelline queen that he'd be right back, which she didn't look happy about at all.

Mike followed me outside to the parking lot and before I could start, he began trying to explain his side.

"Look Kel. I did not intentionally take Mikayla around Melody. When I picked her up from your mom's house that day, Melody called and wanted me to go shopping with her . . ."

I cut Mike off and said, "So wait a minute. You let a bitch come between your daddy-and-daughter time? Please tell me that's not what you're trying to tell me. Then when I asked you to keep her tonight, you said no. Obviously it was for this same hoe!"

"Can you please refrain from the name calling?"

I got closer to Mike's face to make sure he heard me loud and clear. "No, I can't refrain from the name calling because I call it as I see it! Anyone who gets between my baby and her 'daddy' is a bitch, hoe, slut, or whatever else I choose to call her!" At that point I was shouting, and felt like beating the shit out of Mike.

"Calm down, Kel," Mike said, looking around and still trying to remain calm. "I'm sorry that this made you so upset, and believe me, no one can come between me and Mikayla. That hurts for you to even say. You're right. I should've told Melody that I couldn't go shopping with her that day. But tonight, I had already made plans. Any other time wouldn't have been a problem and you know that."

I looked around at all the colorful, bright signs and lights, then at all the traffic of the Chicago nightlife, trying not to look at Mike. I was angry . . . no, I was mad! I didn't know what else to say, but my tears spoke for themselves. Mike grabbed me and gave me a hug.

"I'm sorry for what I did, but I'm not sorry for having a life," he said as he held me close.

"Are y'all done? I heard a voice behind me say."

Mike released me and walked towards his date. Jada stood right behind her, still looking like she was down for whatever.

He grabbed Melody's hand, looked at me and said, "We're done here, right Kel?"

I nodded my head and felt like I had just lost one of the most important battles of my life as they walked back into the bowling alley together. Jada didn't know what to say, so instead of saying anything, she did probably the best thing she could've done. Gave me a hug and told me it would be okay.

After that episode, I didn't even wanna go back in to face Mike and Melody, so Jada went back in to grab the rest of our things and pay the tab. While I waited, so many things went through my mind. I wondered if she had been kissing on my baby. I knew Mikayla had gotten some bumps on her fat jaws a day or two after Mike had taken her shopping. They probably came from Melody's nasty ass! I also wondered how long Mike had known her. They seemed really comfortable with each other. It didn't seem like they were only on a third or fourth date at all. I also wondered how deep his feelings were for her.

Jada came back out and said, "Come on girl. Let's get out of here."

Upon leaving the bowling alley, Jada asked if I wanted to go hang out somewhere else. I told her no. I just wanted to go get Mikayla and go home. She offered to drive me to my momma's house to pick her up, and I felt that was best, because my mind was in too many other places to be driving.

"You know you could've told me about you and Mike," Jada said.

"I know. I'm just a private person, and I don't like putting my problems on others."

"Is that what I do? Put my problems on you?"

"No. Not at all. People deal with things in different ways. I just keep things to myself until I'm ready to share. I've been burned a few times after sharing information, so I sometimes keep my guards up, even though I know you wouldn't do that to me."

I told Jada that I knew she wouldn't do that to me, but honestly I didn't know. After Tif did what she did to me, it was hard for me to trust anyone. She was one of my best friends, and we had been friends for years, so I was never too sure.

"Why did you two end your relationship?"

"It was just the right thing for the both of us."

"I know there's more to that, but I can tell you don't wanna answer anymore questions about that, so I'm just gonna say one thing, then I'll leave it alone. Y'all belong together. Every time I've seen the two of you together, it has been beautiful. Even tonight, under the circumstances, when I walked out there with what's her name, and saw y'all hugging, I could see the love. Be sure this is the right thing. If not, go get your man!"

Jada was right. I didn't wanna answer anymore questions, and who the hell was she to try to give me relationship advice when I was fuckin' her man? I was just really ready to get out of that car. I loved Jada, but the longer I was in that car, the angrier I became, and I didn't know if I was angry at Mike, Melody, Jada, Ty, or myself. Ty texted me the whole time I was in the car with Jada. I told him that I was with her, and he still continued to text. He had become so nonchalant with the whole situation with Jada. It was almost like he didn't care if she found out about us, but I did. I had a lot of thinking to do, so that at the end of the day, I would do the right thing for everyone, but especially, Mikayla and myself.

Chapter 22

I was in a deep sleep when all of a sudden I heard bees buzzing in my ear. I began throwing my hands all over the place, when I finally realized I was dreaming, and the buzzing sound was actually the sound of my phone vibrating next to my pillow. It was hard for me to go to sleep the night before, which resulted in me not falling asleep 'til around four in the morning. The good thing about it was Mikayla was having a bad night and wouldn't stay asleep anyway. I would've been pissed if I had been tired as hell and she wouldn't go to sleep. While playing with her and rocking her all night, I thought long and hard about where my life was going long term. I thought about all of the possible outcomes and consequences of everything that was going on, and my actions. Even though I thought about all of that, I still hadn't come up with a plan. My life was like playing a difficult game of chess. I didn't know what move to make next.

I answered the phone, still half way out of it.

"Hello," I said.

"Hey. I didn't mean to wake you. I thought you would be up with Mikayla."

I jumped straight up in my bed as soon as I heard Mike's voice on the other end. I didn't say anything. I just waited to hear what Mike had to say. It was seven in the morning, so I knew he wasn't trying to see Mikayla that early.

"You there?" he asked.

"Yeah, I'm here."

"I don't even know where to begin . . ."

"Just say what you wanna say."

I could hear Mike taking deep breaths through the phone.

"I couldn't sleep last night," he began. "That whole thing last night was a mess. I hate that that happened. Kel, I don't know who you're seeing, but whoever it is, I can tell it's pretty serious. You're wearing his ring, which hurts like hell."

Mike paused after almost every sentence to take a deep breath. I could tell he had been thinking hard about what he wanted to say to me.

"The fact of the matter is, after I held you last night, I couldn't think about anything or anyone else but you. I wish I could control who I love, but I can't. I'll admit, trust is an issue with me, but I'm willing to work on that if you would be willing to give us another try and help me to trust you more. I know you cheated on me, but I wanna move past that. Like I said, I know you're in a relationship, but I know what we had has to be a lot more deeper than what you have with this other person. No one could possibly love you more than I love you except for God, and if I could love you more than God, I would."

As I listened to Mike, I silently cried relentlessly. I cried because what he said was beautiful, but I wasn't sure that what Ty and I had was any less deep than what Mike and I had. I honestly believed that Ty loved me just as much as Mike, and I didn't want to hurt either of them.

"Mike, I don't know what to say."

"Say you'll give us another try."

I was silent. I didn't know if that was the right thing to do. I had vowed that I would do my best to make all the right decisions from this point on, so I was being very careful as to what I agreed to.

"Kel, do you love me?

"Yes," I said without hesitation. "But am I in love with you should be the question."

"Well, are you?" Mike asked curiously.

"I don't know. I know I've done things to you I shouldn't have, and I ask myself, 'Do you treat people you're in love with like that?'"

"We all make mistakes, Kel. I'm not trying to force you into anything, so you think about it, and I'll be here if you wanna talk."

"Okay."

"Talk to you soon," Mike said sounding hopeful.

When I hung up from talking to Mike, I felt some kind of way, but couldn't describe it. I wanted to call Mike right back and tell him that I am in love with him and I don't know what I was thinking, but something was holding me back from doing that. I felt as though I had my good conscience sitting on one shoulder trying to get her point across, and my bad conscience sitting on the other shoulder, persuading me to do the opposite.

I spent the rest of the morning cleaning my house and listening to some good music, hoping that the answer would just come to me. As I cleaned and listened to a whole lot of love songs, which wasn't intentional, I began reminiscing about Mike, from the time we first met, 'til now. I saw his smile over and over again in my mind. I remembered his sexy wink that always made me smile and him lifting me up and spinning me around like he did each time he saw me, until recently. Last, but not least, I remembered how I felt every time he looked at me. He always made me feel like nothing less than the most beautiful, sexy, intelligent, and important woman in the universe. It had really hurt me the night before to think another woman could be taking that spot.

I also reminisced about Ty. He was hard on the outside, but he had a soft spot for me. I felt our bond the first moment we met and that first dance we took. I knew Ty would've done anything for me then and now. I loved Ty and, like Mike had said when I was on the phone with him, you can't help who you love. The problem was Ty was living that crooked ass life, which I really had gotten past, but it was still something I had to consider while thinking about the lives of me and my daughter. The other problem was he had someone who loved his dirty draws, and unfortunately, that person happened to be someone I loved like a sister. I didn't wanna hurt either one of them, but whichever decision I made, someone was gonna get hurt, so I knew what I needed to do.

"Hey, Mike," I said, when he answered, sounding happy to hear back from me so soon.

"What's up sweetie?"

"Let's go out tonight and just do something fun, and then we can talk about what's next."

"Sounds like a start. Where you wanna go?"

"I'll think of something. Just pick me up at eight."

I had no idea what I wanted to do, but I wanted to make sure it was something that would lighten things up between us, and prepare us to open up and really talk to each other. I wasn't making any promises about anything, but I was willing to be open and see what happened. My momma didn't know at the time, but this was the perfect weekend she had asked to keep Mikayla. I had some business to take care of.

Ty called to tell me he was gonna come by later to see Mikayla. Unfortunate for him, I had to tell him that tonight wasn't a good night.

"What you mean tonight ain't a good night? What you got goin' on?"

I was tired of having to lie all of the damn time and I wasn't about to lie this time. Especially to someone who wasn't officially my man, so I told Ty the truth.

"Mike and I talked, and we decided to go on an outing."

"Outing? You tryna tell me y'all goin' out on a date?"

"If that's what you wanna call it. We're going to have a good time and do some talking."

"So, you plan on fuckin' him too?"

"Did I say that? Quit putting words in my mouth. I'm going to do exactly what I just told you. I'm not obligated to tell you that much, but I thought you did deserve the truth."

"So, are you plannin' on gettin' back with him?"

"I don't know what's gonna happen. I'm taking it day by day. This is just the beginning so I can see what I really want. I'm going in with an open mind. "

"That's bullshit, Kel. You know exactly what you plan on doing, and me and you better be in the equation somewhere."

I didn't know what else to tell Ty. I tried telling him the truth, but he didn't wanna accept that, and wanted to add all his little adlibs to change around what I was saying, to what he believed the truth to be. Nothing was set in stone, but obviously he thought it was, and was afraid my decision didn't involve him. I could hear the anger in his voice as we continued our conversation, and I wasn't feelin' his vibe. Shit, I would've been better off lying to his ass, but it was too late for that. Once the truth was out, it was out. Ty finally ended our conversation by telling me he had some work to do and he'd talk to me later. I was actually relieved to get off of that call, and I had never felt that way about Ty. All I could think was maybe God was trying to reveal some things to me to help me make my decision.

Later that evening, Mike texted me, asking what he should wear since I hadn't told him where we were going. I just told him to wear something casual dress. I had decided we were gonna go this night club I had never been to called "Rumors." I put on a white party dress that came right above the knee, and had pretty diamonds across the top. I was hoping I would be lucky enough not to spill anything on it before the night was over. I wore my hanging diamond earrings and necklace set that Mike had bought me, and wore my hair up in a high classy bun. I made sure to take Ty's ring off, and put it back in a safe place. I glanced at Mike's ring, but decided against wearing that one too. Lastly, I made sure my makeup was blended perfectly. I wanted to look more beautiful than Mike had ever seen me, and I think I was successful.

Mike rang the doorbell at seven fifty-nine. When I opened the door, he immediately picked me up and twirled me around.

"You look gorgeous," Mike said, winking at me. "You ready to go?"

" Yeah, let me get the rest of my things," I said as I went upstairs to grab my purse.

As I came down the staircase, I looked at Mike standing there, and there was no question that he was a beautiful creature. I could tell that he had just shaved because his perfectly defined jawline was even more noticeable. He wore a pair of straight leg jeans, a button down shirt, and blazer. I guess he was trying to look the best I had ever seen him too, because boy, was he lookin' good!

We headed out the door, arm in arm, looking like the world's hottest couple. Jay-Z and Beyoncé didn't have a thing on us that night, besides their money!

"So, where to?" Mike asked.

"Do you know where 'Rumors' nightclub is?"

"Yeeeaaaah . . . What about it?"

"That's where we're going."

"Really?" Mike asked, sounding surprised.

"I said we're gonna have a good time, so come on! Let's go and do something different from what we've ever done before!"

"Okay. Whatever you say," Mike said as he pulled off from in front of the condo.

It was almost a half hour drive to the club, and of course I couldn't just sit there without conversation, so I decided to bring up Melody, hoping I didn't spoil the mood.

"So, Mike. How long have you and Melody known each other?"

"I met her a couple of days after you and I split up. I met her at the grocery store of all places. Yesterday was only maybe our forth date. I didn't call her for a couple of weeks after she gave me her number. I was waiting to see what would happen between us."

I couldn't believe Mike was so open about it, so I continued to talk about it.

"Oh, I thought y'all had known each other a lot longer than that."

"Why did you think that?"

"Just from the rapport you had with each other. It seemed like the two of you meshed well."

"She was cool, but nothing like being with you. You and I have excellent rapport," he said, then looked over at me winking and showing off that million-dollar smile.

"Did you have sex with her?" I asked without any type of reluctance.

Mike didn't answer the question as fast as he had answered the others, so I knew what that meant. I figured he had, but I was just hoping I was wrong.

"Kel, I did, and I hate that I did, but believe me when I say it meant nothing. I just needed some companionship. I missed you."

"It's okay. No need to explain," I said, trying my best not to be irrational.

After that last question, I considered the question and answer segment to be over and in the past, but I guess Mike felt it was his turn.

"So who's the man you're sleeping with?"

"How do you know I'm sleeping with someone?"

"Because men just don't give out big ass diamonds like that for nothing, and believe me, I know all about that pot of gold you got. It can make a man jump through fire. I just wish it all belonged to me. So who is it?"

"Believe me when I say you'll know the whole truth before the night is over. Just not now. Okay?"

"Okay, but I'm gonna hold you to that."

"I promise," I said with a grin.

I had decided that I was gonna get everything out in the open. I was gonna tell Mike who Silas really was and how I had been seeing him. What ever happened after that would depend on Mike's reaction to such a heavy load I was about to throw on him. All of my baggage was about to come out, and how Mike was able to deal with it would determine how I would proceed. The last few minutes of what seemed to be the longest drive ever, Mike and I both remained silent, listening to Eric Benet's "I Wanna Be Loved."

The parking lot was crazy packed at "Rumors". I had heard great things about it, and always wanted to go. I guessed a whole lot of other people heard the same great things I had heard! It was supposedly a very classy nightclub where you could still have fun, but none of that ole ghetto bullshit was going on up in there. I heard people joking about it saying that they have the whole damn Chicago Police Department walking around up in there.

We ended up parking directly across the street from the club, where there was a parking lot that looked like it was about a block long. Before getting out, Mike grabbed my hand, kissed it, and told me he loved me.

"I love you too. Never stopped," I replied.

"I never will stop lovin' you," Mike said and kissed me with the softest lips God ever made.

After Mike made me melt inside, he got out of the car, and came around to let me out. As soon as he opened my door, I heard him say, "Silas?"

I looked through the driver's side window and saw Ty getting closer and closer. Then I saw someone else in the distance running up behind him, but they were too far off for me to tell who it was.

"Naw nigga. You know me as Silas, but yo girl know me as Ty and my baby know me as daddy!"

I saw Ty draw his gun and before I could move, I heard a loud explosion and saw Mike hit the ground.

"No!" I screamed in anguish, and jumped out of the car, falling to the ground right by Mike's side. My thousands of tears fell all over his non-responsive body. "Silas!" The person behind him screamed. Ty turned around, and without thought, fired again.

People were all over the place panicking, not knowing what to do. Blood was gushing from Mike's chest, as I screamed, "Somebody call an ambulance! Please!" While I tried to press on the bullet hole in Mike's chest with one hand, I felt around in his pockets for his cell phone. I didn't know where mine was, but I had to call 911.

I finally found Mike's phone in his jacket pocket, and dialed 911. The dispatcher said that a few people had called and reported it and there were officers already on the scene and an ambulance was on the way. As soon as I got ready to cuss her ass out and tell her there were no officers on the scene, a group of officers came running out of the club with their guns drawn.

"Come on, Mike. Help is coming. Please don't leave me. I couldn't handle that. Fight for both me and Mikayla! Please!"

It wasn't looking good. Mike made no movements whatsoever, and it didn't look like he was even breathing. As the police moved in the direction of Ty, who was already on the ground, the ambulance pulled up and three EMT's jumped out. There was a black woman and two white men. They told me to get back and began working on Mike right away. One of the men felt for a pulse, and he shook his head at the other two. My entire body started shaking uncontrollably. I couldn't believe what was happening. If I hadn't been so concerned with Mike's well-being, I would've walked over there and killed Ty myself! Another ambulance pulled up, and I could see the police officers who had their weapons drawn, signaling for the ambulance to come over where Ty was kneeling. I squinted my eyes to see a little further, and Ty was holding up someone's head, as they lay there motionless, just like Mike. I blinked a few times and saw Ty crying miserably, and then saw the grueling sight of blood coming from Jada's mouth. The person coming up behind Ty had been Jada, and he panicked, not knowing who she was and shot her!

I began crying even harder and turned back around towards Mike. He was on a stretcher and two of the EMTs were lifting him into the ambulance.

"How is he? Is he gonna make it?" I asked nervously.

The female, black EMT said, "Ma'am, to be honest, it's not looking good. We got a faint pulse."

"That's good, right?" I asked trying to sound hopeful.

"Very faint, Ma'am, but we have to go and get him to the hospital asap!"

"I need to be with him!"

"You can meet us there. We're headed to North General."

She jumped in the back of the ambulance and slammed the door in my face. I scrambled on the ground, searching for the keys to Mike's Porsche. I finally found them with his blood all over them. As I stood up to get in the car, the other ambulance was pulling off with Jada inside. Ty was handcuffed and being read his rights. His bloodshot eyes caught mine, and he was no longer the same Ty that I had fallen in love with, and he never again would be. He had just shot two very important people in my life who I loved, and I would never be able to forgive him for that. I jumped in the car and sped off, hitting the Dan Ryan, heading to North General.

Chapter 23

It was a dark, dreary, rainy day on a very sad occasion. The sadness in my heart became even worse when I entered the doors of the chapel with Mikayla laying across my shoulder and my momma by my side. It had been a week since the whole shooting incident, and I had probably only gotten a total of five hours of sleep, and it wasn't even peaceful sleep. I was so miserable that I couldn't even care for Mikayla on my own. The whole episode kept playing over and over in my head. I blamed myself for everything that happened. If I would've never given Ty any indication that we were gonna be together, this whole thing would've never happened. I should've ridded myself of him, and made him go on with his life, and continued on with my life as it was. It didn't matter now, because there was no going back in time, and no matter how much I thought about what I should've done, it wasn't gonna bring anyone back. All I knew was that the person laying up in that casket didn't deserve to be there.

I was reluctant to view the lifeless body of the person that loved and who meant so much to me. My momma told me I would regret it later if I didn't and forced me to go. I couldn't believe what I was looking at. The past week, everything had been so surreal, as if none of it really happened, but now it was reality. This was not supposed to happen like this! I burst out crying and shouting, "Oh God! Please let this be a dream!" My momma grabbed Mikayla from me, so that I wouldn't accidently drop her in the midst of my emotional outburst. She rubbed my back as we headed back to our seats. From the time the pastor began speaking, 'til the end of the funeral service, I cried the entire time, and Mikayla could tell something wasn't right because she cried right along with me.

I had taken so many people in my life for granted, but I knew this tragedy was one that I would truly learn from and would haunt me for the rest of my life. It was just so unfortunate that it took for this to happen for me to understand how important some people in my life were. I didn't know how I would ever get past this, but I had to for everyone else around me who loved me. After everything that happened, I ended up having to tell my momma the entire truth. There was no hiding it, especially after it was all over the news, and the headline in the newspaper read, "Lover's Jealousy Turns Deadly." It seemed as though every time I tried to keep everything so quiet, it still ended up creeping out with a bang.

Even though I could tell my momma was disappointed, she was still there for me. She saw how much I was suffering, and I could tell she just felt bad for me and didn't want me to go through even more. I wondered if I would be able to eat, sleep, or even live a normal life again. I never thought Ty would've gone to the extremes that he did, but one lesson I did learn out of the ordeal was to never put anything past anyone, and when someone says they'll do anything for me, to take it literally. I knew Ty felt like he was doing what he did out of love, but he didn't think about anyone else before he acted on impulse. The truth of the matter was my baby's father was now a murderer and would be locked up for a very long time, if not sentenced to death.

I had my mind set on getting up and saying a few words, but when the time came, I couldn't bring myself to do it. I stood, but suddenly felt weak in the knees, and my tears started flowing once more. Listening to everyone else's stories and comments made me realize how much of a impact one person can have over so many lives, including mine. After the service was over, my momma and I ran into Tasha and Lem. Tasha was always there for me and I loved her for that. She ran up to me, giving me a hug, telling me to let her know if I needed anything. I just nodded my head, knowing if I tried to speak a word, the crying would start all over again.

At the gravesite, the lowering of the casket was too much for me and I begged my momma to just take me home. I couldn't take anymore. As we walked away from the crowd of people standing around, throwing red and white roses on top of the casket as it went lower and lower into the damp ground, I turned around one last time and blew a kiss, hoping that my angel caught it.

My momma pulled up in front of my house, and I stared at Mike's Porsche that sat there motionless. My last memory in that car was flying to the hospital, not sure what the doctors were gonna tell me about Mike and Jada once I got there. I just knew I had to be there for the both of them. I could feel tears welling up in my eyes again just thinking about that night and I knew that was my cue to tell my momma I'd talk to her later.

"Baby, you sure you don't want me to stay for a little while?"

"No, I'll be okay. I'm gonna try to get some rest."

"You want me to take Mikayla with me, at least?"

I knew I probably needed some time by myself, but honestly, I was afraid to be alone. I didn't want my momma to stay, but at least Mikayla would give some company and keep my mind occupied.

"No. I think we'll be okay."

"Girl, get you some rest, and I promise I'll bring her back when you tell me to."

My momma grabbed my hand and squeezed it, and I knew she was right.

"Everything's gonna be all right Kel. You will be able to move on from this. It's just gone take some time and a lot of prayer, but you're strong."

I gave my momma and Mikayla a kiss goodbye, and slowly headed into my building. As soon as I walked in the house and set my keys and purse down, I heard a noise coming from upstairs. From the lower level, I couldn't see anything or anyone, so I grabbed a knife out of the kitchen drawer and headed up the stairs.

Once I got to the top, I looked both left and right, and went towards my bedroom, which was where I could precisely hear the noise coming from.

Cautiously turning the corner to enter the bedroom, I screamed and started swinging the knife with my eyes closed, not knowing what I had run into. I suddenly heard a voice and felt someone grabbing my hand that had a tight grip on the knife.

"I'm not gonna hurt you baby! Calm down!"

Breathing hard, I opened my eyes. Mike carefully grabbed the knife out of my hand, dropped it on the floor, and hugged me tight. I firmly wrapped my arms around his neck and sobbed on his shoulder. He kissed me on my forehead and repeatedly told me everything was gonna be okay.

When I finally caught my breath enough to speak, I said, "What are you doing here? I thought you weren't getting released until tomorrow. I wanted to at least make things comfortable for you."

"Everything is comfortable enough. The doctor said I healed like a champ and it was okay for me to go home, so I called my sister to pick me up. I knew you were at the funeral. I wish I could've been there for you."

I sat down on the bed, thinking, once again about Jada. How could such a young, beautiful person, inside and out, life be over, just like that? She had so much she could've done and become. She died wearing the pink diamond ring that Ty had given her, promising her that he would always be there for her. She was buried with that same ring on her finger, even though he was unable to keep that promise. I was grateful that God spared Mike's life because I don't know what I would've done if I had lost him too, but I wish God would've spared Jada too. She was such a good person, and I hated that she died hearing Ty telling Mike that Mikayla was his baby and I knew she would never forgive me.

The night of the shooting, I was gonna make sure the whole truth came out. Just not the way it did. No one was supposed to get hurt, and no one definitely was supposed to be killed. When Jada had told me at the bowling alley that she was gonna start following Ty, I told her not to do it, but never thought anything else about it. Since everything took place, I think about that conversation all day

every day, and about how I should've stressed it more. Jada was
surrounded by so many lies, and she never had a clue. She and
Mike were the innocent ones throughout the entire ordeal, and they
were the ones who ended up being hurt.

When I made it to the hospital that night, after speeding after
the two ambulances that were carrying my good friend, and my
love, I nervously sat in the lobby alone for hours. I rocked back
and forth in my chair, and then paced back and forth. Mike's
doctor finally came out with a pen and clipboard in his hand. I
couldn't quite read the expression on his face to have some type of
clue of what he was about to say.

I stood as he said, "Mrs. Travis?"

I told them I was his wife when I got to the hospital because I
knew they wouldn't have given me any information if I would've
told them that I was only Mike's fiancé.

"Yes, yes!" I said frantically. "Is he gonna be okay?"

"Well, he did lose a substantial amount of blood, but he's very
strong and has a strong will to live. He seems to be doing good so
far, but the next twenty-four to forty-eight hours are very critical,
so he'll stay in intensive care so he can be observed closely."

I was so ecstatic, I hugged the doctor and said, "Thank you,
thank you, thank you for saving his life!"

I was hoping to hear the same kind of news from Jada's doctor,
who I had told I was Jada's sister. We looked so much alike that he
wouldn't have known the difference anyway. I waited so long for
her doctor to come out that I had fallen asleep. I felt a nudge on the
shoulder, and opened my eyes to the male Indian doctor who I had
spoken with earlier about Jada. I quickly sat up and waited for
good news to come out of his mouth. I knew it wasn't good when
he sat down next to me.

"I'm so sorry, ma'am," the doctor began with his heavy accent,
"the bullet hit some major organs, and we couldn't stop the
bleeding. Your sister hemorrhaged to death. We did all we could
do."

I sat there in shock. What the doctor had just said hadn't sunk
in, and I sat there for hours without saying a word and staring at
the wall. When I finally came to, I ransacked the lobby, throwing
magazines, books, remotes, and whatever else I could get my

hands on, screaming, and shouting. That was when they admitted me, giving me a dose of Valium, and called my momma. From that day 'til now, all it ever seemed like I ever did was cry.

I knew that Mike and I would eventually have to have a long conversation, since I never got to explain everything to him that night, but I was sure by now he had a pretty good idea of what happened. Right now, he didn't seem like he wanted to talk about anything. I thought he was probably just happy to be alive just as much as I was happy that he was alive. The rest of the day we held each other, and knowing he was there with me, I was able to get some rest.

Chapter 24

I woke up the next morning in a cold sweat. I had dreamt about Jada and it was so real. She asked me why didn't I just tell her the truth and she would've been able to accept it. She told me how she thought I was wonderful friend, and it hurt her so much to know that our entire friendship was a lie. She began crying, asking me why, and at that moment, I saw the bullet that killed her soaring through the air. I saw myself screaming, and running towards her, trying to jump in front of the bullet before it reached her, but before I could get there, I saw the impact of the hit lift her off the ground. I saw the pain in her eyes as she stared at me while her body lunged to the ground in slow motion.

I quickly lifted my head up off my pillow and looked around, not knowing where I was. Tears were in my eyes and my heart felt like it was gonna jump out of my chest. I awakened Mike with my sudden movement and he asked me if I was okay. I lied and told him I was fine and got up and went in the bathroom. After being in the bathroom for a few minutes, trying to calm myself down, I heard Mike in the bedroom talking, and I thought he was talking to me until I heard him cursing.

"Man, are you fuckin' kiddin' me? You really have the audacity to be calling here after you killed Jada and almost killed me?"

I ran out of the bathroom and quickly grabbed my cell phone from Mike, and when I put the phone up to my ear, I heard Ty saying, "Trust when I say, I didn't mean to kill her! I loved her, but I did mean to kill yo ass! Now put my baby momma on the phone, nigga!"

"Ty! What the fuck do you want?" I said as I looked over at Mike and saw him sitting there looking at me with disgust on his face and shaking his head.

"I need to talk to you," Ty said, sounding desperate.

"What could you possibly need to talk to me about?"

"Can you please come see me? I need to talk to you in person. It's important."

"Oh, hell no! I'm not coming to see you!"

Mike jumped up out of the bed reaching his hand out for the phone. I shook my head, letting him know I had it. He walked out of the bedroom and slammed the door. I knew he was upset, but I was in between a rock and a hard place. Even though I hated him for what he had done, he was still my child's father.

"Please Kel. After this one last favor, I promise I won't ask you to do anything else for me."

I remained quiet for a minute, contemplating on what I should say, until Ty said, "Kel, you gone do it or not? I only have a couple more minutes."

"When?" I asked.

"Today, at three."

I couldn't even imagine what Ty needed to talk to me about, but I knew it had to have been important to him for him to even have to nerve to call me after everything that had happened. I agreed to go to the prison to see him that afternoon, but trying to explain it to Mike was gonna be the hard part.

After hanging up from with Ty, I went downstairs and sat at the kitchen island and watched Mike at the stove cooking pancakes. He didn't even turn around to acknowledge my presence, so I sat there, waiting until he got done. He would have to turn around sooner or later. When he finally did, I stared at his bare chest that was steel bandaged up from his gunshot wound, and said, "I need to talk to you."

"About what?" he asked nonchalantly.

"Ty wants me to do something."

"Why the hell would you even talk to him? Do you even care that he plotted to kill me, and killed your good friend? Doesn't that bother you at all, or are you still putting your own feelings first?"

"I can't believe you just said that! I live it over and over again, wishing there was something I could've done at that moment to prevent it! I blame myself everyday! Yes, when I decided to keep the truth from both you and Jada, that was a mistake, and I had no idea of the seriousness of it all and all of the emotions that were involved. I'm sorry! I wish I could bring Jada back, but I'm also happy that you're still here because I realize now that I can't and don't wanna live without you." I cried.

"It took for someone to die and for me to be seriously injured for you to realize you want to be with me?"

"Is that really all you got out of everything I said?"

"I'm sorry. I'm just angry, but I have every right to be. You lied to me for no reason. You could've just told me who Silas really was, and it wouldn't have been an issue, but you didn't want me to know because you were being selfish. You didn't want me to pay attention to the interaction between the two of you in each other's presence because you knew you still had feelings for him and knew I would figure it out. I thought we were better than that, but I can't even express how I feel any more than I already have, so tell me, what does 'Ty' want you to do?"

"He wants me to come see him," I said in a low tone, ashamed of what I was saying.

"What?!?! And you're actually considering it?"

"He said it's the last favor and he'll never ask me to do anything else. I'm not doing it for him or me. I'm thinking about Mikayla. I know what he did, but he's still her father."

"Fuck, Kel!" Mike shouted, and threw his glass of orange juice against the wall.

I jumped in fear, not ever seeing Mike that angry, but I knew, like he said, he had every right to be. He paced the floor, balling up his fists, then turned and looked at me.

"Do what you gotta do . . . But I'm going with you."

My eyes got big, not knowing what to say. I could've either told him no, and risked losing him again, or let him know that I was now an open book, and had nothing to hide. He looked at me, waiting on an answer, and I nodded my head.

"We need to be there by three," I said as I walked past him, grabbing a piece of bacon before going upstairs to start getting ready.

On the way to the prison, Mike asked me was I sure I was ready to face Ty. I told him I was, and asked him was he sure. He seemed pretty confident that he was. Before we arrived, I wasn't sure what to expect, since I had never visited anyone in jail before. I could only go by what I saw on movies. I was glad that I had switched purses, because if I had taken my larger Coach purse, the officers would've been all day going through it. Mike and I were patted down, and had to go through metal detectors. It wasn't a comfortable experience at all.

We were finally taken to the room where we would soon be face to face with Ty. We sat on a bench in front of a glass window. There was a telephone with no buttons conveniently located on the ledge in front of us. After sitting there for about five minutes, we saw the door on the other side of the window opening, then Ty appeared in an orange jumpsuit, with two officers escorting him to his seat. He sat down, and the officers moved back towards the door, and remained in sight. I picked up the phone and put it to my ear. Ty sat there, with his eyes focused on me, then they moved over to Mike, and focused on him.

Ty finally picked up the phone and said, "What the fuck is he doin' here?"

Mike obviously read his lips and tried to grab the phone, saying, "She my woman. Not yours. When the hell you gone get that through your head!"

An officer came up behind us and said if Mike didn't calm down, he would have to leave. I nodded my head, and gave Mike a stern look. Mike looked at the officer and apologized. I put the phone back up to my ear, and Ty looked at Mike and told me to give him the phone. I handed Mike the phone, not knowing what this was all about, but I was hoping Ty didn't try to provoke Mike. I stared in Ty's mouth and read his lips.

"I'm not good with apologies and shit, but I do apologize. I let my emotions get the best of me and look where it got me. Right back where I vowed I would never be again. I'm gone be here for a much longer time, so you don't have to worry about me. I'm just askin' that you give me a few minutes with Kel."

Mike looked at me, and I could tell he didn't wanna do what he was about to do, but he stood up, and talked to the guard, asking for him to let him out.

"I'll be waiting for you in the car," he said.

After Mike left, Ty told me how much he loved me and Mikayla, and how angry he was that he messed up any chance of having a relationship with his only child, but he wanted to be some part of her life, so he wanted everything that he worked so hard for to go to her.

"What do you mean?" I asked, kind of knowing what he was saying, but needed clarity.

"The safe that's in my house. I want you to get it out of there before somebody else get in there and take it. It should be enough in there for her to live off of for the rest of her life. I'm gone give you the combination."

"Ty, I can't take that. We'll be fine."

"It's for my baby, and what can I do with it? I'm fucked! I want to be able to say I did something for her. She already won't remember me."

"Yes, she will. I'll bring her to see you as much as I can," I said, becoming emotional.

"No! I won't allow her to see me like this. Just do what I'm telling you to do. Please," he begged.

"Okay. I need a pen."

"No, you don't. It's five, twenty-four, eighty-eight."

I became even more emotional after Ty revealed that his combination to the safe that held his whole life savings was my birth date. He then told me where I could find the spare key.

"You think you can remember that?" he asked, grinning only showing a few of his teeth.

He was miserable, and I could see the remorse in his face and hear it in his voice, but there was nothing that could be done. He was charged with one count of second-degree murder, and one count of attempted murder. His sentencing hearing was a week from today, and it was all over the news that he was facing seventy years to life in prison. Either way, Ty would more than likely be spending the rest of his life in jail.

After I assured Ty that I would do what he asked, it was time to say goodbye. He put two fingers to his lips, then put them up to the glass. I did the same, placing my fingers directly in front of his. Ty told me he loved me once again, but I couldn't bring myself to say it back. I was sure that the tear that rolled down my face said enough. I watched as the two guards who brought Ty in, walked up and grabbed him by both arms to escort him back to his cell.

I wasn't sure how Mike would feel about me going to Ty's place, and getting the safe, but I would soon find out. When I got in the car, Mike was leaned back in the driver's seat, listening to Avery Sunshine's "Ugly Part of Me." As soon as I put on my seatbelt, he sat up and put the car in drive. It was quiet, but I didn't know how to begin the conversation that Mike and I needed to have, so I just waited for him to initiate the dialog. It took a while, but he finally did.

"So, what was that all about?" he asked curiously.

"Ty wants to do something for Mikayla."

"He can't do much from where he is."

"That's why he wanted to talk to me. He needs me . . . Really, us, to do something."

Without asking what Ty wanted us to do, Mike waited for me to tell him whatever it was. I told him what it was and how much it meant to Ty, as if he really cared.

"So what do you think?" Mike asked.

"I think it's a good gesture. We could put money away for Mikayla's college fund, amongst a lot of other things."

"I'll be able to pay for her to go to college. That'll be no problem at all."

"I know it won't baby, but Ty just wants to do something good for Mikayla since he won't be able to be a father to her."

I could tell Mike hated the thought of accepting anything from Ty, but he also didn't wanna feel like he was taking anything from Mikayla that rightfully belonged to her, so he gave in. He said, he didn't know how heavy the safe was, but he knew he that would need some help since he couldn't do a lot of heavy lifting yet. I told him I would help, and we'd be fine.

Since Mike had made up his mind, instead of heading home first, we headed to Ty's house. We told the guard at the gate we were there to take care of some important business for Silas Cooper, and he let us through, probably only because he had seen him in the news and knew he was locked up. We pulled into the driveway, and Mike stared in amazement.

"By the looks of things, Ty should've been in jail a long time ago!"

We got out of the car and walked up the marble driveway. I walked behind the perfectly trimmed bushes, and pulled out one of the bricks on the house that was slightly sticking out, and attached to it was a key. I snatched the key off and let Mike and myself into Ty's mansion. Mike's eyes, not being able to focus on one thing because there was so much to look at, were big as ever. I didn't know what he was expecting, but I was sure he wasn't expecting to be in the home of a millionaire.

Mike followed me up the dual staircase, and into the double doors of the master suite. I looked around and it brought back so many memories. I looked towards the closet, remembering being locked in there while I watched my friend and my lover go at it on the windowsill. I looked at the bed that looked as if it was freshly made, and saw the picture of Jada, with her beautiful smile sitting on the nightstand. I could still smell the scent of her perfume lingering in the air, which brought tears to my eyes. I had to shake it off and do what we had come to do.

Mike and I entered the walk-in closet, and saw the huge safe sitting towards the back. I tried to keep my focus off of all of Jada's clothes and shoes everywhere in sight.

"Kel, there's no way I'm gonna be able to move that. Not even with your help. I can tell that steel is solid, just by looking at it."

I went and put the combination in, hoping Ty wasn't trying to set me up some kind of way, and to my surprise, it worked. What I saw was too much for my mind to handle, so I ran past Mike, who was still standing in the doorway, and stood in the middle of the bedroom floor, taking long, deep breaths.

"What's in there?" Mike asked.

"Too much! I can't take that."

"Look, you made me agree to this, so don't back out on me now. You have his child, and he told you he wants her to have it, so it's not like you're stealing. Would you prefer that it all go to someone who doesn't have any rights to it? If the state comes in here, that'll be the end of it."

I thought about what Mike said, and I went downstairs to the kitchen and grabbed the garbage bags so we had somewhere to put all the bundles of hundred dollars bills and expensive jewelry that were inside the safe. There were also bricks of cocaine in the safe, which Ty hadn't told me about, and I shole wasn't about to put those in the car with us so we could just so happen get pulled over and Mikayla would be parentless with all three parents locked up! After we filled almost six large bags, we had emptied the safe and carried them down one by one to the car. Even though I didn't really feel like I was doing anything wrong, something just didn't feel right, but I couldn't put my finger on it.

After a long day, Mike and I finally made it back to my house, counted the bundles of money, and were in awe of how much it actually was. I didn't know what other types of drugs Ty was selling besides cocaine, and who he was selling to, but he was doing huge things. I saw for myself why he was addicted to his lifestyle and didn't wanna let it go. Greed obviously had a hold on him because we counted four-hundred fifty million, and got tired of counting! We found a semi-safe place to put everything, at least until I bought a safe of my own, or somehow got the safe from Ty's house to mine. Mike and I also finally took some time out to talk about me and Ty's relationship. He wanted to know everything, so I told him everything. I could tell he was hurt by it, but respected me for finally being honest with him.

The next day, Ty called again, just wanting to make sure that I had done what he asked. This time, I answered the phone, and he was very short with me. The only other thing he said was that he was sorry, and me and Mikayla meant the world to him. Before I could say anything, he hung up. I didn't know if he was being rushed off the phone, but what I did know was that he didn't sound like himself.

My first day back at work after the shooting was the very next day and it was a strange feeling. I thought it would be good for me so I could try to keep other things off my mind. I felt like everybody was being cautious around me, but at the same time watching my every move. Like I said, you had to have been dead not to know what happened, but no one was bold enough to ask me anything about it. Cameron did ask me if I was okay, and to let me know if I needed anything. I tried to carry on normal salon conversation, but the whole atmosphere was just uncomfortable.

As I styled my client's hair, and carried on a conversation with her, I looked up at the TV where the Wendy William's Show was interrupted for breaking news. I blinked a couple of times to make sure I was reading the text at the bottom of the screen correctly. It read, "Silas Cooper Found Dead Inside of Cell From Apparent Suicide."

I was still in disbelief, thinking my eyes were playing tricks on me, until I heard the news anchor say, "Silas Cooper, who was the shooter outside of a nightclub a little over a week ago was found dead inside of his cell early this morning by one of the guards. He apparently committed suicide. Updates will be available as soon as we get more information."

Everyone in the shop looked at me with pity. My entire body became numb, and I dropped my comb where I stood. I cried uncontrollably. Almost as hard as I had cried after the shooting. Cameron ran and grabbed me, holding me tight, burying my head in her chest, and shushing me like a baby. The other stylists all came over in a huddle and started praying over me. I appreciated all the love, but it was just too much for me. I cried the whole way home, and in Mike's arms the rest of the night.

Ty didn't have any family, and since he had left us with so much money, I felt obligated to pay for his funeral and make sure Mikayla's biological father had a proper burial. I was glad that Mike was, or acted like he was cool with everything. I knew this had to be just as hard on him as it was on me. Especially to see me cry over another man, and take on the responsibility of having a funeral for him. The service was nice, short, and simple. I made sure he was dressed in his best suit and tie, and chose the best funeral home so he would look as much like himself as possible. Mikayla laid eyes on her father one last time before he was put six feet under. I didn't cry as much as I thought I would at the funeral. I figured I had done so much crying the week prior that I didn't have any more tears left in me.

After the funeral was over and we made it home, someone came to the door. I wasn't expecting anyone, so I asked who it was through the intercom.

"Marisol Luna," the woman responded.

"I'm sorry. Do I know you?"

"No, but I'm . . . was Silas Cooper's Attorney. He told me if anything happened I could find Kelicia Armstrong here."

I buzzed Marisol up right away, and as I was opening the door, Mike came down from putting Mikayla to sleep. Marisol shook both me and Mike's hands and showed me her business card. She held a large brown folder in her hand that looked like it contained some important documents. I led the tall, beautiful Hispanic woman, who reminded me of Eva Mendes, to the sofa to have a seat while I waited to see what she needed with me.

"I hate to bother you, especially right after the funeral, but Silas was very clear about how he wanted things done if anything ever happened to him, and I gave him my word."

Mike and I sat on the couch across from Marisol, oblivious to anything that was going on, as she began taking papers out of her folder while we watched her. She stood up and handed me a document and watched me as I read over it. I was still clueless as to what it was, but obviously Mike wasn't.

"Are you serious?" he asked Marisol.

"Yes. Absolutely!"

Mike explained to me that Ty had signed a document stating if anything happened to him, all of his assets, which were paid in full, would belong to me. I had already taken the money for Mikayla, but I definitely didn't feel right about accepting Ty's house and cars. It wasn't fair to Mike for me to be accepting anything from another man.

I handed the paper back to Marisol and told her I couldn't accept it.

"Silas told me you would probably say that, and told me not to leave until you changed your mind. All you have to do is sign the paper and it's all yours. What you do with it is none of my business. I would've done my part. If you don't take it, it'll just go to the state. You don't want that, do you?"

I didn't know where me and Mike's relationship was going, but I was trying to make sure I began including him in any major decisions that I made. I didn't want him to feel uncomfortable in any way. Before I could ask him what he thought, he told me to sign it. Marisol handed me a pen, and I put the pen to the paper, hesitating before I signed my name as owner of Ty's estate.

"Thank you very much Ms. Armstrong. I know this makes Silas happy. Take care of that little girl. He loved her."

Marisol handed me the car keys and another set of house keys. She also said she had one more thing for me and pulled a small white envelope out of her purse that was addressed to me in Ty's handwriting.

"I almost forgot about this. This was found in his cell when they found him."

As I let Marisol out, she told Mike and I to have a good day as if what she had just done was nothing big at all. She probably did stuff like that all day every day. I didn't know what to say to Mike. It shocked me how understanding he was being throughout this whole ordeal.

"Are you sure you're okay with all this, Mike?"

"I just want it to be over. Whatever that takes. Whatever it takes for people to quit knocking on our door bringing up the past. I'm just ready to move on with just you, Mikayla, and me. That's the only thing that matters to me right now. I'm ready to move my stuff in and sell my house, if that's okay with you of course. I want this to be my permanent domain."

"After all this, you still wanna be with me? I don't understand."

"You think I'm gonna let you go now after I've helped you unpack most of your baggage? Not saying I'm happy about what happened to Ty, but he was, and probably still will hold us back for a while until you get closure. That's the rest of the baggage we have to work on unpacking."

Mike gave me a kiss as he held my hand and we headed upstairs to our bedroom. I walked towards the bathroom and told Mike I'd be right out. I sat on top of the toilet seat and pulled the folded envelope that Marisol had given me out of my bra. I admired Ty's beautiful handwriting on the outside of the envelope where he had addressed it to me. I sniffed the envelope, hoping I could smell just the smallest trace of his scent, but there was nothing. When I opened it, there was a letter.

Dear Kel,

I know you probably thinkin' I took the cowardly way out, and I agree, but I just couldn't handle all this pain at once. I'm so disappointed in myself and I couldn't face you not one more day. I almost killed the love of your life, and killed the woman who loved me to death. I loved Jada. I didn't realize how much I loved her 'til she was dyin' in my arms. That was the most pain I ever felt in my life next to losin' you. I wish I could've traded my life for hers cuz she didn't deserve what she got. Mike didn't deserve it either. I punished him for lovin' you. Maybe one day he'll forgive me. Maybe you can convince him that I wasn't such a bad person. (smile). Anyway, I couldn't live the rest of my life thinkin' about what I did to Jada while rottin' in that cell. Every time I closed my eyes, I saw her face, and it was complete torture. I knew how much pain I had caused you and I didn't want you to go through that any longer either. I made a mess of your life twice, but you don't have to worry about me no more. I want you to live your life with Mike and give him your whole heart. He a good man. I can admit that now and he's gonna take good care of you and Mikayla. I don't want Mikayla to know anything about me. I want her to grow up knowing Mike as her daddy. I approve. She don't need to feel that shame that she'd feel to know her real daddy was a drug dealin' murderer. Move on with your life and be happy. Don't be sad for me. I did what I wanted and I was content with my decision. Just know I loved you from the moment I laid eyes on you and always will. Thank you for bringing my daughter in the world so I could at least leave a piece of me behind. I will forever be grateful to you for that cuz the time I spent with her was the best time of my life. You two will always be the two ladies of my life.

Love, Ty

After reading the letter, I released what I felt like were my final tears for Ty. I felt a huge burden be taken off of my shoulders and knew that was exactly what I needed in order to completely move on.

"Kel, you cool?" I heard Mike say on the other side of the door.

"Yeah. I'll be there in a minute," I said with my voice sounding like it was drowned out in tears.

When I finally opened the door, Mike was still standing right outside with a concerned look on his face. I grabbed his face with both hands and gave him the longest, most passionate kiss I had ever given him.

"What was that for, babe?"

"I just finished unpacking the rest of the baggage," I whispered and smiled.

The End